THE VAMPIRE
AND THE CASE OF THE
WAYWARD WEREWOLF

HEATHER G. HARRIS & JILLEEN DOLBEARE

PUBLISHED BY HELLHOUND PRESS LIMITED

HELLHOUND
PRESS

Heather's Dedication

For my husband, always. For my awesome supporters on Patreon, with special mention to Amanda Peterman and Melissa. I am so grateful and humbled by your belief in me. Thanks to my Patrons who join me on live Q&A's – seeing your faces brightens my day. Your enthusiasm buoys me up, I am so grateful for our chats together. Thanks to my ARC team and street team, you guys are the best! Special mention to all the keen eyed typo-spotters. As always, a million thanks goes to my dear friend, Beba. Thank you for all you do for me, and for indie authors everywhere. You are a legend.

Thanks to Jill for making this such a blast. I've had so much fun building this world together. Bring on the next book!

And finally thanks to you, my readers, my Hell Hounds. I literally couldn't do it without you. I will forever be thankful for your faith in me.

Jill's Dedication

I dedicate this book to my husband and family for putting up with a lot of lost time and endless questions.

To the best co-writer in the world, Heather who is utterly amazing and will roll with anything.

Thanks to the great state of Alaska, for not just having great folklore, but for the endless forests, wilds, and more than enough material for a million books!

To my parents, who taught me to read and love sci-fi and fantasy—I wouldn't be anything without you!

To my fellow FAKAs, thanks for everything! And to all my alpha, beta, and ARC readers. Thank you all!

Content Warnings

Please see the full content warnings on Heather's website, www.heathergharris.com, if you are concerned about triggers.

The *Portlock Paranormal Detective* series has poor language and scenes of violence.

Please note that all of Heather's works are written in British English with British phrases, spellings and grammar being utilised throughout. Jill has suffered through adding extra 'u's and shoving 's's everywhere instead of 'z's.

If you think you have found a typo, please do let Heather know by emailing her at: heathergharrisauthor@gmail.com. Thank you!

Chapter 1

I was going to throttle Timmy when we found him. It was pissing down with rain and absolutely freezing. The cold didn't bother me as much as it had when I was human, but wet was harder to ignore. My trousers were drenched, my hair was dripping, and water was dribbling down my neck; I was soaked to the skin and struggling not to feel grumpy about it.

I thought longingly of the London clubbing scene. I was as far from that as humanly – and inhumanly – possible. Never in a million years had I thought I'd end up in the bumfuck wilds of Alaska. But then, I never thought I'd be a vampire either.

I belatedly pulled up the hood of my borrowed coat. So much for my vaunted observational skills, with all the stress I'd even forgotten I had a hood.

I called the name of the missing lynx-shifter again and again until I was hoarse. If this kid was just having a nap somewhere, heads would roll. Unfortunately, though, he wasn't the first to go missing; Timmy's was the third disappearance in the last week and the atmosphere in the town was tense. I grimaced; we *had* to find Timmy.

After I'd walked what seemed like thirty miles in the woods in the pouring rain, Timmy leapt off a tree stump right at me. I let out an undignified screech and fell backwards into the mud. The lynx kitten landed on my stomach, driving out my breath in a whoosh. So much for my sharp vampire reflexes. Man, I was the worst vampire ever.

'For fuck's sake, Timmy!' I yelled when I could speak again. 'Don't pounce on people!' As my brain connected to my mouth, I winced. Timmy was five years old, so swearing was probably a no-go. Crap. I hoped I wouldn't get fired from my new job before I'd even completed a full week.

The lynx scrambled off me and shifted into a small boy who was sitting naked in the mud. 'For fuck's sake,' he said delightedly.

I winced. 'Don't use those words, little man. They're only for adults.'

He grinned at me. 'Fuck's sake.'

I blew out a breath. I knew nothing about parenting; my own parents didn't know much about it, either, which was why I'd been raised mostly by a nanny.

I utilised one of mum's few parenting techniques: bribery. 'I'll give you chocolate if you stop saying the naughty words.'

Timmy tilted his head, considering, then held out his hand. 'I don't have it now,' I explained.

'For fuck's sake,' he muttered, folding his arms grumpily.

Heaven help me.

He looked at me curiously. 'Who are you?'

Who are any of us, I wanted to reply, but philosophy was probably beyond a five-year-old. 'Elizabeth Octavia Barrington.' I grimaced. 'But everyone calls me Bunny.'

'Why?'

I smirked and lied smoothly. 'I once organized a flash mob of people all doing the bunny hop.'

Timmy's eyes widened. 'Cool. You ran the mob?'

Before I could correct his misconception my boss Gunnar Johansen, the supernatural chief of police – the Nomo – joined us. He must have heard us chatting. I hoped he'd missed the gist of our conversation; supernatural hearing could be hellish sharp, and I wasn't especially proud of the bribery thing.

The Nomo was a huge burly man with long reddish-blond hair, a prodigious beard and bright-blue eyes that could see too deeply. His ready smile brightened when he saw Timmy. Effortlessly picking up the boy in a huge hand, he said, 'Here you are! You gave your mama quite a scare.' He cuddled him close. 'And the rest of us,' he murmured under his breath.

'Sorry, Uncle Gunnar.'

'Don't apologise to me, it's your mom you'd best be showing your belly to,' he chastened lightly. 'You'd better get furry, my boy, it's cold out here.'

'Yes, Uncle Gunnar,' Timmy intoned respectfully as he shifted back into his four-legged form.

Gunnar tucked him under his arm and offered me his other hand, which I gratefully accepted. He hauled me out of the squelchy mud. 'Good work.'

I hadn't done much besides getting pounced on and accidentally swearing at a small child, so I smiled awkwardly and brushed off my trousers as best I could. After a day doing paperwork in the office, I was woefully underdressed for a rescue mission in the forest. Live and learn; administrative assistant or not, always dress for adventure.

My suit trousers were ruined; I definitely had the wrong wardrobe for Alaska. I'd left my London home in a hurry, eager to escape one hundred years of servitude to the Vampire King. He hadn't been keen to let me go, so I'd done everything I could to get away – including stabbing his son Franklin in the bollocks. Franklin was the one who had turned me, and the bastard had done it without my permission. I knew now that he'd been in breach of vampire law, yet somehow *I* was the one being punished whilst he got away scot-free. Bloody nepotism.

Talking of punishment... I shifted uneasily. Better to confess to my current sins than be ratted out by Timmy. I cleared my throat. 'I might have said some choice words when he jumped on me,' I confessed nervously.

Gunnar laughed. 'Wouldn't be the first time – he's a bit of a rascal.' A 'bit' seemed like an understatement. Lauretta, Timmy's mum, had looked wrecked when she'd come into the Nomo's station, though for all I knew the messy bun, dirty joggers and bleary eyes were entirely normal for her.

'He called you uncle. Is he your nephew?' I asked curiously. Lauretta bore no resemblance to Gunnar; she was svelte and blonde, and their only similarity was in their eye colour.

'Just an honorary title.' He ruffled Timmy's lynx head affectionately.

I trudged on beside Gunnar, grateful to have the mountainous man by my side. He'd stuck to me like glue because he feared I didn't have bushcraft, which I didn't. I hadn't yet told him about my eidetic memory, though; having the ability to recall scenes I'd just seen perfectly meant that getting lost was something I'd never experienced.

Still, he was right: I had no business being out here alone, especially not when people kept disappearing. But with Timmy's safe return we were back down to only two people missing, and that was better, right? That could be a coincidence.

As we crashed around the woods I heard all sorts of freakish noises, none of which seemed *normal*, for lack of a better word. I wasn't ready to encounter a chupacabra or something similar right now; I was tired and I wanted a cup of tea and my bed. In that order.

Close to town, Gunnar pulled out his phone and let Lauretta know that we'd found her wayward son. I heard the cried 'Thank fuck!' down the line. Maybe Lauretta wouldn't be too bothered about her son's latest saying. One could hope.

We reached the office shortly afterwards, and Gunnar got Timmy clean, dried and dressed. The kid sat on the plastic waiting-room chair kicking his legs with a hot chocolate in hand. He looked entirely too happy, considering the trouble he'd caused. Gunnar had offered me a hot chocolate too, but I was bone tired and wanted to head home.

The sun was due up soon. I fingered the charm around my neck. It allowed me to walk in sunlight without getting burned to a crisp, but it did nothing to stave off the daytime exhaustion that wracked me and pulled at my bones. 'Here,' I said, starting to shrug out of the borrowed jacket. 'I'm heading home to bed.'

Gunnar frowned. 'If you wait a bit, I'll walk you home. Better safe than sorry.'

'I'll be fine. I'm a vampire, after all.'

'Newer than a week-old lamb,' he muttered. 'And being a vamp didn't stop Kivuk from going missing.'

I smiled politely. 'No one is going to be interested in me. I'm a nobody – I'll be fine.' I held out the jacket.

Gunnar shook his head 'You keep the jacket and the boots,' he said gruffly. 'No doubt you'll be needing them again before long. My wife has plenty of spares.'

'Oh, I couldn't,' I started awkwardly, but the truth was that I was poorer than I'd ever been in my entire life, including my recent rebellious years when I'd been cut from my parents' purse strings and survived by working as a waitress. I'd subsisted on tips. That had all changed when Franklin had been paid a cool £50,000 to turn me into a vampire. I still didn't know why or by whom, but I was determined to find out.

Gunnar waved away my weak objection. 'Keep them,' he repeated. 'My wife wouldn't let me hear the end of it if I didn't give them to you.'

I swallowed past the sudden lump in my throat. The kindness of others still took me by surprise. My parents had assessed people's worth by the amount of cash in their bank accounts, and kindness hadn't mattered a damn to them. But I was trying to find my own way in life – especially now my life was eternal – and I needed to find out what mattered to *me*.

The swearing incident aside, helping Timmy had felt good. Maybe in this new life I could craft a new Bunny, a better Bunny. Elizabeth Octavia Barrington had officially died a week ago, so maybe it was time for some of my shittier attitudes to die with her.

I had a new start. I wasn't going to waste it.

Chapter 2

I waved goodbye to Timmy. He waved back and called loudly, 'For fuck's sake, Bunny!' Gunnar's guffaws chased me out of the door. It turned out that even when you were undead you could still manage a small blush when you were absolutely mortified.

I dragged myself home, anxiously fiddling with the charm around my neck. It was *so* close to sunrise. I tried to pick up my pace but, just as I did, the sun burst through the clouds, streaming in over the trees and mountains. I reeled back but, instead of burning pain, it was pleasantly warm like when I'd been human. My heartbeat thudded once with joy. As a vampire, I had a heartbeat but it was sluggish and slower than two sloths racing.

I lifted my face. God, the sun – I'd missed it so damn much. The things you take for granted. Before I'd spoken to Sidnee, Gunnar's mermaid assistant, I'd thought I would never see it again. I'd only lived in perpetual darkness for a couple of weeks, but I was surprised by how emotional I was at seeing that golden orb again. Even though it made my eyes ache, I gave a happy twirl, kissed the charm pendant around my neck and gave thanks to whoever had created it.

I wanted to spend time basking in the sun but exhaustion was crippling me. Besides, I wanted to check on my new dog, Fluffy. I approached my house, still not quite believing my luck.

This house was small by most people's standards but okay by mine. After I'd rebelliously moved out of my parents' mansion when I was twenty-one, I'd lived in a shitty studio apartment. It was all I could afford on my waitress's salary, but it had been mine, and I'd loved it even though there wasn't enough room to swing a cat in it. In comparison, my new home was almost palatial. It had a bright blue door and was clad in white clapboard, exactly how I'd imagined a house in America would be.

This was my first visit to the States, and hopefully I wouldn't be moving again. I'd come to Portlock, Alaska, and I wanted to stay. Here almost everyone was supernatural and no one had to hide who or what they were. After two decades of dealing with social airs and graces, that openness was refreshing. I just hoped that I'd fit in. I hadn't met a single vampire yet, but there had to be more bloodsuckers in town.

To defer to the nocturnal residents of the town, most places on the high street opened from 4pm to 4am; that way the residents who wanted to do their shopping in daylight hours could do so, but vampires and the like had the cover of darkness. The Nomo's office was the only place open 24/7. Lucky me: I'd got the one job that pulled long-arse shifts, but I wasn't complaining because my job even came with this house!

I unlocked my front door and called, 'Fluffy, I'm home!'

There was a happy bark and he ran in, skittering on the wooden floor in his excitement. Fluffy was a German Shepherd I had found in a bin back in England, discarded, smelly and emaciated. Someone had thrown him away – and that had struck a chord with me. I'd rescued him not long after I'd been turned and we'd adopted each other. After a week of four square meals a day he'd put on a lot of weight and his fur shone, but he still had a way to go before he regained the muscle mass he should have had.

'Hey, boy!' I greeted him, giving him a full body rub. 'Were you okay without me?' He wagged happily so I took that as a yes. German Shepherds are known to be smart, and he was certainly far more intelligent than Arabella, my mum's vapid Pomeranian.

I made myself a cup of tea and downed it whilst it was still scalding. I'd needed that.

'Let's get you some fresh air,' I murmured as I went to the back door. I let Fluffy out then leaned heavily on the doorframe, struggling to stay awake. Fluffy tinkled in the garden and immediately came back to me.

I locked up and was halfway to the bedroom when there was a knock at the door. I contemplated ignoring it but I was new here and I needed desperately to fit in. If I didn't, I had one hundred years of servitude waiting for me in London. Despite my exhaustion, I went to make nice.

I opened the front door. A stranger was standing there with a large basket in his arms, looking away from me. His hair was dark, almost black. He was dressed in jeans, boots and an untucked flannel shirt with the sleeves rolled up to expose well-muscled forearms. Even in profile he looked great. I suddenly felt self-conscious. I was more mud and rain than human. Vampire. Whatever.

The man turned to face me. Like me, he wore a charm around his neck – a fellow vampire! I looked up from the charm to meet his eyes – and got stuck there. We were still staring at each other in silence when he thrust the basket at me. I took it without thinking. I'd probably have accepted a bomb if he'd passed it to me in just the right way.

He cleared his throat. 'Welcome to Portlock. I'm Connor MacKenzie, the vampire leader here.' I was aware that he was speaking but I was still busy gawping at him, my jaw slack. Connor MacKenzie was model beautiful; in fact, he had to be the most handsome man I'd ever seen.

I realised I was staring. Fuck. *Say something, anything.* 'You're Scottish?' I blurted out. As soon as the words left my lips I realised he hadn't got a Scottish burr, just a flat American accent. His name might be Scottish but he wasn't.

He looked a little nonplussed. 'My family originated from there but I've lived in Alaska my whole life,' he said finally.

'Oh, right.' I was usually good at small talk but exhaustion had me firing on empty. I belatedly realised that I needed to introduce myself. 'I'm Bunny, the new vampire in town.' I'd have held out my hand to shake, but my arms were full of the basket he'd thrust at me.

'I know. That's why I'm here.' He pointed. 'With a welcome basket.'

'Oh, right. Um, thanks.'

'I won't keep you. Daytime exhaustion must be pulling at you.' He cleared his throat. 'Someone from my office will send you an email about check-ins and paperwork. Welcome to town.'

'Wait! Did you know Kivuk Sakari?' I asked.

He turned back and suddenly the loose, friendly vibe was gone. He frowned at me. 'What's it to you?'

'I'm working at the Nomo's office. I was studying his file when the call came in about Timmy going missing.' I was grateful I wasn't stuttering under the power of his glare. Oof, the welcome wagon had done a total 180-degree turn.

He tensed even more. 'Someone else is missing?'

'Only temporarily,' I assured him. 'A shifter kid. We found him messing about in the woods.'

Connor grimaced. 'Idiot pup. He'll get killed out there.' He shook his head. 'Stan needs to get his house in order,' he muttered to himself.

I noticed that he hadn't answered my question about Kivuk. Without another word, he turned on his heel and walked away. He moved with a grace I could only dream of attaining, yet there was something faintly predatory about it.

I couldn't help feeling that Connor MacKenzie, like Timmy, could pounce at any time.

Chapter 3

I plonked the welcome basket on the floor; I didn't have the energy or inclination to unpack it right now. 'Don't eat anything,' I ordered Fluffy. 'It might be poisoned. We can't trust anyone. He was pretty, and the pretty ones are always shifty.'

He barked and gave me an innocent look that I didn't buy for a second, but I was too shattered to care. I dragged myself to my bedroom and fell on the bed fully clothed. Fluffy jumped up, turned around three times and settled next to me. I felt oddly safe having him there so, regardless of the fact that this house was still a little strange to me, I was out in an instant.

I woke as the sun was setting, some sort of primordial vampire instinct telling me that this was *my* time. I was utterly rejuvenated, which was a relief after my earlier weariness. My exhaustion had been so strong, so all-consuming, that I'd wondered if something was wrong with me. The shitty handbook I'd been given hadn't covered this and it seemed a somewhat glaring omission. Connor had mentioned daytime exhaustion, though, so it had to be something that was normal for vampires. For once, I wasn't a freak.

Fluffy ran out as I hopped in the shower. I hoped he didn't need to pee too badly because I *had* to wash off this grime first. Once I was clean, I dried, dressed and did some basic makeup. I found my hairdryer and went to plug it in then paused; I still didn't have a damned adaptor. Air-drying it was.

I'd grown up watching American TV and I'd expected America to feel pretty much like the UK but, to my surprise, I felt like I was in a foreign country. Things were different, like the plugs and the toilet flushing in a different way. Still, it was my new home and these weird discrepancies would soon become the norm. I felt like a fish out of water, but I'd find my feet soon. I had to. I squared my shoulders.

Downstairs Fluffy was waiting patiently by the door. I let him out and collected the welcome basket that I'd dumped by the front door. I put it on the dining-room table, unwrapped the bow and pretty cellophane and checked out the contents.

There was a mix of Alaskan products – smoked salmon, crackers, caribou-meat sticks, salmonberry preserves – and a weird looking knife with a tag on that told me it was an ulu. Who gave someone a knife as a welcome present? Talk about mixed messages.

My cupboards were still bare so it wasn't hard to find space for the gifts. When I was done, I was left with a pretty wicker basket with a handle. It was too beautiful to throw away and I decided to repurpose it as a laundry basket in the bathroom.

It was still early so I cooked the breakfast of champions for Fluffy and me: sausages, beans and toast. Whilst it was cooling, I chugged a lukewarm cup of blood. It didn't taste anywhere nearly as disgusting as it should have done, but it didn't hit the spot the way a cup of tea did. For me, blood was a necessity rather than a craving; if I tried to eat regular food without drinking it first, I vomited everywhere and it wasn't pretty. Luckily, I could drink anytime I wanted; it was just solid food that required blood first, as if somehow I had to warm up my body to handle real food.

As part of living in a magical town, Sidnee had set up a blood delivery service for me. It was like a milk delivery, but with haemoglobin. Every few days an insulated cool box of blood was deposited on my doorstop. For obvious reasons, Portlock didn't want its vampire contingent getting nibbly. The Nomo's office had a contract with a local blood bank and the cost of the blood was taken directly from my wages. Lucky me.

Fluffy and I ate companionably. I'd never been so grateful to have a four-legged friend; I might be on the other side of the world, but I still had a dog to love. When we were done, I attached his collar and lead. Fluffy gave me a baleful look. 'I'm sorry, but I don't know the dog-walking laws here,' I explained. 'Better to be safe than sorry. Let's go investigate the town a little.'

We wandered down neat, uncracked pavements past tidy gardens and well-cared-for homes. A few people were out exercising, hurrying to work or returning home. I got several friendly waves, and a few people stopped to fuss over Fluffy. The place felt wholesome and everyone seemed so friendly; if it wasn't for the two people who'd gone missing, I'd have wondered if any crime actually happened here. Maybe they were star-crossed lovers who'd run away together.

Working for the police might be dull in a small town like this but, dull or not, I was here for the long haul. Gunnar had extracted me from the UK and servitude, so I owed him big time. He had my undying loyalty – unless he proved himself unworthy of it.

A few vehicles passed by, mostly big trucks or SUVs. In comparison to the cars in the UK, these vehicles seemed huge, like cars hopped up on steroids. Everything in America seemed to be supersized; even the streets were wider.

I'd have to ask Sidnee or Gunnar about things to do in Portlock; I'd need something to fill my days besides working, watching TV, howling at the moon and sucking down cups of blood. Maybe there were some sort of paranormal games I could join in or a team I could support. The Yanks were big on sports, right? Go Portlock Poltergeists!

As I walked, I looked around. I knew we were near the ocean because we'd flown over and landed in it when I'd arrived. There were mountains and lots of woods. The twilight was long because the mountains blocked a lot of the sun. This was a place carved out of the wilderness and I felt tiny and insignificant, but in a good way. If I was small, then so were my mistakes.

I took Fluffy home and put out fresh water and some dry food for him to nibble on, ignoring his disdainful look at the latter. I gave him a big cuddle and promised I'd be back soon, but he still watched balefully as I walked out of the front door.

This time I had the rubber boots in a bag, spare leggings and a top, and the waterproof jacket under my arm. This Bunny learned from her mistakes.

I walked briskly to work. There were still a lot of people out and about; the town seemed to have come alive in the growing darkness. I wondered how many of the supernaturals were nocturnal – was it just the vampires, or were the werewolves night creatures, too? Didn't they have a thing about the moon?

I walked into the office to see a line of people waiting at the desk. I looked at the queue in horror and double-checked the time on my new phone. I wasn't late – I wasn't even due in yet.

Gunnar and Sidnee were standing at the high counter. The mermaid's dusky skin was set off perfectly by her maroon top, and her silky dark hair tumbled artfully over her shoulders. She always looked immaculate, which was more than I could say for Gunnar. His beard looked like it might still have his breakfast in it.

'I am so sorry!' I apologised, eyes wide. 'Am I late? I thought I wasn't due in until 8pm!'

Gunnar chuckled. 'You aren't late. The booze flight came in early, and people are desperate for their liquor.'

I looked at them, confused. 'Sorry? What?'

He turned to Sidnee. 'I'll deal with this for a minute. Can you explain what's going on and show her the ropes?'

'Sure thing, boss.' She flipped him a cheeky salute, grabbed my arm and pulled me into the break room. Once the door was closed, she explained, 'Portlock is a damp town.'

That meant nothing to me. Did she mean it suffered from mould? I shook my head to show I didn't understand, though my blank expression had probably told her that already.

'In Alaska, we have dry towns, damp towns or regular "no-limit" towns when it comes to alcohol.'

'What?' I exclaimed. In the UK, pubs and bars sold alcohol, some of them round the clock, and so did shops. The concept of a dry town conjured up images of 1920s' speakeasies. I had no idea that some areas of America were still living in the prohibition era.

Sidnee continued. 'No alcohol is allowed in a dry town – it can't be sold and it can't be brought in.'

Even though my mouth was hanging open, I nodded. You couldn't even bring it in?

'In a damp town, no alcohol can be sold so there are no liquor stores and no bars, but you can order some for personal use. In our case, we arrange for it to be flown in and the Nomo's office controls distribution. Everyone can order a certain amount per flight, depending on the space on the plane. It's not a problem when we have daily flights, but things can get ugly if there are delays.'

I was still stuck on the whole no pubs and bars thing; if there were no bars, that meant there were no clubs. 'What do people do for fun?' I asked, although frankly my last clubbing experience had left a lot to be desired. I'd been out partying with friends when that knobhead Franklin had bitten and turned me.

Sidnee laughed at my horror-stricken expression. 'We don't live in caves!' she assured me. 'We have parties, game nights and get-togethers, just not in public places. We have lots of community events as well. We socialize, but with less alcohol.'

I was a Brit: alcohol was as much a part of my culture as having a monarchy. Though the younger generations seemed to have a much greater emphasis on healthy living, the older generations – and mine – still partied hard, and binge culture was still very much a thing.

'Any questions?' Sidnee asked. 'We should get out there before the crowd gets unruly.'

'What do I need to do?'

'You'll pick it up,' she assured me. 'Just watch for a few minutes and when you feel comfortable, jump in.'

Training in the Nomo's office seemed pretty hands-on. For once, I was grateful for my eidetic memory. Surely even I couldn't fuck this up?

Chapter 4

Sidnee was right: it wasn't complicated and I picked it up fast. My old job in a bar had made me used to demanding customers and slinging alcohol across an expanse of wood. My job now was to check each person's slip against our invoice then give them their alcohol. With the three of us working together, we soon whittled down the queue.

When the last customer had gone, I had to enter everything on the computer and file the hard copies. I couldn't believe my luck: for the amount of pay I was getting, not to mention the perks like the lovely house, the sunlight charm and insurance cover, this job was child's play. It was certainly much easier than waitressing – and so far no one had grabbed my ass. Total bonus.

To be honest, bar the Timmy incident, it had seemed a little boring. I'd had all sorts of pre-conceived notions as I'd flown halfway around the world to become an administrative assistant to the chief of police. I'd daydreamed about car chases and arresting malodorous werewolves, and relished the thought that now that I was a vampire I could do a lot more damage to a sleazebag than just dumping a tray of drinks on them.

I felt my fangs drop a little at the thought and covered my mouth. I looked around, but luckily no one was around to see me fanging out. I took some deep breaths and eventually they retracted. Stupid things: I still had no real control over them.

With nothing else to do, I dug into the two missing persons' files. The vampire, Kivuk Sakari, had been missing for three days. His age was listed as unknown, and his residence just said *See Kamluck Logging*. Calling the file sparse was an understatement.

In comparison, the other file was thick. Jack Taylor was human, with no supernatural skills. He was only twenty-three and still lived with his parents. He hadn't come home from his shift at the Pizza Kodiak Kitchen where he worked as a waiter. There were pages of testimonies from friends and family, all saying how unusual his disappearance was. He'd been missing for weeks – before I'd even arrived in Portlock.

Gunnar had the CCTV footage from the Pizza Kodiak Kitchen storefront. Although it showed Jack arriving for his shift, it didn't show him leaving. The property had a rear exit that wasn't covered by cameras, and Gunnar's notes surmised that he'd left that way. That was the last time he'd been seen nearly four weeks ago.

None of his friends and family had known about a planned trip, no one said he'd been acting weird or edgy, and none of his credit or debit cards had been used since he'd gone missing.

To all intents and purposes, it was a cold case. Gunnar wanted me to look through it so I could familiarise myself with witness statements, documents and how a case was handled. He also had me look through a few completed files. A lot of the issues in the town seemed to end in violence. Tempers were high, arrests for assault were common – but prosecuting them was not.

My stomach growled at midnight when it was time for my 'lunch' break. I was allowed to leave the office, so I dashed home to check on Fluffy. The streets were busy; midnight was rush hour here.

'Fluffy, I'm home!'

He raced towards me, overjoyed to see me, and his unconditional love was like a balm to my soul. After I'd said hello, I warmed and downed my blood, had a quick sandwich and took him out. When it was time for me to leave again, he started giving me full puppy-dog eyes. My heart twisted.

'Don't worry, boy.' I patted his head. 'The office seems pretty relaxed so I'm going to ask Gunnar if you can come to work with me sometimes. It's worth a try – he can only say no!' Fluffy cocked his head, wagged his tail and his intelligent eyes lit up. He thought so too.

I gave him one last cuddle before I jogged back to the office. I'd just walked in when the phone rang so I raced to my desk. 'Nomo's office, Bunny speaking,' I answered in my best phone voice, although the effect was slightly ruined by all the panting. Note to self: don't jog to work and answer phones.

'Let me speak to the Nomo,' a gruff voice ordered.

I looked at Gunnar's office, but the door was shut and the light was out. 'I'm afraid he's out on a break. Can I take a message?' I chirped pleasantly.

I could hear a ruckus on the other end of the line. 'For fuck's sake! Find him and tell him to get his huge ass down to the hardware store. Frank Wakefield is plastered and tearing the fucking place apart.' The caller hung up.

I recognised the name: Frank had been one of the people in the queue for drink. I hastily found Gunnar's cell number and called it. Someone tearing up the place seemed like something I should interrupt his break for, right?

His phone rang a few times before he answered. 'What's up, doc?' he laughed. Was that a Bugs Bunny joke?

'We have an issue.' I relayed the message briskly.

'Damn it, Frank,' Gunnar muttered, all traces of amusement gone from his voice. 'Okay, Bunny, I need you to go into the file room and grab the black bag there. I'll meet you at the hardware store.'

Me? He wanted *me* to go? I'd dealt with plenty of drunks before, but they were usually trying to grope me. I doubted a knee to the bollocks would stop this guy if he was some sort of supernatural. I wondered what type he was, but Gunnar hung up before I could ask.

I ran into the back room. It took me a minute to find the black bag but finally I slung it over my shoulder and headed out. Halfway to the front door, I realised I had no fucking clue where to go. Google to the rescue! I hastily searched the maps on my phone; luckily, there was only one hardware store in town, in a row of shops next to a diner and the pizza restaurant. There was a small supermarket just down from it, next to a funeral home, and a florist. This little town really had everything you could need; caskets, coffee and carnations.

I made my way there double-time. Gunnar had already arrived and he nodded his approval when he spotted the bag over my shoulder. I felt a warm glow: at least I was doing something right. There was quite a crowd gathered outside; I guessed in such a small town, this kind of thing counted as entertainment. Some kids were snickering amongst themselves; the red eyes and blown pupils told me these teens were high as kites.

We were about ten yards away when two men came flying through the front window of the shop. I ducked instinctively as glass sprayed everywhere, and the crowd stepped back with a collective gasp. The men were going at it, whaling at each other. One of them was a dark-skinned man I remembered from the liquor run at the office – Frank Wakefield. He had long, shaggy hair, and his clothing was torn and dishevelled. He was roaring like an animal, though he still *looked* human. Maybe he was about to change into something else.

The man grappling with him was Connor MacKenzie. I gaped at the sight of him trading blows. He'd seemed so civilised and urbane when he'd given me the welcome basket; seeing him like this was giving me a whole other view of the man. A really *nice* view. Damn, but those jeans fit him well.

Whilst Frank was throwing wild punches, Connor's were calculated and precise. My own strength had grown exponentially since I'd become a vampire, so I could tell straight away that he was holding back. He might look a little wild, but he was in control of the situation. He probably didn't need me and Gunnar to wade in.

Before I'd met Connor, my sole experience with any vampire leader had been with the King of Europe, who definitely never grappled in the street; he had people to do that for him.

Needed or not, Gunnar strolled over and stood, arms akimbo, towering over the two men. Crap. I was on his team, right? I waded into the fray, braced my feet and helped him separate the men. Gunnar picked up Frank and set him on his feet, whilst Connor shrugged off my hands and did a neat flip to standing. He was still ready, though, and his eyes were coolly assessing Frank.

Gunnar held back Frank and gave him a firm shake when he started to lunge at Connor again. 'Are you gonna control yourself?' he asked coolly. 'Or am I gonna control you?' His voice was threatening enough to break through Frank's alcohol-induced haze.

Frank's eyes widened. 'I'm good.' He held up his hands. When Gunnar released his grip, he immediately started swaying.

'I doubt that,' Connor muttered not quite under his breath. 'I had it handled, Nomo.'

'You might have had it handled, but could the town take much more of the handling?' Gunnar gestured to the broken glass littering the street.

Apparently Frank's state of drunkenness level was way past steaming, and he was still making bad decisions. I could relate to that; I'd made one or ten when I was drunk, too. As he started back towards the store, I trotted after him. 'Hey, big fella, you're not going back in there, are you? Come this way.'

He was so shitfaced that he let me turn him around. 'You're real pretty, you know? All that blonde hair,' he said dreamily. 'Shame you're a vamp.'

Gunnar guffawed. 'Don't let your wife hear you say that. You're going to have to come with me to sleep it off, Frank.'

Frank let out a low growl and suddenly the affable waster of a moment ago was gone. 'I'm not going anywhere,' he yelled. He planted his feet firmly on the sidewalk.

Gunnar pinched the bridge of his nose. 'The hard way it is, then.'

I strengthened my grip on Frank, in case he decided that bolting was a good idea, while Gunnar put the bag on the ground, opened it and dug through it. 'Let me go, pretty girl,' Frank growled.

'Nope,' I said cheerily. He growled again so I tapped him on the nose, like I'd do to a dog. He gaped at me.

Once Gunnar had found a pair of green plastic zip cuffs, he relieved me of my charge. 'Frank,' he said calmly, 'you're under arrest.' He read the man his rights and expertly cuffed him as Frank continued gazing at me in disbelief.

The second the cuffs touched his skin, he sagged into an unconscious puddle in the street. I stared. Handy piece of kit!

'Green plastic zip cuffs are magic-cancelling,' Gunnar explained. 'They also cancelled his buzz – and apparently his consciousness.' He grinned. 'I guess magic was all that was keeping him upright.'

Connor stalked over. 'I thought he was banned from the alcohol run, Nomo. He was plastered. Did Barrington accidentally give him alcohol?'

I felt my fangs drop. Firstly, I was Bunny, not Barrington, and secondly, no I fucking didn't! I made sure my lips were fully closed to hide my sharp teeth. Man, they were so embarrassing but luckily, my outrage at Connor helped me ignore my self-consciousness. I was seething at the accusation that I'd done something wrong when I was trying so hard to do everything right.

I cast my mind back and relived the moment – thank you, eidetic memory. *The scent of coffee filled the air. I smiled at the man before me who told me his name was Frank. I found his invoice, told Gunnar what he needed then marked it off as Gunnar had passed the alcohol to the customer.* Yes, I'd filed Frank's paperwork, but I hadn't handed out the goods. That was Gunnar. Any mistakes here weren't mine.

Gunnar frowned at Connor and his tone held a mild rebuke. '*I* dealt with Frank. He picked up his booze earlier. He must have drunk every damn drop in an hour.'

'Even with a limit, there's no way a brown bear shifter could be that blitzed,' Connor insisted.

'He must have padded it with some 'shine. I'll talk to the Grimes brothers. Might as well let *Bunny* meet a few more of the town's personalities.' Gunnar laid clear emphasis on my correct name, which calmed me down enough to make my fangs retract. At least *someone* was in my corner, even if it wasn't my local vamp leader. 'Now Connor, I'm not pressing charges against you for the scuffle with Frank, but next time call me. Don't deal with it yourself.'

Connor grunted but promised nothing. He finally looked at me and my breath caught at his ridiculously chiselled cheekbones. *Danger, Will Robinson!* I said to myself. But beauty or not, he was being a right asshole. His glance was one of dismissal, a quick up and down and then move on. I didn't try to hide my answering glower.

Connor ignored my glare. 'It's reaching boiling point, Nomo. Frank needs to dry out for good.'

Gunnar sighed. 'I'll put him on the no-booze list. He's gonna be pissed as hell when he wakes up.'

Another man shoved forward. 'What's going on?' He was brown haired, handsome and *huge*. What did they feed the men in this town?

Connor's voice was dangerously calm. 'What's going on, Stan, is that once again I'm cleaning up your shit. Get your shifters under control.' The air was suddenly tense and the propensity for violence hung in the air. Just like that, my fangs snicked down again. What did they think *I* was going to do?

'Connor,' Gunnar rebuked softly.

The burly man stepped into Connor's personal space. 'You can fuck right off, Connor. At least I haven't lost one of my men,' he jeered.

'Hey!' Gunnar objected, but it was too late: Connor was already swinging at Stan, and this time he didn't pull his punch. Stan went sailing into the store's wall with a solid thump. He stumbled to his feet; he was dazed but in seconds he'd shaken his head and was alert and growling. He dropped to a fighter's stance.

Gunnar stepped forward. 'Stan, my boy, no. Tempers are frayed. Come on, now. Connor helped me with Frank.' His voice was low and soothing.

Grimacing, Stan righted himself. His glare was still fixed on Connor but the violence was gone.

Gunnar kept talking. 'I'll be taking Frank in now. And Stan? That's it – he's dry. Maybe you could go tell Martha for me.' He looked between Stan and Connor. 'No one wants to press charges for this little scuffle, do they?'

Stan grimaced but shook his head. The edge had faded from the air, and we all looked down at the man crumpled on the street; he was pathetic, not a threat. It seemed Stan's rage had dispersed too. Connor's anger was still simmering, but he'd stepped back. He shook his head.

The crowd was dispersing now it was clear that there wouldn't be an encore. Glass still littered the pavement. A man, presumably the shop owner, was standing inside the shop behind the shattered window. He put his hands on his hips and huffed as he glowered at the unconscious Frank.

'Ernie,' Gunnar called, 'I'll be back to take a statement about the damage. Let me just get Frank secured first.' Ernie nodded and disappeared back inside the hardware store.

Gunnar quickly searched Frank for weapons. Finding none, he hauled the huge man up in a fireman's lift and ambled effortlessly back to the office. Stan went towards the clinic, presumably to notify Frank's wife that he'd been a bad boy again.

As I picked up the black bag and turned to follow Gunnar, Connor's reached out to touch my shoulder. I jerked away. He'd tried to blame the whole Frank thing on *me*. 'I don't know how things work here, but in England you don't touch a lady without her permission,' I bitched. It might not have been smart to piss off a vampire who had just sent a huge man flying through the air, but I was done with being a wallflower.

I stalked away, head held high, and I didn't look back to watch his reaction. He might be the vampire leader or whatever, but I'd dealt with innumerable jumped-up assholes who thought they were worth more than me. I'd accepted that attitude a lot back home, but I wasn't doing it any more.

Nobody puts Bunny in the corner.

Chapter 5

Apparently the Nomo's building also had a small jail. I hadn't been past Gunnar's office because it seemed private and I had no need, but beyond it was an unmarked metal door leading to a reinforced concrete room with four cells. Inside each cell was a bunk, a toilet and a sink; because of the cold, each bed had a blanket, too.

Frank was the only occupant. After Gunnar dumped him in one of the cells, he came around with a groan and sat up. 'Seriously, Gunnar?' he complained as my boss removed the cuffs. 'How long will I be banned this time?'

'No more chances, Frank. You're done. Dry.'

'Dammit!' Frank surged to his feet. 'Don't do that to me!'

'You did it to yourself.' Frank sagged back down again. 'I think we'll look at a three-day stay,' Gunnar went on. 'Unless your old lady will come and get you sooner.'

'You know she won't.'

'It's probably safer here for you anyway,' Gunnar smirked.

Frank sighed. 'You're probably right. She'll have my hide for messing up the store. I'm gonna have to pick up an extra job to pay for the damage. She'll *love* that.'

We left the jail room. Back in the office, Gunnar paused. 'Give me a minute. I've gotta call my wife Sigrid and tell her we have a customer. She handles meals, and she'll step in to monitor the cell while we're out visiting the Grimes brothers. You gotta monitor drunks more than most – you don't want them choking on their own vomit, or deciding that pounding their heads against a wall is preferable to explaining to their wives.'

'I thought the cuffs sorted out Frank's buzz?'

'They may have killed the fun side of the drink, but they'll leave him with a hangover.'

'That sucks.'

'You're not wrong. Once Sigrid is monitoring him, we'll go see the Grimes'.'

Why was I going to see the town's moonshiners? If this town was damp surely a moonshine operation was illegal? Were we arresting them? I was starting to realise that my job involved far more than being an administrative assistant and the prospect excited me. Filing was boring.

Gunnar came out of his office a few minutes later. 'Ready? Sigrid is monitoring the cell so we can go.'

'I am absolutely ready.' I waited a beat. 'What am I supposed to do exactly?'

'Just watch. This is part of your on-the-job training,' he said ambiguously.

He took me around the back of the building to an SUV with the Nomo symbol on the side. I'd seen the police insignia on paperwork: it was a shield with the word 'Alaska' curving at the top and 'Portlock Nomo' at the bottom. The shield was split into four with one symbol on each segment: a moon, a sun, the sea and a tree.

Gunnar swung into the car and I got in the other side. It was weird climbing in on the driver's side then riding as a passenger; I was well aware that Americans drove on the opposite side of the road to us Brits, but it felt strange not having the steering wheel on my side of the car. 'Is it far?' I asked, more to make conversation than a real desire to know the distance.

'A few miles out, but it's in the mountains and the roads are rough.'

Great, off-roading. I was grateful that I'd put on sensible clothes for the day; tottering up a mountainside in heels would have looked ridiculous. When I had some spare money, I'd buy myself a pair of kick-ass boots. The rubber ones everyone wore around here were monstrously ugly, a crime against fashion.

Gunnar flipped on a radio channel and we listened in companionable silence. As we drove, I noted that the town was bigger than I'd first thought. Along the water were various businesses and warehouses, but then we turned up towards the mountain. There were neighbourhoods scattered along the main road; in the distance I could see some bigger, more expensive places looking down on the water, and others higher up where the view would be even better. Most of them were ablaze with lights.

I thought, perhaps ungenerously, that Connor probably had one of the swankier houses. I sniffed; they were nothing compared to the mansions I'd been paraded around at home. The square footage of some of those places had even amazed my socialite mother.

We turned a few times, but my brain kept a mental map. Finally, we turned onto a narrow, dark, dirt road. Tree branches scraped the vehicle, and we bounced along like we were at a rodeo over the huge ruts and bumps. If I were still human, I'd be checking my kidneys the next day to see if they were still in the right place.

The ride seemed to go on for ages, but finally we pulled up to a ramshackle shed twenty-eight minutes after we'd gotten in the car. It seemed to be made of corrugated tin, rusted in places and covered with tree litter and moss. I looked at it warily. Surely this couldn't be our destination? It looked like a good sneeze would make the whole thing collapse.

'This is a residence?' I asked dubiously, wrinkling my nose.

Gunnar barked a laugh. 'It isn't what it seems. Come on, I'll show you.'

I suppressed a sigh. I was rapidly learning that nothing in this town was quite what it appeared to be.

I'd fit right in.

Chapter 6

The woods around the Grimes' residence were dark and creepy. There were lots of unnerving noises that I recognised from the Timmy incident, but I still couldn't tell what was making them. Between the unusual sounds were bone-deep silences that made my skin crawl. I reasoned that it was just the lack of traffic that was disturbing me; I was a city girl used to constant noise. In the arse end of nowhere, there was no traffic, no shouts or laughter, no sirens.

I shivered as I felt the wilderness staring at me and stuck close to Gunnar. He was gentlemanly enough to pretend he didn't notice that the big bad vampire was quaking in her trainers.

We walked up to a door secured on the outside with a padlock and he pounded on the wood. I frowned: if someone was inside, they were locked in. I was about to point that out when a voice bellowed, 'What do you want? We're closed.'

'It's the Nomo. Open up, or I'll huff and puff and blow the door down!' Gunnar winked at me. He was enjoying himself and that helped ease some of my tension. He wouldn't be cracking jokes if we were in danger.

'Gunnar?' Sounds slid out, punctuated by obscenities. 'I'm coming. Give me a goddamn minute,' a gruff voice bit out.

Despite the padlock, the door swung open. How the heck did that happen? Light and warmth poured out framing a man dressed in a vest and a pair of ratty joggers. He had at least three days of beard growth and rumpled greasy hair. He squinted up at Gunnar. 'You here for the akpik 'shine? Just got a new batch made.'

Gunnar bought moonshine? I'd have to be careful when I asked him whether that was legal; I didn't want to imply anything, and maybe I was misunderstanding the situation. Damp towns and moonshine were all gobbledygook to me.

'Nah, Larry. I'm here about Frank Wakefield.'

'Why? What'd he do?'

'He tore up the hardware store. I'm gonna have to tell you not to sell to him anymore. He's banned.'

'That stupid son of a bitch. He never learns,' Larry grumbled. 'Fine. I'll let Lenny know.'

'That's all I wanted to tell you – and I'll take two bottles.' Gunnar paused and looked at me. 'Can't let the wife know.'

I mimed zipping my lips and Larry laughed. 'Give me a sec,' he said. 'I'll go get 'em.'

I was totally out of my element; I'd thought Gunnar was straight-laced but now I wasn't sure what to believe.

Since Larry was no longer standing in the entrance, I peered nosily inside. I spied a large living room with a gigantic TV showing some kind of sports. I looked back at the outside of the building: it was an old twelve-by-twelve metal shed but inside was a spacious, normal-looking house. Well, that was cool.

I'd never heard of any magic like this, but to be fair I'd been pretty ignorant of the supernatural world before I'd been turned – you could probably count the facts I knew on one hand. But I was here to learn and, with my memory, once I learnt a thing it was in the vault forever.

Amused, Gunnar watched me looking at the house. He could see the wonder on my face.

Larry came back and handed him two large bottles of clear liquid. 'Who's the girl?' he asked as if he'd just noticed me for the first time. Rude.

'This is my new assistant, Bunny. She's a vampire.'

'Bunny, huh?' Larry scratched his beard. 'How does a vamp get a silly name like that? I thought they chose fancy, sophisticated names when they turned?'

They did? No one had told me that, and I hadn't read it in my stupid vampire manual. Well, my name was Bunny and I'd gone by it since I was a girl. It wasn't the first time I'd been asked to explain it – far from it. 'I had extra-long ears when I was born. I had to have them cut off, but the name stuck,' I said with a straight face.

Larry squinted at me as he tried to assess the veracity of my statement. 'I call BS,' he said after a beat. 'But I like the story – it had mutilation, so what's not to like?' Jeez. 'So, vampire named Bunny, you like 'shine?'

'I've never had any,' I answered truthfully.

'Hold on.' He returned a few minutes later with a small bottle. 'Local flavour. Akpik – salmonberry if you're from out of town, which I can tell you are from your accent.'

'Akpik,' I said firmly. 'I'm joining the town.'

He smirked. 'Lucky you. Portlock is something else. Let me know what you think. First one's free!' He was just like a drug dealer.

I looked at Gunnar, who smiled benignly. 'Uh, thanks.' I tucked the bottle under my arm.

'Night, Larry,' Gunnar said warmly. 'Thanks for these two. And remember, Frank is banned.'

'Yeah, yeah. I got it. See you Gunnar, Bunny.'

We climbed back into the SUV. Once we were heading back down the mountain, I couldn't hold back my questions any longer – enquiring minds *had* to know.

What the heck was up with this moonshine shit?

Chapter 7

I cleared my throat before I started my rookie interrogation. 'So isn't it illegal to buy and sell moonshine? I thought Portlock was a damp town and people could only get liquor through our office?'

'You'll find that some things fall into a grey area. Legally, the Grimes brothers are a little outside my jurisdiction. Don't get me wrong, if they were selling to minors or peddling in the streets it would be different. But they make a good product and they'll listen when someone like Frank is banned. They provide a service. There could be a lot more problems for us to deal with if they didn't exist. You understand?'

I thought about the little I'd learned in school about the United States and the prohibition era. I imagined that was what he was hinting at: people could get their booze, feel a little dangerous as they did it, but were actually completely under control. Especially if the Grimes brothers were willing to listen to and abide by the Nomo's rules. 'Yeah, I got it,' I replied.

'You'll have to let me know what you think of the akpik,' he said.

'I will.'

The car juddered as we went over a particularly big pothole. The stretch of road was awful and we bounced around so hard I nearly struck my head. 'I guess the local council doesn't maintain these roads,' I muttered.

Gunnar shook his head. 'No, they're privately owned. The Grimes brothers are more focused on earning their income rather than spending it on upkeep.'

That reminded me of the shambolic looking house that was clearly anything but. 'Talking of which, what gives with that house?'

Gunnar laughed. 'I wondered whether you'd ask. The Grimes are witches with a gift for illusion. They don't want anyone breaking in, so they disguise the place.'

'But doesn't everyone know where they live if they're coming to get their moonshine?'

'Nah, they don't do business there. They have a proper shop down the mountain a-ways. But I figured they would have closed up and gone home at this time of night.'

I fondled the small bottle. 'Can vampires even get drunk?'

'Everyone can get drunk if they're determined enough. It just depends on how much you drink and how fast. You'll have to figure out what works for you. Are you a big drinker?'

I thought about it. I had always liked to club and party; a therapist would probably have said I was trying to fill a void caused by my frequently absent parents – or maybe I just didn't have enough hobbies. The thought of being in a dry town had filled me with horror but damp I could handle.

My last experience of alcohol had soured things a little because I'd been drunk when I'd been made undead. Drinking to excess no longer seemed like a good idea, though maybe I was shutting the barn door after the horse had already fucked off. 'I used to be,' I said finally. 'I don't know if I still am.'

'Fair enough.' He didn't pry further and we travelled in silence for a few minutes.

Since we'd been chatting about non-work stuff, and I didn't know when I'd get the courage again, I asked about my dog. 'Gunnar ... would you mind if I brought Fluffy to work sometimes?' I rushed on before he could refuse. 'He's a good dog and he's alone in the house. I feel bad leaving him locked up all the time. He won't be a bother – he can sit at my feet at my desk. He might even be an asset. He's super smart.'

Gunnar glanced at me, his expression serious for once. 'How is he around people?'

'He's great unless I'm threatened,' I admitted honestly.

'If you're threatened, they deserve what they get.' He tapped his fingers on his steering wheel whilst he thought about it. 'I don't mind. I like dogs. As long as he doesn't bite anyone who's *not* threatening you, he's welcome. We'll have him in on a trial basis.'

'Oh thank you so much!' I grinned happily. I'd felt awful leaving him for so many hours with only a brief bathroom break here and there; he'd be happier with me – and I suspected I would be too.

Finally Gunnar pulled into the parking lot behind the Nomo building and turned off the engine. I put my hand on the handle to get out. 'Bunny,' he said softly. I stopped and looked at him. 'You're doing a great job. I know it's not easy without clear-cut rules or instructions, but you seem to take everything in your stride. I just wanted you to know. Great job.'

I felt a stir of pride, the first I could remember in a long time. 'Thanks.'

'Since you're doing so well, I'd like to introduce you to the council. This Friday is our monthly meeting. You won't normally have to go unless you want to or you have to fill in for me, but you should get a feel for it. It's at the mayor's office at 8pm.'

'Sure.' I paused. 'What's the council?'

Gunnar chuckled. 'You've fit in so well I sometimes forget you've only been around supernats a couple of weeks. As you know, Portlock isn't a typical human town, although we have a mayor and law enforcement like any regular town. It is actually comprised of a group of supernaturals of all different types trying to get along and keep a civilized society. In the wider world, all supernaturals are hidden. Everyone keeps themselves and their abilities secret, and it can be a real strain. There are supernatural towns all over the world where we can live openly. We use magic to keep most of the humans away and we live in peace and harmony.' He threw me a grin that told me they did anything but. 'In those supernat towns all the factions have to work together. To facilitate that, we hold monthly meetings.'

'Factions?'

Gunnar nodded. 'Yup. There are the magic users – witches, shamans, druids, necromancers, etc. Then there are the land shifters like Stan, Frank, and Timmy and his mum, Lauretta. The sirens are water shifters, like our Sidnee, and there's a huge variety of them –

mermaids, selkies, kelpies, nymphs, salmon shifters – basically anything you can think of that swims. The vampires are a group too, as are the few humans we have.'

'Like Jack Taylor, the missing guy? He was human, right?'

Gunnar sighed. 'Yeah, like Jack Taylor. We have a few humans who know about supernats – most are related somehow to one, and they've agreed to keep a lid on it. Frankly, we couldn't survive without them because we need people to keep our connection open to the rest of the world. We do like to use Amazon Prime in Alaska.' He winked.

I laughed. 'That makes sense.'

I still wasn't sure precisely how things worked. Jim, the pilot who'd flown me in, had explained that there was a magical barrier around Portlock. At the time, I hadn't thought to ask who or what the barrier protected it from. I had assumed it was from humans, but if there were humans here then maybe I'd been wrong.

'How many other vampires are there in town?' Glancing at someone was no guarantee that you could tell what race they were from – I still had no idea what Gunnar was. And I assumed there were other vampires running around town with daylight charms, the same as me and Connor, so people keeping to the hours of darkness wasn't a sure sign either.

'I'm sure Connor will fill you in.'

Connor. So far he'd given me a welcome basket and insulted me in the street, so the jury was out on him! I was sure he'd check in on me, but when or where was a complete mystery. He'd mentioned that someone would be in touch but no email had arrived. I guessed he was still hip-deep in trying to find the missing Kivuk.

Being so new to the undead life, I'd assumed that someone would be watching over me, but maybe they trusted Gunnar to do it? Was *he* a vampire? He didn't *look* vampiric. 'Are you a vampire, Gunnar?' I asked, hoping the question would spur him to tell me what he actually was.

He guffawed. 'Definitely not! Come on, let's *hop* to it. We got paperwork to complete.'

I was learning that when he said 'we' and 'paperwork', he meant me. I wasn't complaining; at least I wasn't the vampire king's slave. Anything was better than that – even paperwork.

Chapter 8

It turned out that I'd had no phone reception when we were up the mountain – something to remember for next time. Now that I had a signal again, my phone pinged repeatedly. In the hour or so that we'd been gone, there had been a slew of messages. Job one: writing them down and prioritising them.

The night was wearing on and we weren't expecting walk-ins at that hour, so Gunnar locked the door. 'How come you're locking up?' I asked. It was the first time I'd seen him or Sidnee do that.

'Trouble's coming. I feel it in my bones.' He frowned then disappeared into his office. Well, that wasn't reassuring in the slightest.

I started to listen to the messages, making notes as I went. Thanks to Gunnar's cryptic comment, I felt jittery. Most of the calls weren't pressing, but we had a few that required action. There was a possible break in, a fender bender and a fox in a chicken coop. The latter hardly seemed like police work, but I added it to the pile before gathering up my notes.

There was a thud at the glass front door. I looked over – and was momentarily paralysed. I knew that werewolves existed, though I'd never seen one, and there was no doubt what this was. Like in the movie *Underworld*, it was huge, hairy and bipedal. It threw all eight feet of itself against the door again.

My mouth was hanging open – but my fangs were nowhere to be seen. 'Gunnar!' I shouted in panic. 'Werewolf!'

The creature drew back. Next time it hurled itself against door, the frame cracked and the bulletproof glass rattled. Gunnar ran out with two shotguns and a machete. 'Try not to kill him,' he instructed, passing me one of the guns.

'I don't know how to shoot!' I said in panic. 'Brits don't have guns!'

'Well, how do you scare off the bears?'

'There are no bears!'

'Didn't you go clay-pigeon shooting?' he demanded. 'Posh Brits do that.'

'My mum believed in teaching me cross-stitch and singing. Shooting isn't ladylike.'

The werewolf let out a howl that made the hairs stand up on the back of my neck. It wasn't enjoying our banter; it wanted all the attention. 'Come on now, son,' Gunnar called loudly. 'What's the matter? Let's talk this out.'

The voice, when it came, was growling, garbled and dark. 'You ... must ... let... us ... in.'

Oh fuck. Erm, no thank you. Absolutely not doing that. My knees were knocking and I was grateful Gunnar had locked the door. It would hold, right?

'Who are you, son?' my boss demanded. 'Tell me your name. I don't recognise you.'

The werewolf gave a hacking laugh. 'Lower... the... barrier.'

Gunnar tensed. 'Oh boy,' he murmured. 'This isn't good.'

'No shit!'

He passed me the machete. 'There's no time to hit the alarm for backup, by the time they arrive, we'll already be dead. You're a vampire, so you're fast and you're strong. I'll distract him. When you can, cut his head off with this.'

'What? What happened to trying not to kill him!'

'The stakes have gone up,' he barked. 'Be ready! Here he comes!'

'Huff...' the werewolf growled. 'Puff...' Only a short time ago, Gunnar had made the same joke. Now, it was terrifying.

The werewolf pulled back. For a moment I thought he was going to walk off and leave us alone, but then he turned back and ran full force at our door. This time, it banged open.

I screamed.

Chapter 9

I wanted to run like my rabbit namesake, but I held my ground. The werewolf thundered in, not towards me but towards Gunnar.

Gunnar lifted his shotgun. 'One last chance, son! Let's talk this out!'

'Lower ... the ... barrier!' the werewolf snarled and leapt towards him. I heard shots; the werewolf grunted but didn't stop.

Gunnar was using the shotgun to push against the beast, holding the werewolf at distance as the beast's claws and maw tried to savage him. 'Anytime now would be good!' he shouted to me.

Fuck. He needed me. An alien heat suddenly burned in my stomach; it felt like flames were licking at my insides. This was no time for indigestion! I ignored the feeling, pushing it down. Instead, I drew a deep breath, lifted the blade and moved. I leapt onto the desk next to the werewolf and then, with my added height, brought down the weapon with all of my might.

It turned out that all of my might as a vampire was quite a lot of might. The werewolf's head separated from his shoulders with a sickening squelch, and the force of my forward momentum buried the machete into the hard wooden floor. Yikes. Too much might.

The head bounced once then rolled to a stop. For a moment, the werewolf didn't realise he'd been beheaded and his limbs flailed, then his body collapsed in a heap. There was blood everywhere.

Gunnar pushed him away. 'Well,' he sighed, 'this is a mess.'

My heart was pounding. I had *killed* someone. A crazy, murderous threatening someone, but even so. I worked the machete carefully out of the floor. I took several deep breaths, watching the blood drip from the huge weapon.

'Bunny!' Gunnar said, his voice urgent, 'Are you okay? Should I call Connor?'

I frowned at him, 'Why would you do that?'

'All this blood... you must be battling bloodlust?'

I blinked. 'Erm, nope. I'm good.'

His mouth dropped slightly. 'You're good?' His eyes scoured me for signs that I was about to descend into a murderous haze. 'You don't feel like going on a killing spree?' he asked with a hint of amusement. The tension eased from him as he studied my slightly bemused face; he was obviously relieved at what he saw there because he shrugged. 'I guess not.'

'Honestly, I'm fine. No lingering murderous urges. Is that weird?' I still had very little idea about my own kind. The 'manual' I'd received when I'd been turned had lacked any real information, probably in case it fell into any non-magical hands.

'It's unusual, for sure.' Gunnar scrubbed at his beard. 'I've never met a vampire less affected by blood.'

Great: even as a vampire, I was a freak.

I blew out another breath and focussed on the dead body before me. The body that I had *made* dead. Fuck. 'Will I be arrested?' I asked tremulously.

Gunnar's eyes softened. 'Of course you won't. You followed my orders. This was a lawful kill.'

'Will I have to see a psychologist or something?'

He snorted. 'Not unless you want to. This isn't the ped police, Bunny.'

'Ped?'

'Pedestrian – normal, non-magic folk. Sometimes brute force is needed. You did the right thing. You're not going to be punished for it.'

'But there'll be a note on my file?'

He grinned. 'You don't have a file. Relax. We just need to notify Stan we had a rogue, then we'll take it from there. I'll get a body bag, we'll pop the body in that and move it to the morgue.'

'What about the investigation?'

'There is no investigation, Bunny. This werewolf attacked us, we defended ourselves. End of story. There will be no repercussions. You did your job.'

'Are you saying I have a licence to kill?'

'Only when it's warranted, but yes. You're on the side of the law now, and the law will protect you.'

And *that*, I thought, was the motto of bent cops everywhere. I *liked* Gunnar, he'd saved me from hell on earth, but I wasn't stupid. First the moonshine, then this? Who was Gunnar – and which side was he on?

We moved the body to the truck and Gunnar drove it to the morgue whilst I cleaned up the blood. He gave me a potion from a secure vault to use on the carpet and in moments all signs of murder were gone. Handy for both cleaners and criminals.

The front door was still busted but we couldn't do much about that for now. I waited impatiently for my boss to return, keeping one eye on the door in case the crazy fucker wasn't running alone. No other werewolves appeared – but it was the longest twenty minutes of my life. Tomorrow, I was *definitely* bringing Fluffy with me; he could be my emotional support dog, if nothing else.

I surged to my feet when Gunnar walked in. 'They'll start trying to ID the body,' he said.

'Doesn't it, you know, shift back?'

'Nope, but we can still do fingerprints. They're the same for werewolves.'

'Well, that's something because I guess dental records don't match.'

'No siree. A werewolf's muzzle and teeth are very different from human ones.'

'So I saw,' I muttered.

'Okay, so those phone messages?' Gunnar asked calmly.

I stared at him. 'Are you serious?'

'Of course.' He looked amused. 'Did you want to wail and gnash your teeth a while longer?'

I folded my arms. 'Yes, I do. I haven't done nearly enough gnashing.'

He laughed. 'Well do it in the car on the way to our next case. This is a small town but it's supernatural. We're never doing nothing for long.'

He looked through the phone messages quickly. 'We'll go check this one first.' He handed me the one about the break-in, then held up the second one and shook his head in exasperation. It was the fox message.

'This is Gertrude. She hates her neighbour who's a fox shifter. She's been trying to get me to arrest him – or shoot him – for years, and in return he torments her. He runs around her yard in his fox shape until she comes out with the shotgun and starts blasting away. We'll have to visit before we get lots of noise complaints and old Remmy loses his tail.'

'What about the fender bender?'

'They can fill out a report online. They didn't request me directly, so it can't have been serious. The notification is more about their insurance requirements than a request for assistance.' He stood up with a groan. 'Looks like it's gonna be a crazy night. Fetch the black bag again.'

Going to be a crazy night? Like it wasn't already?

Chapter 10

I hurried back to the break room where I'd left the bag after the Frank Wakefield incident. I wondered if we should check on him before we left, especially with the front door less than secure. I put the bag on my desk and turned to pick up my jacket, but before I had a chance to put it on a woman breezed through the busted door. She didn't even blink at its state.

Gunnar came out of the back room carrying a plywood board to secure the door. He grunted a greeting to the lady but clearly he was busy. He held the board up to the wrecked door. It fit perfectly, and I wondered how often the damned thing got busted that he had the right-sized piece to hand. He got his drill out.

'Who are you?' the newcomer demanded. Apparently I was more interesting than the state of the office and Gunnar's DIY skills.

Wasn't that supposed to be my line? I moved to the counter. 'I'm Bunny, the new administrative assistant. Who are you?' I might have sounded a little more aggressive than I intended, but I *had* just been attacked by a werewolf and my adrenaline was still high.

'I'm Martha. Frank's wife. Where's that no-good drunk husband of mine?' She was petite, and her black hair was pulled back in a tight ponytail that hung limply down her back. She was dressed in scrubs, so she probably worked at the local clinic. She looked tired and pissed off.

'He's in the lockup,' I said.

She grimaced. 'Now I'm here, I guess I'd better go see him.' Waves of displeasure cascaded over her features and I felt a moment of sympathy for poor Frank.

'Just a moment, I'll get the Nomo,' I said. Gunnar couldn't hear over the whine of the drill as he fixed up the door, but I wasn't sure if there was a protocol for letting in visitors. I was sure spousal visits were fine, but it was best to check.

Before I could get Gunnar's attention, Martha had walked around the desk and was heading for the lockup. She knew exactly where it was: Frank was obviously a *very* naughty boy.

'Ma'am! Just a minute, please!' I put up a hand to stop her, but she shoved me out of the way. I let her because the last time I'd used my full strength heads had rolled. I didn't want to do that again anytime soon, and definitely not by accident.

I ran to Gunnar and touched his shoulder to get his attention. 'Gunnar, there's a woman here for Frank. She just let herself into the lockup!'

'That'll be Martha,' he sighed. 'Well, he knew this beatdown was coming. I guess I'd better save him.' Gunnar hadn't just put plywood over the door; he'd even installed a new lock. Apparently he was a man of many talents.

'I tried to stop her,' I said lamely. 'But I didn't want to cause an incident by hurting her, especially after the whole...' I made a chopping motion with my hand and grimaced.

Gunnar clapped me on my shoulder. 'Better to stop the tide,' he mumbled. He opened the door to the lockup and a stream of angry Spanish came pouring out. 'Martha, my apologies but visiting time is over. Bunny and I have to head out on a call, so we have to lock up.'

Martha glared angrily at him. 'This is *your* fault. You know he can't handle his drink, yet you still served him.'

Gunnar was unruffled. 'He's a grown man responsible for his own actions. Regardless, he has now been banned.'

She looked at her husband whose head was hanging. 'Good,' she bit out. She glare at her husband. 'This is it, Frank,' she snapped out. 'We got booted out of Bayocean because of your drinking and brawling. Portlock is the last supernat town that would take us. You are *not* ruining this for us. You are *dry!* You hear me, Frank?'

Frank nodded, his head in his hands. He heard her.

'Good because if you go rogue again, I'll be calling the MIB on you.'

Then, as requested, she stormed out. Frank was sitting on the bunk, head in his hands and shoulders slumped. Poor guy, he'd gotten some jabs from Connor and now a few verbal ones from his wife; I bet I knew which had hurt more.

'Sigrid will bring you some food in about an hour,' Gunnar promised.

Frank raised his head. 'Appreciate that.'

'Let's go, Bunny.'

We headed out. 'How will your wife bring the food if you've put a new lock on the front door?'

'She'll come in the back, she always does. The back door doesn't get busted much so I don't have to change the locks so often.' Apparently the caller who'd left a message wasn't the only one who suffered from break-ins. Wonderful.

'Who's the MIB?' I asked Gunnar curiously. 'The Men In Black?' I joked.

'The Magical Investigation Bureau.' His glare told me to take this seriously. 'They call themselves 'special investigators' and they get all sorts of powers we don't like.' His jaw worked, 'We're all but certain that there are black sites specifically built for supernat containment.'

I swallowed hard. Screw the boogeyman. Toe the line or the MIB will get you. And you'll never be seen again. No wonder Frank had blanched.

We went out to the car park; wherever we were going, it was far enough that we needed to drive. I definitely needed my own car, though for now I was happy to ride shotgun. I plunked the black bag in the back seat and climbed in.

As Gunnar cranked the engine, he rang Stan on the hands-free. 'I was sleeping,' Stan answered grumpily.

'Lucky that one of us is. We've got a problem.'

'What?' All traces of sleepiness were gone from Stan's voice.

'The Nomo's office was just attacked by a werewolf. I need you to contact all of yours and account for them. Make sure they're okay.'

The shifter leader was silent for a beat. 'You don't think it was one of mine?'

'No, I don't.'

'Why not?'

'Because his eyes were red and he was growling about the barrier.'

'Oh fuck.'

'That's about the size of it,' Gunnar agreed. 'Check on your werewolves, confirm it's none of them, then we can start trying to identify this wayward one.'

'You got it. I'll call you when I've spoken to them all.'

'Appreciate that.' Gunnar hung up.

'His eyes were red? Is that not normal?' I asked.

'No. Normally a werewolf's eyes are the same colour as their human ones.'

'What does it mean when they're red?'

'Nothing good, Bunny. Nothing good.'

Chapter 11

We drove along the coast for about six miles then pulled up another dirt road. This one wasn't so narrow and it was populated by ten or so small houses. The one we pulled up to was the last in the row, set back in the trees.

Gunnar eyed the trees warily and I looked around as well. The moon was high; though it was only a little over half full, it still cast a good glow of light on the surrounding area. Even so, there were shadows within shadows. I squinted into the bushes, checking for werewolves with red eyes, but I couldn't see anything other than trees, brush, weeds and grass.

As I scanned, a small section of the undergrowth caught my eye. It looked like it had been tamped down a bit, like someone had come in from the woods. A chill ran down my spine and I hastened to catch up with Gunnar.

He knocked briskly on the front door. After a few beats, an old woman answered – she'd clearly been waiting for us. She was elderly, with a full head of white hair and her back bowed by time. She stooped as she leaned on an intricately carved cane. 'It's happening again, Gunnar,' she warned, her voice querulous.

'We don't know that,' he tried to reassure her. 'It could be lots of things.' But he grimaced and I didn't quite believe him. The woman's mouth tightened; she didn't either.

I'd seen the unease on Gunnar's face; no matter what he said, he was worried too. He'd faced a raging werewolf with a shotgun and a grin – so what the heck were they so afraid of?

'Come in,' the old lady said firmly. 'I made tea.'

My ears pricked up. Tea was just what I needed to settle myself after cutting off someone's head. Tea solved everything ... except shitty family dynamics. I'd had many high teas with my mother and they'd solved fuck all. Tea was something we'd used to gloss over the cracks, and it had turned out that it wasn't terribly good as putty.

The old lady led us into a small living room, all flower prints and doilies like something out of a history book. Everything looked *old*. I guessed she didn't believe in modernising, but each to their own and all that.

Before we sat, Gunnar introduced us. 'Mrs Wright, this is Bunny. Bunny, Mrs Wright is our oldest resident.'

'I've been here since 1793,' she said with a smile. Apparently so had her furniture.

I guessed she wasn't human. I tried to school my features, but my eyebrows had already risen of their own accord. I pulled them back down and tried to look unfazed. She chuckled, pleased to have gotten a reaction from me. 'I'm not what I seem.'

Evidently. 'Are any of us?' I asked lightly.

She smirked. 'Rarely. You've got a point there, dearie. Just bear with me one moment.' She popped into the kitchen then returned carrying a silver tea service. Her warning glare as she came in told me an offer of help would not be kindly received; she was obviously fiercely protective of her independence.

We waited patiently as she put the tray down and started pouring. She didn't ask us our preferences; it looked like we were all getting tea, white, no sugar, which was perfect for me. Despite her age, her hands were steady.

When we each held a delicate, flowered teacup and saucer, we settled in to chat. Gunnar looked faintly ridiculous as he tried to handle the fragile cup in his massive hand. She might as well have given him a thimble to sip from. 'Why do you think it's happening again?' he asked.

I was mystified, but no doubt I'd piece it all together – or, more likely, Gunnar would fill in the blanks afterwards. I couldn't help but feel that the werewolf at the office and whatever this was were connected, and I suspected Gunnar did too. For whatever reason, he was downplaying it.

Mrs Wright lowered her cup. 'I heard it out there.' She looked at the wall of her house, staring into the woods behind it.

'You're sure it wasn't an animal?'

She scoffed. 'I know the animals in these parts. It wasn't anything we know.'

'What did it sound like?' Gunnar moved to the edge of his seat, his tea forgotten.

'Impossible to describe.' She grimaced, but tried to describe it anyway. 'A wailing, crying scream. You won't know it until you hear it for yourself.'

'A banshee?' he offered.

'I know a banshee's wail when I hear one!' she objected indignantly.

'Hmmm. You said there was a break-in. What happened?'

'It's better if I show you.'

I reluctantly set down the tea and followed Mrs Wright out of her back door. We crossed the garden, which was surprisingly well-kept for someone who appeared so frail, to the edge of a low fence. She stopped. 'Gunnar, you know I'm at the edge of the barrier here.' She pointed at something with her cane.

I had excellent vision even in the dark, and Gunnar must have had the same because he didn't squint. His intake of breath let me know he saw precisely what I did.

Mrs Wright's cane pointed unerringly to a rock cairn. Even in the dark, I could see that it was a new formation. No moss grew on the stones and there was no dirt; the stones were freshly cleaned and recently placed here. My neck and scalp prickled.

The cairn was a perfectly formed pyramid and at the top was a twisted wooden figure, a crude doll with a sharp stick through its middle. I shivered. No mistaking the meaning.

It was a threat.

Chapter 12

I swallowed hard and took an inadvertent step back towards the house. One raging werewolf was enough for me to deal with today. If a small creepy girl came out of the woods singing a tune, I was swimming all the way back to England.

Gunnar peered through the trees around us. The night was silent, the wind utterly still. Nothing moved – and it should have. I was close to peeing my big-girl pants. He grunted, 'Let's go inside.' He didn't have to tell me twice.

When we got back to the house, we didn't sit back down but went straight to the front door. I looked longingly at my half-finished cup of tea. Next time, I'd know to down it.

As we left, Gunnar told Mrs Wright, 'I'll let the council know.'

'Be quick about it, Gunnar.' I got the feeling that she was used to having the last word.

We climbed into the SUV and drove off. For once, I didn't ask any questions; I found I didn't want the answers.

The next stop was the fox place: Gertrude, Gunnar had called her. When he knocked on the door, a skinny woman with short spiky hair and a pinched face answered it. 'About time, Gunnar!' she bitched. 'That bastard is at it again. This time you need to take him in!'

'Has he done anything illegal?' Gunnar asked with admirable patience. It was clearly a question he'd asked multiple times before.

Her lips pinched further. 'He's trespassing!'

'Is he a fox or a man?'

She spat the words in disgust. 'He's a fox.'

'You know I can't do anything but talk to him. There are no laws to prevent animals trespassing.'

'There should be,' Gertrude huffed. 'If I see him again, I'm shooting him. I can shoot any fox that goes after my chickens!'

'Not in town, Gertrude,' Gunner said firmly, his jovial tone gone. 'We can't have citizens blasting away, and there's houses and families on either side of your yard.' She sank away from him and he softened his tone. 'I'll go talk to him, alright?' She nodded, but the look in her eyes said it wasn't all right in the slightest.

We walked to the fence gate and let ourselves into her backyard. 'Remmy!' Gunnar bellowed. Instantly, a silver fox came trotting over. 'That's enough,' Gunnar snarled. 'You're going to cause Gertrude to shoot someone. Go home, or one day I'll let her take a chunk out of you with her shotgun. I don't want to be called here again. Do you understand?'

The fox blinked its luminous eyes at him and gave a single nod.

'Well, go on then.'

The fox trotted off and slithered under the fence to his own yard, I presumed. 'That seemed easy,' I remarked.

'Until he gets bored again. Let's hope it lasts longer than a week this time.' Gunner's tone was grim. 'One day soon I'm going to get called to a body here – but I don't know whether the corpse will be Gertrude's or Remmy's. I'll drive you home,' he offered.

'Thanks, that would be great.'

When he pulled up to my house he turned to me, his expression serious. 'Well, you've had your first real taste of what it means to work with the Nomo. What do you think? You want me to arrange a transfer for you to somewhere else?'

Panic lanced through me. 'I can't go back!'

'Not to London,' he assured me. 'I wouldn't hand you back to that piece of crap. Flouting the rules like that.' He shook his head in disgust. 'No, if you don't like this work, I'll get you a place in another supernat town. Most aren't quite as ... wild as ours.'

'I don't want to go,' I said softly, and I was surprised at how true that was. 'The werewolf attack thing was a bit of a surprise, but mostly it's foxes and dolls, right?'

Gunnar barked a laugh. 'I won't lie to you; I'd say it's fifty-fifty, kid. You handled yourself well but this position isn't for everyone. Sidnee doesn't ride with me for a reason. But I need a number two, and I think you could be it. If it'll be too much, I'd rather you say so now before I invest my time and heart into you.'

God, but how I wished someone would invest their heart into me. 'It's not too much,' I blurted. 'And it's like anything, right? You get used to it?'

'Some do, some don't.' He assessed me. 'I reckon you will.'

'Good, because I'm all in, Gunnar. You're not getting rid of me that easily. Werewolf schmerwolf.'

Tension eased from his shoulders and he beamed at me with genuine warmth in his eyes. 'I'm glad to hear it, Bunny, real glad.'

I smiled back. I was as stubborn as they come. I'd decided Portlock was going to be my new home and it was going to be, dammit. And if something was going on in this town, I wanted to find out what.

Chapter 13

I lost track of the days that followed in a flurry of mundane events and paperwork. Stan had spoken to his werewolves and the corpse in the morgue wasn't one of his. It remained a John Doe whilst we waited for his prints to be processed. In the movies the results took minutes, but in the real world it took days. Until we had a name, the body and the case were on ice.

I was starting to love my job. As he'd promised, Gunnar spent a lot of time and energy showing me the ropes, and I also enjoyed those few hours when Sidnee and I got to work together because usually we were ships in the night. Between the three of us, we provided twenty-four-hour cover for the Nomo's office.

As far as I could tell, Gunnar didn't need sleep and rarely seemed to go home. His wife, Sigrid, must have been a tolerant woman, though I hadn't yet managed to meet her. I was beginning to doubt whether she existed.

Fluffy loved coming to the office, and catching sight of him always made Gunnar smile a little wider; he really was a dog person. On the second day, a brand-new dog bed appeared next to my desk, together with a bowl of water. Fluffy seemed to enjoy his new job and faithfully followed me around the office as I went to the photocopier and the filing cabinet and back again.

Before I knew it, Friday rolled around and it was time for the supernatural council meeting. I was nervous but trying to hide it. The shifts I worked with Gunnar were long and they never seemed to go quite as planned so I hadn't had much downtime or met many locals, other than the few I'd run across as part of the job. The council would be full of people I didn't know, supernaturals I hadn't yet encountered. Here's hoping Mum's years of etiquette training meant that I wouldn't make a complete fool of myself.

The meeting started at 8pm but Gunnar and I were going in early to set up the snacks and handle the security as people came in. That made me more nervous: I didn't want a machete flung at me. Before Portlock, the most fighting I'd done was to take down a few handsy guys at my old club, and that one time I'd defended myself against the creepy vampire that turned me. Of course, I'd kneed him and then knifed him in the balls, so maybe I had a gift for knife wielding. Who knew?

I had no idea what kind of 'security' I could offer, other than my keen powers of observation, but Gunnar seemed more than capable of handling it. Hopefully I'd only be there to pick up the paperwork slack. If there was one thing you could say about Gunnar, it was that he despised paperwork.

The council room was a standard government room with mottled grey-and-blue carpet, padded plastic chairs and light-grey walls – boring and depressing as fuck. For some reason, I'd expected something *more* from the supernatural council, but I guessed discreet was the supernats' watchword.

Sidnee had laid out refreshments: a large coffee decanter, as well as hot water for tea, thank all the gods. I looked through the sad-sack tea bags and wrinkled my nose: I could at least upgrade those before the next meeting. Maybe these Americans would like tea if they drank a better quality.

Gunnar arrived and had me move to the main doors. He had a table blocking the way in with an assortment of strongboxes under it. The boxes were solid and had some runes painted on them. Whatever they were for, they were heavy duty.

I frowned. 'What's with the boxes?'

He grinned, his white teeth flashing under his copious facial hair. 'For securing weapons.' He winked. 'You're in for a treat.' He really believed in learning by doing, but sometimes his lack of instruction or prior warning was annoying.

This was America; would everyone come in carrying ten guns each? In England, you needed a licence to carry a gun, and it was difficult to buy one.

Here it was much easier; having said that, the only guns I'd seen since I'd arrived were Gunnar's shotguns. Most people probably concealed them.

Gunnar checked his watch. 'Any time now,' he said confidently.

The show was about to commence. I fiddled restlessly with the charm around my neck. My mouth was bone dry because I was so nervous; I was about to meet the leaders of the supernatural community and old insecurities were looming large.

Mum had always put so much pressure on me to impress the *right* people, to be accepted into the *right* circles. All that had happened was that I'd tried too hard and no one had liked me so I'd had a lonely childhood. My best friend had been my nana. As I'd grown up, I'd collected superficial friends but I doubted that any of them had batted an eyelid when I'd fallen off the radar. I'd had no texts, no missed calls, nothing. At best, they'd been fair-weather friends. Now I'd ditched my phone so they couldn't reach me if they tried, but it was hard to feel like it was a loss.

If I didn't fit in here, would I be sent away? How secure *was* my job? I chewed my thumbnail. I couldn't go back to Europe, not for one hundred years. If I did, I'd be imprisoned and nothing more than an indentured servant, given to my slimeball sire as a plaything. All the nopes.

I tried to level my breathing and act cool. Fake it till you make it, right? Hell, I'd beheaded a rampaging werewolf – I could handle anything they threw at me. Probably. I pulled back my shoulders and tried to drown out my mother's voice harping on about the importance of good posture.

'Stand here,' Gunnar instructed, gesturing to a place by his side. 'Us supernaturals are nothing if not predictable. We carry our chosen items around with us like comfort blankets. Your job is to note who brings what so we can give it back at the end of the meeting.' It sounded simple enough and I gave him a thumbs-up.

'Here we go,' he murmured. 'Look lively, kid.'

As a man approached the table, Gunnar raised his voice and announced briskly, 'Mafu Finau, Mayor.'

I searched for his name on the list, feeling a little stressed when I couldn't immediately find it. Why the fuck wasn't the list alphabetical? I bet Gunnar had written it. Nope, paperwork was *not* his strength.

I finally found the name and gave it a tick. The Mayor handed over a long wooden stick about two inches thick and two feet long, not short enough to be a wand, not long enough to be a staff. For all I knew, it could have been his dog's favourite stick. Gunnar placed it in a lockbox and I wrote 'big stick' next to Mayor Mafu's name. Gunnar's lips twitched when he saw my notation.

I took a moment to study and memorise the list; with my superior recall, the next name wouldn't be so panic-inducing.

Mafu was clearly Polynesian, although I didn't know from precisely where, and he was massive; he had to be six-foot five or six, and he was heavyset to go with it. It was hard to tell if his bulk was made of muscle or fat, but either way I wouldn't be sassing him. He was dressed in a suit jacket, shirt, tie, and a native kilt with grass flip-flops on his feet. The skirt thing felt out of place, but maybe it was his formal dress. I was woefully ignorant of indigenous culture, something I'd be rectifying soon. Mafu had manicured fingers and pedicured toes; he was a man who took care of himself – so muscles rather than fat.

'Liv Fox, Magic Leader,' Gunnar announced a few moments later as a woman swept in wearing a smart suit, shoulders back, head at a haughty angle. I found her name instantly and ticked her name off before looking up to see what weapon, if any, she was carrying. Apparently Gunnar was wondering the same thing. He waited, arms folded, face impassive, and simply stared at her.

I took her measure. She was tall and dark skinned, with dark eyes and wide lips in a perfectly symmetrical face. Her beauty was startling; it was rare that anyone was *truly* symmetrical. Atop her head rested a beautifully maintained Afro with a silver streak that arched from her right temple past her ear. It was distinctive and my eyes were drawn to it. For a moment, I couldn't look away from her, but then she caught my eye and smirked. Her dark eyes were ancient, cold, and calculating.

I had a sudden vision of ancient sands and sweltering sun, and I saw her standing on a dais like an empress or a goddess with thousands of people bowing before her. She was dressed in white and gold and wore an elaborate headdress. She met my gaze and smirked again.

I blinked and the vision was gone as suddenly as it had arrived. Was it something that she had sent me – or something else? I shook my head to clear it, trying to ground myself in the room. What had she done to me? I didn't know whether to feel pissed off at the thought or afraid. I settled somewhere in the middle and made sure not to meet her gaze again. Something told me that she was not to be fucked with.

Gunnar pointedly cleared his throat. Liv Fox handed him an object disdainfully and sighed, as if it were all a massive imposition. I saw a flash of blue and black, then Gunnar placed the item in one of the boxes. He looked her over again but this time he seemed satisfied. He stepped aside to allow her in.

He gestured for me to lean in and murmured, 'One magical scarab.'

I dutifully wrote that down next to Liv's name. My head still felt strange so I cast my mind back to the moment when she'd walked in and recalled the exact memory. I re-examined it and focused on Liv: she'd been fingering something in her pocket as she'd looked at me. The scarab. She'd definitely sent me that vision – but why?

Chapter 14

I was still feeling a little dazed when Connor MacKenzie sauntered in. That was enough to shake me out of my weird funk; no way was he seeing me unless I appeared to be in full control of my faculties. He already seemed to have decided I was flighty; I didn't need to give him any more ammo.

Sheer churlishness made me wait until Gunnar announced, 'Connor MacKenzie, vampire leader,' before I ticked off his name. Connor appeared to have made little effort with his appearance and he was still dressed as a lumberjack. Damn the man for looking good in plaid, but you'd think he'd have at least made an effort for the council.

Without being prompted, he pulled a handgun from the back of his jeans and a knife from his boot. I recorded them as Gunnar placed the weapons in a different box. When I looked up, Connor had already gone into the main room without so much as a 'hey, how are you doing?' to his latest vampire. I guessed he was one of those hands-off leaders. That was fine; I didn't want his hands anywhere near me anyway.

I could hear voices in the council chamber and they didn't sound happy. My anxiety spiked. I tried to focus on my task. The shouting wasn't anything to do with me. Hopefully.

Next in line was the most ethereal woman I'd ever seen. Thin and lithe, she moved with a sinuous grace. Her skin was a warm brown but she had the palest sea-blue eyes; her hair was also blue, though a darker shade, and I wondered if it was natural or dyed that colour. It was clear she was not human and never had been – no human moved like that. She had an alien poise and fluidity like a professional dancer's. I tried not to stare but it was hard: she really was something else.

'Calliope Galanis,' Gunnar announced. 'The siren leader,' he murmured to me.

Her hand floated out and deposited something into Gunnar's hand. He held it up so I could see before dropping it into her box. I wasn't quite sure what to write: 'pretty shell' didn't sound professional so I upgraded it to 'pearlescent shell'. She swayed her way in, and her two attendants, a male and female, each handed over two-foot-long tridents for the box.

Fricking tridents! That was insane. I held on to my poker face with effort. Who carried actual tridents around with them? Despite their length they disappeared into the box, and I looked at it sharply. They shouldn't have fit. I guessed I had to leave logic at the door along with any weapons.

There was a scuffle and a few sharp words inside the council room. Gunnar's eyes narrowed and his booming voice rang out. 'Stop that or you're out for the night!' The noise stopped instantly; it seemed that no one wanted to fuck with Gunnar.

Next up was Stan, the shifter leader, the man I'd met during the fight in the street. He'd made an effort to clean up for the meeting. He was tall and well built, with brown hair and piercing hazel eyes; he looked like he had dual heritage, with dark skin and exotic features. Like Connor he wore jeans, though he'd paired them with a long-sleeved dark shirt. The shirt was tucked in and showed off his muscular chest that tapered down to a slim waist and hips. When my eyes made it back up to his face, I found that he was smirking at me. My cheeks warmed.

This time when Gunnar cleared his throat it was directed at me. I mumbled, 'Sorry.'

Luckily, my boss looked amused. 'We'll try this again. Stan Ahmaogak, shifter leader.'

I marked him off and raised my head in time to see Stan looking me over with the same blatant interest I'd accidentally shown him.

Gunnar raised his eyebrows at Stan, tacitly asking for his weapon of choice. Stan shrugged. 'None. *I* am a weapon.' Then that smirk again. No weapon, no entourage; either he was cocky or he was dangerous, perhaps both, though Connor had slammed him into a wall with relative ease.

The queue had dwindled to one. The last person was a bulky indigenous man but, unlike Mafu he wasn't dressed in traditional garb; he wore camouflage trousers and a tight black top that showed off corded muscles. He looked to be flirting with forty; his clear brown skin had a few lines and his short black hair was flecked with silver. He was average height – and he was *solid*. He looked like he could move a mountain if he so desired. There was an energy about him that impressed me, and I wondered what kind of supernatural he was – a werewolf, maybe? His eyes were piercing and I knew that, like me, he saw everything. Damned hyper-awareness.

Gunnar pulled out the last lockbox, this one larger than the others. 'Thomas Patkotak, human leader.'

Human? Of all the people that had come through, I'd have pegged this man as a supernatural. He was focused and intense, and I sensed he was as dangerous as those who had magic. I dutifully ticked his name and waited for him to divest his gun or whatever he carried.

Sure enough, he pulled a handgun from the back of his jeans. I wrote it down and went to put down my pen, but then he pulled out two more guns from places I'd missed, maybe from under his jacket. He didn't stop: he pulled several wooden stakes, three long silver knives, ten throwing knives, a curved blade – a sickle? – two blades that I'd have to ask Gunnar about, and a hatchet. Once he'd finished he held up his hands.

Gunnar looked him over thoughtfully and raised an eyebrow. Thomas grinned and pulled two more knives. Gunnar huffed. With an unrepentant grin, Thomas pulled out a small handgun from his boot. I looked at the pile of weaponry in the box and gawked.

Gunnar double-checked my list. 'Not a hatchet, a tactical tomahawk. And yes, that was a sickle. These knives...' he pointed at the two strangely curved blades '...that look like claws are karambits. The big knife is a Bowie, and that one is...' he picked it up and examined it for a minute '...some type of modified kukri.'

Thomas nodded and looked impressed at Gunnar's knowledge.

I corrected my list and Gunnar placed the weapons one at a time into a strong box. Once he was done, he locked it and put the keys in his pocket. Thomas nodded again and moved inside. Despite the fact that he was now unarmed, he still felt like one of the most dangerous people in the room.

'Why does he have so many weapons?' I asked curiously as Gunnar completed his remaining tasks.

'He's a hunter.'

With all of those weapons, it begged the question, 'What does he hunt?'

Gunnar's smile was grim and humourless. 'Us.'

Chapter 15

After the last council member had entered, we screened about twenty or so locals who wanted to attend. Apparently the meetings were thrown open to keep the proceedings transparent. Only one or two of the locals had weapons; the rest seemed to have left theirs at home. It was a shame the council members weren't as smart – but then they would have missed out on all that posturing and drama, which they'd seemed to enjoy so much.

Gunnar and I went into the council chambers, where everyone had descended like vultures on the food and drinks. My nervousness returned full force: my boss was about to parade me like a prize pony, just like Mum used to do. I wondered how long his introductory speech would last; Mum's had always seemed interminable.

He smiled kindly. 'I'll make it fast then you can get a snack and sit in the back. No one will even notice you.' He locked the door into the council chamber, for security no doubt, but I suddenly felt constrained. I was locked *in* as much as any others were locked *out*.

I smiled back wanly. 'Thanks. I'd be grateful if you could get it over with quickly.'

He chuckled. 'Come on, little rabbit, let's end your suffering.'

I followed him up front to a seventies' style wooden dais. Gunnar fiddled with the mic for a moment until a loud screech had everyone covering their ears in pain. 'Well, that was one way to shut you all up,' he said. There were a few grins in response; he knew his audience.

Gunnar nodded at Sidnee, which was her cue to start taking the minutes, then hit the dais with a small gavel. The noise resonated through the room. 'I call to order the monthly meeting of the Portlock Supernatural Council. Presiding, Mayor

Finau. Temporary speaker, council member Gunnar Johansen. Minutes by secretary and treasurer, Sidnee Fletcher.'

He adjusted the mic a little. His voice was so loud and booming that I couldn't be the only one who wished he wouldn't use it at all. 'Before we begin, I wanted to introduce my new assistant.' He looked at me and gestured for me to step forward.

'This is Bunny Barrington, and she's working in the office and the field. She's a new vampire, so don't be tempting her with any spilled blood tonight.' There were a few titters from the crowd at what was obviously meant to be a joke. I caught Connor's eye; he was frowning and looking at me intently. Well, *almost* everyone thought it was a joke.

'She's from London, England, so go easy on her with your wild Alaskan ways.' Gunnar's tone was jovial but there was a hint of warning in his eyes: *go easy on her, or else*. It warmed me; nobody had had my back like that in a long time, not since my nana had passed.

There was a polite round of applause and Gunnar dismissed me. That was it? God, it had been virtually painless compared to the rambling introductions I'd endured at Mum's hands.

I walked away from the dais with a sigh of relief, grabbed a pastry and sat in the back row behind Sidnee to watch the room. Gunnar went through some council business first and, just like he'd said, no one was even looking at me. I sat and munched quietly, a cup of tea cooling on the empty chair next to me.

I tuned in again as Gunnar started talking about the missing people. 'I'm sorry to say that we are no further along in finding Jack Taylor, though I have some news to give you in a moment that might have further bearing on the issue.' He sounded grim. 'Connor, do you have any update on Kivuk Sakari's disappearance? He was last seen at his residence. No further sightings have been documented.'

Connor stood up. Obviously frustrated, he said, 'Nothing further to add. I have spoken to all of my people. Kivuk hasn't been seen.' His jaw worked for a moment but then he sat back down.

Gunnar licked his lips; he looked almost nervous. 'Mrs Wright appears to have had a visitor to the edge of the barrier. She says she heard it.' Noise exploded into the room and Connor surged to his feet. Gunnar banged his gavel and reluctantly the crowd settled. 'I know this is scary news, especially with Jack and Kivuk missing. It's a reminder to be vigilant, more so than ever.'

'Are there any rips in the barrier?' Stan asked grimly.

Gunnar shook his head. 'None yet. I undertook a full sweep after my meeting with Mrs Wright and I didn't see any tears or fissures.' He paused. 'But in some areas it looked ... thinner.'

People started muttering again and the room filled with a tense hubbub. Finally one of the townsmen, a man called Ahote, raised his hand. Gunnar nodded at him. 'What proof does she have?' Ahote shuffled as he spoke; he looked restless, worried.

Gunnar scratched his jaw and looked like he wanted to be somewhere else. Anywhere else. He cleared his throat. 'There was a cairn with a stick doll perched on top at the edge of the barrier. It was speared through.' He cleared his throat again. 'There's more. Bunny and I were attacked in the Nomo's office by a werewolf. Stan has confirmed none of our werewolves are missing.'

The silence that fell was absolute until Connor broke it. 'You think the mutt came through the barrier?'

'Either that, or someone is making new werewolves in town.'

The room filled with voices again. Connor spoke over them. 'Do we have an ID for the werewolf? I presume it's on ice now?'

'Bunny dispatched it,' Gunnar confirmed. Everyone swivelled to look at me, their disbelief obvious. I gave an awkward finger wave and they turned back to Gunnar. 'No ID yet,' he said, 'but we should get the results of the prints any day now.'

'What do we do?' someone shouted over the noise.

Gunnar grimaced; he didn't have a plan of action. 'For now, nothing. We watch, we assess, we stay vigilant. Stay inside the barrier and make sure everyone you know does the same. I want it clear to all factions that no one is to go wandering about. Be alert; be safe. I'm not imposing a curfew.' The unspoken 'yet' was clear.

Chapter 16

Gunnar changed the subject. 'On to other matters. Stan, you're up.'

The shifter leader took the podium, looked around then addressed someone in the crowd. 'We agreed to hold off until the fish plant raised their prices on salmon, but *Smoky Bay* is out fishing.' He was looking at one of the seats but I couldn't tell at whom.

A man's voice answered, 'We don't have the funds like PBE. We *have* to fish.'

'I'm talking,' Stan growled. 'Wait your turn. If we don't work together, we'll all lose money. If we don't get them over 375, we'll all be tightening our belts.' Stan nodded. 'Now I'm done.'

There was further muttering in the crowd, but this time the noises were of assent. Gunnar's eyes were roving over them all, poised for trouble.

The mayor took the stand. Stan stood to one side but didn't leave the stage; I realised that was probably why Gunnar was presiding over this meeting – the mayor was involved in this disagreement.

Mayor Mafu spoke firmly. 'Smoky Bay is just starting out. We have to fish and sell at whatever price we're given or we'll go under. Asking us to hold out is killing the business.'

There were a few 'hear, hears' in the crowd. I leaned forward. 'What is going on?' I whispered to Sidnee.

She turned and whispered back. 'Fish. Apparently, the processing plant isn't giving a good rate on gutted and gilled salmon per pound, so they want to drive up the price artificially by not bringing them fish.'

'Oh.' I tuned back in. The debate was getting a little more heated.

Stan was yelling, and Calliope and Liv had joined in. Was everyone involved in the fishing industry here? I was going to have to bone up on my fish knowledge; I knew a little about caviar, swordfish and bluefin tuna, but apart from that I wasn't much of a pescatarian – I leaned towards juicy steaks. I guess that would have to change since I was evidently living in a fishing village.

'I'm not pulling my fishermen,' Mafu said firmly. 'We'll keep fishing.' He folded his arms across his vast chest. His feet were spread wide; grass skirt or not, it was clear he meant business.

Stan squared up to him. Tempers were fraying. The two big men were chest to chest yelling at each other, then Stan prodded Mafu. Tension ratcheted up. A few men and women in the crowd were standing up now, and virtually everyone was shouting. 'You're killing our economy,' Stan growled.

'I have to feed my family!' the mayor yelled back.

'Feed 'em fish, you line-jumping bastard,' Stan bit back sharply.

'Enough!' Connor roared. 'The barrier is weakening, we have people missing, we have a rogue werewolf attacking people – and you're arguing about fucking *fish*?'

Stan glowered. 'You would, too, if it was your livelihood. Just fuck off and polish your wood. Leave us to discuss real men's work.'

This *wasn't* what I'd expected of a council meeting.

Connor snarled and his fangs flashed. The Nomo banged the gavel again. 'Meeting dismissed.' Everyone ignored him and continued arguing. Stan had turned his attention back to Mafu and the two were fronting up to each other. Stan pushed Mafu, Mafu pushed back.

Gunnar rolled towards them. 'Stop,' he barked. They didn't. Stan reared back and threw a punch; that seemed to be like waving a flag, and fights broke out all over the room. I stayed well back.

'What *is* Gunnar?' I asked Sidnee. 'He said he's not a vampire, but he's strong.' He certainly wasn't intimidated by the two big men fighting in front of him.

'Demigod,' she answered.

'You're joking!' I scoffed.

She shrugged. 'Nope.'

Huh: I hadn't even known that demigods were real. I guess there was a lot I didn't know was real. 'So Connor's not in fish?' I asked.

'Nah, he's in logging.'

'Logging?' I asked. 'Like an actual lumberjack?'

Sidnee smirked. 'It's not exactly like you are picturing.'

I grinned and sang the line, '"He's a lumberjack and he's okay"!'

She looked at me blankly. 'What?'

'*Monty Python*,' I said. She still looked blank. 'British comedians,' I explained. 'They did a sketch about lumberjacks. I'll play it for you some time.' I brought the conversation back to Connor. 'Anyway, how do you know what I'm picturing?'

'Nowadays lumberjacks use chainsaws and heavy machinery. You're picturing a sweaty guy with an axe.'

I was – and without a shirt, too. And maybe some high heels. I grinned.

'That one,' she tilted her head toward Connor, 'owns the company. He isn't swinging an axe anymore.'

More's the pity; he'd look good doing that. 'Does everyone else in town work with fish?' I asked curiously, because there certainly seemed to be a lot of people shouting about it.

'We have three main industries – fishing, logging and mining. The mining isn't so big, and the shifters are all over it. But fishing? That's the biggest.'

I looked up in time to see the mayor sail into some chairs as people scrambled out of the way. Snarling, Stan rumbled in after Mafu, then they were rolling around on the floor. Individual fights were escalating in the crowd, and I could suddenly smell blood in the air.

Gunnar looked over at me. *Stay back,* he mouthed to me. I gave him a thumbs-up. Looking relieved that I wasn't going to wade in, he and Connor joined the melee. Gunnar grabbed Stan and Connor pulled up the mayor. 'Enough!' the Nomo bellowed.

Like a switch had been flicked, the whole room fell deathly silent. The brawlers paused mid-punch and everyone froze. Was it out of fear or, as a demigod, did Gunnar have some other sort of magic?

'I said, meeting *adjourned*,' he ground out. 'You'll come pick up your weapons at the office tomorrow. I'm not giving them back now when you're acting like a bunch of hotheads. I'll call you each with an appointment. And don't you dare take this out into the streets or I'll haul your asses in.'

The threat hung in the air. Most people looked a little shamefaced, though Stan was still flushed with anger as he shrugged off Gunnar and stormed out. Liv and Calliope were glaring at each other, both of them with messed-up hair and their clothing askew. Slowly and sullenly, the crowd dispersed.

It was safe to say my first council meeting was a total shambles. On the plus side, I needn't have worried about being introduced to the community; after that shit show, no one would be thinking about me.

'So what was decided?' I asked Gunnar once everyone had filed out except Sidnee and me.

He frowned darkly, 'Absolutely nothing, unfortunately. Mark my words, someone is going to get hurt over this one.'

I felt a shiver of foreboding run down my spine. Something told me he was right, but I didn't know whether he was talking about fish or the barrier...

Chapter 17

The next day, Sidnee invited me over for dinner. It was supposed to be my first night off and I felt a warm glow at the thought of spending it with a friend. I hadn't had a real friend in – well, ever. I'd had social friends, work friends and some girls I wanted to be friends with, but I was firmly discouraged from those because they weren't socially acceptable enough for my mother. She wanted me to associate only with people a degree above us in the social hierarchy. Her narrow views had constricted my social circle to a group of one: me.

She certainly wouldn't have approved of me befriending a half-blood mermaid who worked for a living – scandalous! There again, she probably wasn't that crazy about a vampire daughter who was a failed waitress, either. Distance helped me care less about her views, that and the fact that she and Dad hadn't helped me escape London when I'd asked them to. Dad's business empire relied on a good working relationship with the Vampire King of Europe, so they had encouraged me to embrace my one hundred years of servitude. Weeks later, it still stung that they had chosen Dad's business and wealth over me, their only daughter.

I was surprised when tears sprang to my eyes. Maybe I wasn't over it as much as I pretended to be. I swiped at them, then drank a cup of warmed blood, swallowing the dark liquid down over the lump in my throat.

Fluffy gave a soft whine and pressed his body against my legs in comfort. 'I'm okay,' I promised, giving a shaky laugh. 'I just have shitty parents, I guess. When I moved out, I thought my opinion of them had already hit rock bottom, but it seems there were still some more depths to plumb.'

I stroked his head. '*Now* we're at rock bottom. I'm their only daughter and they're supposed to put *me* first. I know that sounds selfish, but all the time I see these parents who would do anything for their kids and mine wouldn't even lend me the plane fare to get here.'

I dashed at the next few tears. 'I'm okay.' I repeated firmly. 'It doesn't matter – *they* don't matter. I'll probably never see them again.' Why did saying that out loud hurt my chest so much?

'Let's go to Sidnee's,' I said in as light a tone as I could manage. I put a collar on Fluffy and looped his lead around my neck so I could carry it hands-free. He was so well-behaved that he didn't really need it, but I wanted one with me just in case. Then, needing to be prepared for every eventuality, I grabbed a couple of poo bags and shoved them in my pocket.

It wasn't hard to find Sidnee's house; like me, her accommodation was provided by the Nomo's office. She lived only three doors down from me in the row of houses that the council had arranged for its workers. The only difference between our places was that my white-painted house had a bright-blue door and her door was sea-green.

When I knocked, she opened it with a welcoming smile. 'Hey, Bunny, Fluffy, come on in!' Holding the door open, she stepped back. My first social visit with someone in ages. Here's hoping I didn't fuck this up; I could really do with a friend that wasn't a canine.

Sidnee's house was full of pictures, cushions and blankets, making it cosy and charming. In contrast, mine looked sterile and barely lived in. I decided right then that when I received my first paycheck I'd invest in some home décor. I wanted my place to feel like this – like a home.

'I've made some Filipino food,' she said as I kicked off my shoes. 'I hope you like it.'

'I'm sure I'll love it,' I said honestly. My one vice was that I was a total foodie and I liked to try new things – plus it smelled absolutely divine.

Fluffy clearly felt the same because he kept licking his lips and sniffing the air. I gave him a ruffle. 'I don't know how she feels about dogs eating her food, so be patient,' I whispered to him. 'I'll feed you at home.'

I should have given him dinner before we left. Score minus one for my pet-caring abilities.

'I'm more than happy for him to have some,' Sidnee announced loudly. 'I've cooked enough for a small army. Portion sizes are my weakness. Fluffy can absolutely try anything that's not too spicy!'

I guess I hadn't whispered quietly enough. Fluffy gave a happy wag and both of our stomachs growled loudly at the same moment, making Sidnee laugh. 'Poor portion sizes or not, I guess I won't have leftovers!' she said.

I sat at the table and Fluffy leaned against my legs. Sidnee named the dishes as she set them down: first a huge bowl of noodles with vegetables and maybe chicken, 'pancit'; then a veritable stack of chicken pieces on the bone, 'Chicken adobo', and finally a plate heaped with homemade eggrolls, 'lumpia.'

She wasn't wrong about her portion sizes but I was up to the challenge and I ate until I thought I would burst. Fluffy enjoyed his own plate of deboned chicken; when he was finished, he rolled on his back, all four legs in the air, and promptly went to sleep.

It was nice to see him so content. When I'd rescued him, he'd been a terrible state. How anyone could have neglected an animal like that was beyond me.

I pushed back my plate. 'That was the best food I've eaten in months. Thank you so much. Let me help clear the table.'

'Oh no! You're a guest.'

'Please, let me help!'

Sidnee relented, and I stacked the plates and carried them into the kitchen. We talked companionably whilst we washed the dishes together. 'Is Fluffy a purebred German Shepherd?' she asked. 'He's very handsome.'

'Thanks; I rescued him from a huge commercial bin. Someone had thrown him away and locked the lid.' That thought still disturbed me.

'Oh my! How awful. People can be so cruel!'

The image of my sire, Franklin, flashed into my mind. He had kicked Fluffy when my dog dared to defend me and sent him slamming into a wall. At the time Fluffy had been so thin and emaciated that I feared Franklin had killed him. My mind reared back from the violent memory and I pushed it away.

I'd been silent too long and Sidnee was looking at me with concern. 'Yes, they can,' I agreed finally. Whatever had passed across my face had raised further questions but I saw her choose not to ask them.

'So, I saw you admiring Stan, the shifter leader, at the meeting,' she said instead.

'He's pretty good looking,' I responded non-committally.

'Yeah, he is. He was also admiring you right back.'

I flushed. Flattering as that was, I'd soured a little on men. I'd picked up my sire at a club. Things had been getting hot and heavy, and he'd suggested we go outside. There, in a dank, dark alley, he'd turned me. Later, I discovered he'd been paid £50,000 to break vampire law to do it. Turning someone who was unwilling was apparently a big no-no but, as the son of the Vampire King, Franklin felt the laws didn't apply to him. Evidently his father had agreed, because the prick had gotten away with it scot-free.

I'd have to vet any new man thoroughly before I'd even think of dating again. And handsome as Stan was, his temper had put me off. Even so, I could still look even if I didn't touch. 'Was he?' I asked airily.

'Yep. Connor MacKenzie kept watching you, too.'

Did he? I scoured through my memories of the council shitshow. Anytime I'd looked at Connor he'd been frowning, plus, he'd insulted me twice already. He clearly hadn't warmed to me – either that or he hated being saddled with me as a new vampire and I was a millstone around his neck.

'I guess in a way he's my boss. I don't really know what being the vampire leader entails, but he's just keeping an eye on me. So, what about you?' I asked pointedly. 'Are you seeing anyone?'

Sidnee blushed prettily. 'I've been out twice with someone, but I don't know if anything will come of it.'

'Ooh, tell me more!'

She told me a little about her dates as we finished clearing up then retired to her sofa with glasses of wine. She passed me one of her many blankets and I sat with it on my knees. Fluffy jumped up next to me. 'Fluffy!' I said, scandalised. 'Off you get! Just because it's fine at home doesn't mean it's okay elsewhere!' He hung his head and started to get off.

Sidnee laughed. 'It's fine. Up you get!' Fluffy finished climbing down, gave her a grateful lick then climbed up next to me again.

'I'm so glad you invited us over, Sidnee,' I told her. ' It's been wonderful.' Perhaps the sip of wine had loosened my tongue, because I blurted out, 'I've never really had a girlfriend who didn't have an agenda.'

She looked at me with sympathy. 'That sucks. I'm happy to be your first one, though.'

I smiled at that. I wanted to try my best to be a good friend – friends asked after each other, right? 'You aren't off the hook! Tell me more about your guy. You told me about the dates, but how do you feel when you're with him? Is the spark there?' I took another sip of my wine and looked at her expectantly.

She blushed a little. 'You could say that! He's—'

My phone rang and at the same moment hers beeped with a text message. I hastily pulled mine out of my back pocket and looked at the screen. Gunnar. A sinking feeling in my gut told me that my day off was about to come to an abrupt end.

I hurriedly swiped to accept the call. Gunnar's gruff voice was grim. 'I'm sorry to interrupt your evening but I need you to get down to the harbour. There's been a murder.'

Chapter 18

'There's been a murder,' I said as soon as I hung up.

'Apparently so.' Sidnee's tone was grim. Gunnar must have texted her the same message. 'Let's go.'

My first thought was that Stan and Mafu's argument must have escalated, then I wondered if there'd been another werewolf incident. I quickly dismissed that – Gunnar had said there'd been a 'murder' not an 'attack'.

I looked down at my jeans and a jumper – I had no idea what one wore to a crime scene. Sidnee pulled on her rubber boots as I stared at my white trainers. 'Should I stop by my house and grab my boots?' I asked her.

'Yeah, that's a good idea, but quickly.' The bubbly open expression she usually wore had been replaced by grim determination, like she was bracing herself for something. It suddenly occurred to me that, unlike me, she probably knew the victim. That sucked.

I ran to my house and pulled on the borrowed gumboots and a waterproof jacket. I considered taking Fluffy, but since we were going to a murder scene I decided to leave him at home. 'Sorry, bud,' I murmured. 'You'd better sit this one out.' I flicked on the TV, made sure he had water and headed back out.

Sidnee was waiting for me and together we jogged down to the harbour, urgency thrumming through us both. It was dark, but the lights at the dock were bright and the tiki torches had been lit to ward off the mosquitoes. We could see Gunnar's massive form towards the end of the dock and a dark form lying in front of him.

Before we got to the scene, I smelled the coppery tang of blood. It had an odd edge to it. I expected my fangs to drop but nope. My fangs were the worst – they seemed to only drop when I *didn't* expect them to, not when I did like when I smelled food. I was a terrible vampire. Was it something you could fail? Maybe they'd stake me for being defective. Great, something new to worry about.

Sidnee looked over at me, eyes wide in sudden panic. 'Are you okay?' she asked. 'All that blood...'

'I can smell it but I'm fine,' I reassured her.

Eyes wide, she shouted to Gunnar, 'Bunny can smell the blood!'

Gunnar turned and flashed her a grin, 'Don't worry. She's good with blood, aren't you Bunny?'

I gave him a thumbs up, 'All good.'

Sidnee blinked, '*How* are you good? You should be going into a murderous rage right now. You're still so new as a vamp.'

I shrugged helplessly, 'I don't know. I guess I'm a bit weird, even for a vampire. Honestly, you don't need to worry about me. I'm fine. Let's just focus on that poor guy.' I gestured to the prone body.

Frankly, we had more important things to worry about than my liquid diet. Someone was flat out behind Gunnar – and he was very, very dead.

Chapter 19

Freak or not, I was grateful that Gunnar was still willing to let me onto the scene. He gave me a pair of booties to slip on and some gloves, all the while shooting me sidelong glances to check I was still okay.

He clapped me on the shoulder as I got closer to the body. 'You're doing great,' he assured me, which pulled a smile from me. The truth was I had something to add here. I was very observant and my memory was second to none; I could memorise the scene not just visually but with my other senses, too.

I took a deep breath. Blood, yes, but there was something else scenting the air, like a bad taste fizzing at the back of my throat. It might be nothing. Then again, it might be something.

If Gunnar sent me away I'd be beside myself wondering what I was missing, not because I was especially morbid but because I desperately wanted to be an asset to the department. If he made me leave every time blood was involved, I wouldn't be a very valuable resource – exceptional filing skills aside.

Gunnar held up a hand. He was still blocking the view but the scent of blood pervaded the night air together with that mysterious tang. 'Stop just there,' he instructed gruffly. 'I haven't photographed the scene. I got here only a minute or two before you arrived.'

He stepped aside so that we could see the body. My first impression was a wave of blood – it looked like buckets of the stuff had been flung around. Did one body have *that* much blood in it? The end of the dock was soaked in it, the wooden boards saturated.

Then I saw the body itself. It was nightmarish, twisted so strangely that I could barely work out what I was looking at. It certainly wasn't just human: for a start, there was fur.

My eyes must have been bulging as I stared because Gunnar noticed. 'Werewolf,' he said abruptly. 'Partially shifted.'

I'd only seen one werewolf, but it had looked far less nightmarish in its complete form than this human–werewolf mashup.

Its face – it was hard to think of the body as a him, though it was undoubtedly male – was so contorted that I doubted even his own mother would have recognised him. One arm was mostly human, but the other was long and hairy with a huge hand-like paw and claws. His legs were far too muscular and covered in dark wiry hair. The proof that he was male also remained partially shifted; that was a sight I'd happily have bleached from my brain if I could.

A gift of vampirism was my excellent eyesight, so the next thing I noticed were the slashes all over the body – better to focus on those than the half-mutated schlong. If I concentrated on counting then I wouldn't be overcome by horror. I figured that breaking down and sobbing at the scene meant I wouldn't be invited to another one, so I tried hard to calm myself by counting the wounds, focusing on those rather than the fact that what lay before me was a man who had probably loved, who had a mother and father who would grieve.

'Thirty-three,' I mumbled with a frown. That was a lot. There had been a lot of hate here. The wound across the throat had been so deep it had almost severed the head. The amount of blood sprayed around told me that the deadly wound had probably been the last.

'What's that?' Gunnar asked.

'Sorry, I didn't mean to interrupt your thoughts. I just counted thirty-three wounds, though there may well be more that I can't see on his back.'

Gunnar was looking at me with new interest. 'Thirty-three, give or take?' he asked faintly.

'No give or take,' I said firmly. 'There are definitely thirty-three visible wounds but as I said, there could be some on the other side too.'

Gunnar stepped closer to the body, a little way into the pool of blood. He knelt to check for a pulse and I gaped. Surely *nothing* could survive an attack like that? He saw my incredulous look. 'Standard procedure,' he explained. 'You *always* verify death. You'd be surprised what people can survive, especially supernats.' Chastened, I nodded.

He sighed. 'But not in this case.' He stood up. 'Don't touch anything, I'm gonna grab my forensics kit and camera. We'll start documenting the scene.'

'How did it get called in?' I asked.

'An anonymous tip.'

'The murderer?'

'Most likely,' Gunnar agreed. 'Anyone else would have stayed around to give a statement – unless they were a terrified witness.'

'Male or female?' I asked.

He shrugged. 'With AI voices so accessible these days, that doesn't mean a thing – but for what it's worth, it sounded male. Don't touch anything,' he reiterated as he walked away.

Sidnee and I stood frozen in place. Despite being in the open, the stench of blood and death was overwhelming. Neither of us wanted to look at the body for too long, let alone get any closer to it, but

I found it hard to look away. My brain kept trying to make sense of it, like it was a ghoulish puzzle. It was like a train derailment or a car accident, you just couldn't look anywhere else, so I used the time to examine and memorise everything I could see.

The water looked motionless but having Sidnee beside me was a reminder that it probably wasn't as still as it appeared. Mermaids, selkies and all sorts might lurk in its depths. I shivered. The body was close to the water; was there something down there waiting to claim us if we stepped too close?

Curiosity killed the cat, and maybe it would kill the Bunny too, because I found myself inching closer to the water's edge. I peered over the edge of the dock – and immediately let out a blood-curdling scream as I met something's eyes.

Chapter 20

'Holy shit!' I screamed. Sidnee dashed to my side as a trident appeared from nowhere in her hands.

The huge yellow eyes in the water blinked at me, totally unbothered by my cussing. I couldn't tear my eyes away. The thing in the water was huge and it *glittered*! It was like an eel, but the size and length of a whale at least. It was swimming calmly and idly under the jetty. I was surprised the water was deep enough for it, but it must have been because now it was under the boards below our feet. My sluggish heart gave a firm thud as I waited for the *Jaws* moment when the sea-beast leapt up and crunched Sidnee, me, the body and the boards, all in one fell swoop.

Sidnee let out a relieved giggle. 'It's okay!' she called back to Gunnar, who was racing back to us. 'Bunny just saw the water dragon.'

'The water dragon?' I repeated dumbly, still watching the flash of glitter through the slats of the board.

'Yeah, they're ... a guardian of the sea. Nothing to be feared. I imagine they sensed the blood and came to see what's up.' Tension eased from Sidnee's shoulders. 'I actually feel a heck of a lot better knowing they're here. If whatever killed the werewolf was water based, they would be long gone. Only a fool would fight the water dragon.'

'They?' I asked.

She shrugged. 'No one knows their gender. I wouldn't want to piss them off.'

Now that fear had faded, my brain kicked in. 'Can you ask them if they saw anything?'

She shrugged. 'In the same way you can ask God if he saw anything.'

'So...'

'I can ask, but I probably won't get a response. And if I did, most people would think I was crazy.'

Gunnar had headed back to the truck and was picking up all the equipment he'd dropped when he'd heard me scream. Sidnee and I watched together as the water dragon slunk deeper into the depths of the water. They were gone, or at least they were out of sight. Out of sight, out of mind, right? Wrong! I'd be thinking of those golden eyes for a while yet. A freaking dragon – a water one, but even so it counted. It was rare for me to be happy about being turned into the walking undead, but today had ticked off something on a bucket list I hadn't known I'd had.

A howl rent the air and I stepped a little closer to Sidnee. There was an answering howl and the hair on my neck stood up. Dammit, with all my focus on the water, I'd not been monitoring the surrounding area. I turned and hastily scanned the darkness. If another werewolf arrived, Gunnar would need to give me another machete. My heart gave another thud; I was getting quite the cardio-vascular work out tonight.

Sidnee smiled. 'Just a normal wolf,' she reassured me. 'We get them here.' But I noticed she stepped closer to me.

'Sure.' I tried to be calm about the idea of a pack of normal wolves converging on us but, try as I might, I couldn't stop visualising the werewolf as it had burst through the office with its red eyes and murder on its mind.

When Gunnar finally came back laden with equipment, I gave him a sheepish smile. 'Sorry about that.'

He smiled. 'No worries. You're not the first to scream at our water dragon. But they're a guardian, not to be feared unless you have nefarious intentions.'

'I have none of those,' I promised.

'Then you're good. Help me with these, won't you?'

I leapt forward to unburden him. Gunnar stacked everything neatly then pulled out a large camera and proceeded to photograph the scene from every angle. He asked Sidnee and me to collect samples and place them in evidence bags, which he sealed, labelled and placed in a lock box. I guessed that there weren't any crime-scene techs here in the backwaters, just us. Lucky us.

We worked in silence; to talk somehow seemed disrespectful to the corpse. It was impossible not to step in the blood because the whole place was painted with it, and I was glad for the booties. I wouldn't have wanted to get my boots covered in it, even if they were ugly.

'All right,' Gunnar said finally. 'Let's call it a day.'

Thank God for that – I was so done with swabs and blood and death. I was pretty sure I was going to smell it for days. And despite Sidnee's assurances, I still couldn't let go of the image of the other murderous werewolf I'd encountered. 'Do you know the victim?' I asked Gunnar quietly.

'If he's local then I probably do. I know most of the werewolves in these parts, though not all. But if it's another out-of-town werewolf like the one that attacked us, then no. I can't tell who it is with the face half-shifted like that. Once we get the body out of here and cleaned up, I'll get Stan to come by and identify him.'

'Did you find a wallet or a phone?' I asked curiously. I hadn't seen either, but maybe Gunnar had tagged and bagged them while I was doing something else.

'No, but we're gonna have Sidnee go and take a look in the water once we're done.'

I looked at her: she didn't look too happy, though I thought she'd been expecting it. She'd been Gunnar's assistant since before I'd started, but she was still a little green around the gills. 'At least you won't have to smell the blood anymore,' I said to her softly to encourage her. That was the only positive I could think of.

'It's not just the smell,' she grimaced.

I could understand her distress, though I didn't feel the same. The scene was gruesome, but after my initial shock I'd found our work fascinating: first the photos, then setting out the cones by the items of interest, then more photos, then bagging everything up, recording it in the evidence box and locking it away so the chain of evidence was unbroken...

I'd always thought I'd be a good investigator but Mum would have broken out in hives if I'd floated the idea of becoming a police officer. Now I found that I wanted to dive in to investigate this grisly crime and the gore didn't bother me. Maybe it was a vampire thing, or maybe it was because I couldn't have known the victim; either way, I was pleased that I was keeping a level head.

Finally Gunnar said, 'There's nothing else we can do here. It's up to the lab now. I'll call the ambulance to transport the body. Sidnee, go do your thing, please. Check out a hundred yards or so around this spot and head down the channel – say five hundred yards? If you don't find anything at the bottom, then the current has taken them or the murderer has them.'

'Has taken what?' I asked. 'The wallet and the phone?'

'And the murder weapon and anything else suspicious.'

Duh. I hadn't even thought about the murder weapon. I needed to get better at this investigating malarkey. The last thing I wanted was for Gunnar to ship me back to old Blighty.

I was going to be the best damned assistant ever, even at a chilling crime scene.

Chapter 21

Sidnee started to strip off and I whirled around to give her some privacy. Gunnar had already turned his back. 'Would you hold my clothes, Bunny?' she asked.

'Sure,' I said lightly. I squinched my eyes shut, turned round and held my hands out blindly.

She laughed. 'No need to be shy on my account – nakedness is part of my upbringing. But by all means, keep your eyes closed if it makes you feel uncomfortable.'

It absolutely did – but I was new Bunny, and new Bunny wasn't going to be a prude. I opened my eyes but kept them firmly at head height as Sidnee passed me her clothes. Finally she stood naked, her arms crossed over her chest in deferment to my obvious discomfort.

'Isn't the water insanely cold?' I asked. 'Don't you need a wetsuit or something?'

She laughed out loud. 'Mermaid! Don't worry, once I shift I won't be cold.' She gave me a finger wave, then ran and dived off the pier. A tiny splash rippled where she entered the water. A couple of seconds later, her head popped up – only it wasn't the Sidnee I was used to seeing. My mouth dropped open.

In place of her hair was a Mohawk made of tiny tendrils like a jellyfish. Her eyes were significantly larger and totally black. Her skin was no longer the bronze of her mixed blood but two-toned – dark bluish-grey on her back, fading to a lighter shade on her front. Her breasts were gone, fins had sprouted down her arms and she waved at me with a hand that was webbed.

Amazed, I swallowed and waved back. She broke up out of the water like a fish and then dived back down. Her large pearlescent fluke caught the fluorescent lights and then she was gone.

We waited. After about ten minutes, I started to worry. 'How long can she stay underwater?' I asked Gunnar.

He shrugged. 'Far as I know, forever.'

'Oh.' I had assumed that as a mammal she would need to breathe air, but she wasn't just a mammal but a magical creature. Sidnee was so lovely in a girl-next-door kind of a way that half the time I forgot she was supernatural. Hell, half the time I forgot *I* was supernatural. 'How long do you think it will take for her to search the area?' I asked.

'Don't know.' Gunnar stared anxiously at the water. He wasn't as unconcerned as he was trying to appear with his laconic answers.

'She'll be okay with the water dragon, right?'

He squeezed my shoulder. 'You're a good friend. She'll be fine.'

A heavy silence fell again as we waited next to the cooling corpse. A chill ran down my spine as I realised it really was eerily silent: there were no birds calling, no cars on the road. It felt like everyone and everything had had the good sense to vamoose, and only us idiots stood on the dock waiting with targets on our backs.

My fangs snicked down. Great: where had they been when I was confronted by a fricking water dragon? Nowhere, that's where.

The coppery smell of blood invaded my nostrils for almost an hour before Sidnee finally emerged from the water. She landed in human form, naked, on the balls of her feet on the dock behind us. Neat. Ten out of ten for style.

She looked pleased. 'I didn't find the wallet or the murder weapon, but I did find this.' She held out a cell phone; water was pouring from it but I noticed that not a drop remained on her skin. Cool trick.

'Nice work.' Gunnar held out an evidence bag, sealed it and put it in the evidence box.

I passed Sidnee her clothes and she hastily pulled them on as her flesh goose-pimpled in the cold. 'Hopefully the cell is the victim's or the killer's,' she said optimistically.

'We can hope, but realistically, it could belong to anyone.' Gunnar sighed. 'Probably every fisherman from this town has dropped a phone in the drink. Now we're all dressed and on dry land, let's wrap this up.'

He dialled the ambulance. While we waited, we bagged and tagged our booties and gloves in case we'd touched something that later transpired to be important. The ambulance showed up quickly; it was a small town and everything seemed to be pretty close, plus I doubted they had many murders; Gunnar and Sidnee weren't acting like this was any old day.

They walked up to meet the ambulance but I continued to look at the body. Something was itching at the back of my mind, something I was seeing but couldn't put my finger on. It wasn't until the stretcher thunked down on the wooden pier that I realised what it was.

The victim had obviously been stabbed, and I was fairly certain that was the cause of death, but his muzzle was wet and there was a lot of drool around his mouth. His pupils were blown open – in pain, or something else? Were those simply signs of a werewolf shifting or had he been ill.

But I'd read about those symptoms before – and they had all the hallmarks of a poisoning.

I briefly mentioned my suspicions to Gunnar but he didn't look sold. It was probably irrelevant because the body had clearly bled to death – the deck had been soaked in blood. I didn't want to show myself up, but I'd sneak a look at the lab statement and raise my suspicions with Gunnar again if there was anything that supported my theory.

I hugged Fluffy extra hard that night. Sensing that I needed the comfort, he snuggled close.

Chapter 22

The next day, when the body was ready for identification, Gunnar and I went to the hospital's morgue to meet Stan.

I'd already seen that Stan was handsome and today he looked delicious. What was with everyone looking so amazing in this town? Was there something in the water? If so, I wanted a gallon of it. I ran my eyes over his muscular arms and chest and slim waist and hips. When they made it back up to his face, he was smirking at me. My cheeks warmed.

Then Stan seemed to realise where we were and why and wiped the smirk off his face. He was all business as he led the way into the morgue. It was cold inside and smelled of disinfectant and formaldehyde with an underlying scent of human waste. Lovely: sometimes sharp vampire senses were not a gift.

Gunnar pulled back the sheet and Stan stared for a second. 'That's Eric Walker,' he said finally.

I guess Stan had seen him in partially shifted form before, because even Eric's mother couldn't have identified Eric from his twisted face. Unlike shifters, werewolves were made rather than born. Eric's parents might have been fully pedestrian, and seeing their son like this would have been horrific. A closed casket would be necessary.

Now he wasn't coated in blood, his 'otherness' was even more evident. His skin was greyish and pale; the yellow tint around the eyes was still there, just a little less visible.

'Thanks, Stan. Sorry you had to see this,' Gunnar offered.

'No, it's better I do it rather than a friend or a family member.' My stomach clenched. Did Eric have a wife? Children?

'I didn't know Eric had any family.' Gunnar frowned.

'He has a cousin or two, but none in town. I can let them know.'

'I'd appreciate that.'

We left the room. Now we had a name, we could start the investigation in earnest. Before Stan left, Gunnar asked, 'Did Eric have any enemies?'

'None that I knew of. As you know we've been having issues with the fishing, same as usual, but nothing that's affected him directly.' He frowned. 'It's not easy to kill a werewolf. Even with all of those cuts, he should have healed.' His voice turned accusatory, 'I'm thinking it would take a magic user to keep them from healing.'

'We don't know anything yet, no sense guessing or accusing anyone. We need to keep the peace, now more than ever.' Gunnar's tone was placatory and Stan nodded, but he was still frowning. 'Any significant others? Girlfriend? Boyfriend?' Gunnar continued.

'I don't know. He was straight, but I don't know if he had a current girlfriend or a live-in partner. He had a girl for a while that he yo-yoed with – rumour was she strayed with someone else. Not sure what his current status was, Eric generally kept to himself.'

'Is there anyone he was especially close to that I could talk to?'

'He was friendly with Jim.'

'The pilot?' I blurted out.

Stan looked at me like he'd forgotten I was there, 'Yeah.' He looked me up and down, letting his interest show. I did my best to ignore it; now was *really* not the time to get his flirt on.

'Good to know,' Gunnar said. 'If you think of anything else, give me a call.'

'Sure will. Find this bastard, Gunnar. We're on edge with the rogue werewolf, the cairn and the fish plant trying to rip us off. Things are tense. I'm worried that one more thing will set this town off like the fourth of July.'

'I'll do my best.'

'Do it quickly.' Stan gave Gunnar a friendly clap on the shoulder and me another interested look. When he smiled wryly, I raised my eyebrow in question. He shook his head a little and walked off. I guessed he'd realised that this was not an appropriate time for flirting and I was glad he'd got the memo, albeit a bit late.

'So, what's next?' I asked Gunnar eagerly.

'We'll talk to Jim and anyone else who knew Eric. We'll search his house, his car, see if he had a phone and if the one we found was his.'

Gunnar pulled out his own phone and searched through his contacts. He hit dial and a few moments later grimaced faintly as the beep for voicemail clicked in. 'Hi, Jim. I have some news for you. Give me a call when you can.' He ended the call. 'Jim must be flying. Let's go check out Eric's house.'

What would a werewolf's house be like? Would there be steaks and a shrine to the moon? I was eager to find out. This detective shit was *fun*.

Chapter 23

Eric's house looked a little run down, not terribly, but enough to show that the owner either wasn't houseproud or didn't have the money to keep it up. Perhaps it was a bit of both. It needed a lick of paint and the windows cleaning. The garden was overgrown and wild; I'd bet a lawnmower hadn't attacked that grass in a year or more.

There was a small section of gravel for parking with weeds growing through it. The moonlight glinted off something liquid on it. After we'd parked and got out of the car, I surreptitiously touched the shiny patch and brought my fingertip to my nose. Oil: it looked like Eric's car had some sort of oil leak. Shitty things came in threes, and I wondered what the third thing was that had gone wrong in Eric's life – besides death and car problems.

Gunnar knocked on the front door, which seemed unnecessary when we knew that the owner of the property was dead, though there was a chance that someone else was living there. We waited a minute but no one answered. He tried the door: locked. 'Let's check the back, then I'll break in if I have to.'

As we walked around back, a husky-type dog barked at us. He was tied up and his food and water bowls were empty. Gunnar swore softly. 'We'll take care of you, Buddy,' he promised soothingly. The dog stopped barking and started wagging.

I spotted a hose, filled the empty bowl and set it carefully in front of the dog. He immediately started lapping up the water. When he'd had his fill, Gunnar stroked him. 'We'll be back to feed you in a minute, Bud. We just need to go into the house for a second.'

He turned the knob on the back door but nothing happened. After sliding me a glance, he turned the knob again and this time it swung open. He passed me some gloves and a camera. 'This could be a crime scene, so make sure to take plenty of photos as we go.'

'Roger that.'

The dog was still looking at us hopefully. I thought about Fluffy, how he'd been starved and thrown away, and I promised I'd make sure this dog was fed and homed even if I had to adopt him myself. I could start my own kennels: 'Bunny's Barking Boutique – hop in for a paw-sitively delightful stay'. I'd make millions.

'Come on, Bunny,' Gunnar cajoled from the open doorway. I gave him an apologetic smile and followed him inside.

The first thing I looked for was dog food. There was a big open bag next to the door, so Eric wasn't a total arsehole. Gunnar also glanced at it. I had a feeling that the dog wouldn't be sad and lonely for long. 'Can I just feed him?' I asked, 'It won't take a minute.'

Gunnar looked amused but indulgent. 'Go right ahead.'

I took a cup of the dog biscuits to the dog and tipped them into the empty bowl. 'Here, this'll keep you going, little guy.' I patted his scruffy head then went back inside the house again. 'All done,' I told Gunnar.

'Good. Let's get to work.'

I nodded, doing my best to look focused. It was time to find some actual frigging clues.

The back door opened into the kitchen; like the outside of the house, it was old, banged up and grimy. Dirty dishes were piled in the sink and pizza boxes were stacked on the bin. My nose wrinkled at the aroma of rotten food.

Eric hadn't been dead long so the detritus had been there pre-mortem. It seemed odd that a werewolf would be happy living in a stinky environment – or maybe I was making assumptions. Just because they were supernatural and part-canine didn't mean their sense of smell was better than a human's.

I scanned everything, took photographs of the room and looked for anything that stood out as unusual. There was a dog calendar on the wall on which all of the Wednesdays had been circled but no notations. Weird.

Besides the fact that Eric had been a slob, nothing else leapt out at me: there was no knife dripping with blood on the breadboard. We checked the kitchen cupboards, fridge and freezer but they were all pretty bare. Did Eric hunt for food in human form or as a werewolf, because there wasn't a whole lot to eat there? My eyes slid back to the huge sack of dog food. Surely Eric hadn't eaten that? I shuddered at the thought.

With nothing noteworthy in the kitchen, we moved into the living room. This was obviously the place where Eric spent most of his time: firstly, it was a shade cleaner than the kitchen, and secondly, the focal point of the room was an oversized leather reclining chair right in front of a seventy-inch TV. A sofa had been pushed against the wall. There was yet another empty pizza box on the table next to the recliner, this one marked 'Pizza Kodiak Kitchen', the name of the local pizza place. I gathered that Eric ate a lot of pizza but it was better than dog food.

At the side of the room was a log burner. The glass door was closed but through it, I could see a fairly clear grate with no half-burnt logs. The room was cool; the fire obviously hadn't been lit recently.

When Gunnar finished scrawling in his notebook, he effortlessly moved the recliner, checked under it then returned it to its original position. I grasped one end of the sofa, Gunnar took the other and we moved it out a couple of feet away from the wall; no dead bodies or blood-stained knives behind it. We checked under the cushions; nothing. This was turning out to be a disappointment.

We looked in every nook and cranny but there was nothing, zip, *nada*: no phone, no notes, no bills or paper of any kind. That seemed strange because most people had *something*. I was pretty tidy but I had bills or letters stacked in certain places – the top of my microwave was prime real estate for important paperwork. Maybe Eric's paperwork was stored somewhere else or had already been recycled. I immediately dismissed the latter; given the state of the house and the number of cardboard pizza boxes strewn around, it seemed unlikely that Eric was bothered about saving the planet.

We moved down the hall of the single-storey house to explore the three bedrooms. The first was dusty and looked unused. I snapped some pics and then we checked the dresser and cupboards, both of which were empty except for sheets and blankets. We dutifully unfolded, shook and refolded each one then put them back. We checked under the bed and mattress; more dust but no monsters, no wads of cash.

If I were being polite, I'd have said that the next room was used for storage but it was really just a dumping ground. There seemed to be no logic about why anything had been placed anywhere but even so I took a bunch of photos before we waded in. We found car magazines, old photos and a bunch of family papers, but nothing dated within the last three years. Curiouser and curiouser. When we walked out, the room was significantly tidier than when we'd gone in; at least now you could see the floor.

The final room was obviously Eric's bedroom. The bed was unmade – no surprise there. We went through the same process: photos, notes, checking every drawer, every cupboard. We shook out clothes, burrowed in pockets. We found a few dollar bills, some change, a couple of – thankfully wrapped – condoms. There was a charger cord for a mobile phone but no phone; in fact, there was no computer or electronics besides the huge TV, a gaming console and a DVD player. It seemed weird in this day and age not to have a computer, laptop or a tablet.

With some reluctance on my part, we went into the bathroom. Typical of Eric's cleaning style, or lack thereof, it was filthy. The toilet was so caked in old urine, that it instantly made me retch. I snapped some pictures then graciously decided to let Gunnar do the search. 'I'll leave this one to you,' I muttered. I moved into the hallway still holding my nose, but even so the smell was enough to make me gag.

Gunnar searched the area thoroughly and found nothing. Finally he held up a white wicker bin so I could see inside it. It was empty; in fact, it was the cleanest thing in the whole house. Interesting.

A now-familiar scent caught my nose. 'Blood,' I said grimly.

Gunnar whirled around. 'Blood? Where?'

'Under the bin maybe?'

He upended the bin again; sure enough, there was a smear of dark red on the bottom of it. He studied it. 'Dried, old,' he sounded disappointed.

'It's probably nothing,' I agreed.

'Worth sending it to the labs, though.' He marked it with a cone and took a picture. 'We'll get it when we leave. No point toting it around the house.'

Next up was a modest utility room. There wasn't much to search, but we looked around and inside the washing and drying machines. Eric wasn't a tidy boy, yet there was zero paperwork in the house. The only conclusion I could reach was that he'd disposed of it for some shady reason or someone had removed it for him – either before or after his death.

'Is it worth printing the house?' I suggested.

Gunnar gave a wry smile. 'You've been watching too much *CSI*. We don't have the time, money or resources to print the whole house. This place isn't even a crime scene.'

'But the murderer could have come here,' I pointed out.

'So could have every Tom, Dick and Harry in town.'

'Bummer.'

'Yeah. Did you notice anything strange outside?' Gunnar asked me.

I replayed everything I'd seen before we'd come inside: the dilapidated exterior, the wild garden, the lack of a shed or a garage, the dog tied up. 'No vehicle!' I blurted out. Eric's body had been on the docks and there was no car with him. We'd assumed that he'd walked into town and then been attacked; that being the case, his car should have been at his house.

'No vehicle,' he agreed grimly. 'Eric drives a navy-blue Chevy truck that's seen better days. But where is it?'

'Maybe it went up to the great car heaven.' I murmured. At Gunnar's raised eyebrows, I hastily explained, 'You know, he scrapped it. It leaks oil. Maybe he decided to get rid of it.'

He gave me another sharp look. 'Yeah, maybe.' Neither of us was buying that for a minute. 'No truck here or at the harbour, no phone, no computer or tablet. Anything else that could be missing?'

'Besides his wallet and the murder weapon?'

'Yeah.'

'Up-to-date mail and the rubbish from the bathroom bin,' I replied promptly. 'I didn't see another bin in the house besides the kitchen one.'

'Exactly.' He looked at me approvingly. 'You don't miss much, do you, Bunny?'

I resisted the urge to tell him about my weird memory because it always made people uncomfortable. For some reason the idea that I could recall everything they'd ever said – and what they'd been wearing when they said it – made them feel awkward.

Gunnar continued, 'Someone either killed Eric and came back to collect that stuff or took it and then killed him. You can hide small things but there's only so many places you can hide a truck in a village this size with no outside roads. It'll turn up,' he said confidently.

'Do we put out an APB?' I hazarded.

'A what?' Gunnar looked confused.

'In the American cop shows, they always put out an APB when something or someone is missing.'

He guffawed. 'An APB is an all-points bulletin to let law enforcement know someone or something is missing. We *are* law enforcement and we already know. However, we can get eyes looking. I'll call Ernie and have him put it on the radio.'

'Ernie from the hardware store?'

'Yup, the one and the same. In a small town, lots of people do more than one job.' He winked. 'Like you.'

'Admin assistant and general assistant?' I asked lightly.

'This town needs more than one law enforcement officer, so you get to help me out and about.'

I didn't mind the admin part, but the investigation stuff was so much more interesting. I loved being in the thick of it. 'Brilliant.'

Gunnar laughed. 'I'll see if you still think that in a few years' time.'

That made me feel even better. He thought I'd still be working for him in a few years, so he must have been happy with what he'd seen of me so far. That was encouraging.

We'd given the whole house a thorough search. I grabbed the huge bag of dog food to take with us; before being turned, I would have staggered under its weight but now it seemed feather-light.

Gunnar locked the house, using the back door key that hung carelessly by the doorframe, pocketed the key and unchained the poor dog. Buddy was happy to see us and wagged his tail. We loaded him into the SUV and left Eric's depressing home.

Chapter 24

Gunnar had asked me to come into the office early the next day, so I dragged my tired arse out of bed as soon as I could. The daytime exhaustion was kicking my butt, even with a tonne of coffee. Caffeine evidently still worked on me, but not to the same extent.

By the time I sloped off to the office with Fluffy at my heels, the sun was already setting. Sidnee was at the desk, manning the phones. She gave me a wide smile. 'Hey, Bunny, Fluffy. Go on back, he's waiting for you.'

I winced a little. 'Sorry, I'm later than I'd hoped.'

'Hush, you're still early. Just because *he* can operate on empty doesn't mean everyone else can.'

I sent her a grateful smile and knocked briskly at his door. 'Come in, Bunny,' Gunnar called.

How did he know it was me knocking? Good guesswork? He was expecting me, after all. He got straight to it. 'I've been thinking,' he rubbed his beard thoughtfully, 'Stan probably wasn't wrong about looking into the magic users. Killing a werewolf is a pretty hard task – a strike to the heart or decapitation is usually the only sure way.'

The image of the rogue werewolf's head flashed into my mind. 'Do we have an ID on the werewolf that attacked us yet?' I asked.

'No, but I'm hoping we'll get it soon. In the meantime, we need to focus on Eric, Kivuk and Jack, not the dumbass that tried to kill us.'

'Is that the order to prioritise tasks?' I asked curiously. 'Eric, Kivuk then Jack?'

'Eric is dead and his case is still hot. Kivuk has been missing a few days and all we have are dead ends. Maybe he just went on a trip.'

'But you don't believe that.'

He sighed. 'No, I don't believe that.'

'And Jack?'

'Jack's human, and he's been missing nearly a month. He's dead, we just haven't found his body yet.' Gunnar's tone was grim. 'But either way, he's a cold case for now.'

'Why don't you think he's gone on a trip like Kivuk?' I queried.

'Kivuk's an old vamp. He's not going to ask Connor's permission before he ducks out; he'll just go. Jack was a homebody – he would have told his parents, planned a route with them. Besides, being a human it'd be hard for him to traverse the barrier unless he flew out with Jim, and that flight didn't happen. But Kivuk could have gotten through the barrier alone.'

'So you think they're all dead?'

'Yes, I do.'

'Do you think we have a serial killer?'

'Better than hoping we have three separate murderers running around. But now we have something to dig into. Eric didn't disappear – we have a corpse.'

'They're getting cocky.'

'Maybe. Wanting to show off what they've accomplished. They took out a werewolf, without even removing his head. So ... magic user. Somehow they held Eric still whilst they killed him. We'll have to be discreet with our enquiries, or we'll start a lot of rumours around town and rumours in this place have a way of blowing up. We don't need a witch hunt on top of everything else.'

He cleared his throat. 'I talked to my wife. There's a whole array of magic users, but she thinks that it had to be a witch or maybe a shaman. Necromancers work with the already-dead, and druids wouldn't fit. Maybe a practitioner of voodoo, but we only have one, and she's frail and confined to her bed so I'm confident we can write her off.'

I'd have thought voodoo was something you could do lying in bed, but I didn't disagree. Gunnar knew more about this shit than me; if he said the voodoo lady was out, I'd take his word for it – for now, anyway. She was still on my list, just right at the bottom.

I knew next to nothing about witches and shamans. 'How many witches and shamans are there in Portlock?' I asked.

'A few, but according to my wife there are only three that would be strong enough magically to incapacitate a werewolf.'

I wondered if Gunnar's wife should also be on the list, but I kept that thought to myself. 'Is the magic leader a witch?' I asked. The image of Liv Fox flashed into my mind, not as I'd seen her at the council meeting but as I'd seen her in the vision she'd sent me. Odd.

'No, she's a necromancer. Different magic. She'd be top of the list if the deceased had done something *after* he was dead.'

'Maybe the werewolf's killer was an animated corpse,' I suggested. 'Maybe that's how they got close enough to kill him. It wouldn't matter if they were harmed in the attack because they were already dead.'

Gunnar looked at me with interest. 'Great theory, but no. An animated corpse stinks and that stench hangs in the air. All I could smell at the scene was blood. Besides, there was nothing under the werewolf's nails – no blood, hair, muscle or bone. In your scenario, there would have been.'

I cast my mind back and recalled the scents at the dock: fresh, coppery blood; Sidnee's light, floral perfume; the weird tang. There'd been no undead, rotting-corpse smell. In my mind's eye I examined the corpse again, paying attention to the claws. They were clean. 'True.' I conceded. 'But there was a smell of *something*.'

'Something acrid,' Gunnar agreed, looking at me with approval. I basked in it.

I wondered what else we could do. 'Could we have Liv wake Eric up and ask him who killed him?'

Gunnar gave me another measured look; I was getting a lot of those. 'Very good question. Honestly? I don't know. So, let's see what the answer is.' He grabbed his phone and hit speed dial 7. I wondered if he had all of the council members on speed dial or whether it was only Liv. Something to ponder.

He turned it on speakerphone and set the phone on his desk. It rang three times before a sultry voice answered, 'Gunnar.' She all but purred his name. 'To what do I owe the pleasure?'

'Liv, I have a necromancer question.'

A beat of unbelieving silence ensued. Then, 'I believe I'm in shock,' she quipped, amused.

'Well, there's a first time for everything.' He took a breath and said, 'I've got a dead body.'

'It's a complete secret, so naturally I heard.' Humour was still in her tone.

Gunnar rolled his eyes and mouthed, 'small town' to me. 'I need a favour.'

'You sure know how to make a woman's knees go weak.'

Gunnar ignored that. 'What are the chances you can wake the victim and get answers from him?'

She gave a deep throaty chuckle, 'You must be all out of leads, Gunnar.' Her voice sobered. 'It's a possibility, but it depends if his spirit hung around afterwards. Most move on immediately after death, especially if it was a violent end.'

'Are you willing to give it a try?'

Another throaty laugh. 'How can I resist? Colour me intrigued.'

'Meet us at the clinic in an hour?'

'I'll grab my supplies. See you soon, Gunnar.'

Gunnar looked at Fluffy. 'You're going to have to stay here with Sidnee. No dogs allowed in the hospital.' Fluffy barked and trotted over to sit with Sidnee. 'Let's go,' my boss said to me. 'It's time to make a deal with the devil.' It sounded like he was only half-joking.

Chapter 25

My first impression of Liv Fox hadn't been favourable, and I didn't think Gunnar was a huge fan of her either. Her constant, and seemingly unwanted, intimacy was tantamount to sexual harassment. Working in a bar, I'd had enough of that to last me a lifetime. People who harassed others were assholes, pure and simple. If there was no return interest, dial it down or fuck off.

Even so, I was trying to be open-minded about Liv and I was curious to see her work. I wanted to learn as much as I could from *all* the supernatural types. I had years of knowledge to catch up on; my ignorance about their world was so vast it had its own gravitational pull.

She swept into the room wearing heels, tight jeans and an equally tight top. Her leather bag looked like it had cost more than my monthly salary. She looked stunning – and she knew it. She sashayed in, hips swinging hypnotically. Gunnar looked uncomfortable. Poor guy.

She looked at me standing close to him and sent me a look full of malice. As our eyes met, she instantly removed the vitriol and replaced it with a warm smile that I didn't believe for a second. 'Where's the body?' she asked breathily, even managing to make asking after a corpse sound sexy. She threw in a sidelong look at Gunnar from under her lashes.

He didn't reply, just went over and pulled out the cooler drawer.

'Hmm, that won't work, I need him here.' She pointed to the centre of the room. 'Do be a darling and move him,' she purred.

Gunnar's jaw worked a little but he nodded. The body was on a metal and canvas stretcher so it wasn't too difficult to position it exactly where she wanted. Liv plonked her bag on top of Eric's hairy belly and I winced, though I guessed he couldn't feel it. The ick factor was high, but she was probably used to working with corpses.

She pulled several items from her bag – candles, containers and crystals – and I watched curiously. She arranged the candles around the body, then sprinkled what looked like an herb onto Eric's skin. I inhaled surreptitiously. Huh, it was basil, which didn't seem like a magical herb to me – unless it was combined with tomatoes and mozzarella; I had a weakness for caprese salad.

Next Liv placed crystals on Eric: one on his forehead, one on each limb, and one on his belly. 'Before I light the candles and start, stay out of the circle. Don't come in. Got it?'

Gunnar and I nodded and stepped back. I wasn't quite sure where the circle was because she hadn't drawn anything on the floor, but I was staying well out of her way. The last thing I wanted was to accidentally invite slobbish Eric to inhabit my body; after all, technically I was a corpse too, and I didn't want there to be any confusion.

Liv bowed and carefully lit each candle, then stood at Eric's head, lifted her arms and began to chant. The temperature in the room dropped instantly, and the lights flickered and went out. Only the candles remained. She could have turned the lights out first, but that would have been less dramatic and Liv clearly thrived on drama.

I rubbed my arms and turned to Gunnar; he looked a little spooked, too. There was a prickle along my nerve endings and my anxiety level ratcheted up. If I was dead, could she affect me? It wasn't a nice thought. Maybe I should have waited outside. I edged another step backward and the prickling sensation passed.

Liv's arms dropped and the fluorescent lights flooded back on. She looked at us, disappointment pinching her mouth as she extinguished the candles. 'You can come close now,' she said. 'There is no spirit left. He's gone. I could raise the body, of course, but you won't get your answers.'

'Thank you, Liv,' Gunnar said

She nodded at him, no sass left. Whatever she'd done had momentarily stripped the temptress right out of her. She started picking up her things; once she was done, she took one last look at Gunnar and gave a little sigh. He didn't notice because he was already on his phone, tapping out a message.

My sigh matched Liv's. This hadn't gone quite the way that I'd hoped. Oh well, it looked like we'd have to solve the murder the hard way – with determination, grit and hopefully some cool police gadgets.

Chapter 26

We heard Jim's small plane coming in. 'Let's go down to the harbour,' Gunnar said, turning the car in that direction instead of the office.

We parked not far from the waterfront and I followed him down a different dock from the murder site. Jim was unloading totes and boxes from the plane onto thankfully un-bloodstained wooden planks. 'Gunnar,' he said, straightening up. He looked tired and worn; the bags under his eyes were big enough to pack for a trip to the moon, and his shoulders were a little more stooped.

When we were close enough to speak comfortably, Gunnar started. 'I have some bad news for you.'

Jim tensed. 'Is it about Eric?'

'Yeah, how'd you know?' Gunnar asked.

'The voicemail you left – and a bad feeling that's been chasing me since before I left.' Jim ran a hand through his hair. 'I knew something bad was going to happen to him and I told him to come with me, but he wouldn't listen. Thought I was being ridiculous.' He blew out a harsh breath. 'He's dead?' he asked, his tone resigned.

Gunnar nodded. Jim closed his eyes and bowed his head. We remained silent for a moment, letting him process it until finally Gunnar broke the aching silence. 'I'm sorry to ask, Jim, but when did you leave town?'

Jim looked up, giving him a sharp look with grief-stricken eyes. 'Why the heck are you asking that? Am I a suspect?'

'I just need to know when you left. I've got boxes to tick. You know how it is,' Gunnar soothed.

Jim looked him in the eye. 'I've been gone for four days.' Gunnar's shoulders loosened a tiny bit. 'You can check online. My flight will have been recorded.'

Gunnar nodded. 'I'll check Flight Radar 24.'

'I'm not saying another word until you accept that I wasn't here. Pull it up on your phone. Now.' Jim was glaring at Gunnar; gone was the affable man I remembered from my flight into Portlock. I could understand his anger – I'd be mad if someone hinted I might have killed my bestie. Of course, I'd need a bestie first for that to happen.

Gunnar fiddled with his phone for a while then said, 'Yep. You're all clear.'

I sighed with relief. The tension had been building with every swipe of his phone. Jim's shoulders loosened and his lips quirked in a small, relieved smile.

'Now, tell me about your premonition,' Gunnar pressed as he pocketed the phone.

'I saw him the night before I left. He was acting strange, said someone had been tormenting him. When I asked what was going on, he said it wasn't anything he could pinpoint. Weird sounds, things being moved when he thought he'd put them in a certain spot, banging on the house at night when he was trying to sleep. I told him he was stressed because he wasn't getting any work fishing on account of the freeze out, but he insisted it was real. He was going crazy.'

'What else can you tell me about him? Friends? Girlfriends? Hobbies?'

Jim sighed. 'Eric was low on friends. He's been hanging out with some werewolves a lot recently, and that wasn't like him. He's got no hobbies besides walking Loki. He's been dating Virginia Tide a while.' He grimaced. 'I'm not a fan of hers. They do this on-again, off-again thing.' He shrugged. 'Nothing he did was ever good enough for her. They were poorly matched, should have split up permanently long ago.'

If Virginia had been bitching about Eric's tidying and cleaning skills, I thought she had a point.

Gunnar was quiet a moment then he asked, 'Isn't Virginia Tide a human?'

'Yeah. She's as ped as they come.' He looked at me properly for the first time. 'Ped means pedestrian. Normal. Not supernat.' He offered a faint smile. 'Hey, Bunny. Hope you're settling in okay.'

'I'm doing great thanks,' I replied. Better than Eric, that was for sure.

Gunnar ignored our conversation and stuck to the point. 'Virginia didn't do it.'

'Are you sure?' Jim asked, looking eager to hear Gunnar's response.

'Positive. Someone must have used magic to do what they did to Eric otherwise he wouldn't have died.'

'Well, unless it was related to the fishing dispute, I'm all out of suspects for you. Eric didn't have any enemies. He wasn't popular, but he tried his best not to make waves.'

'Do you think it *was* related to the fishing issue?' I asked him.

'Maybe. This town sure gets hot under the collar for fish. It's our main industry, even with the mining and logging growing all the time. The call to stop fishing was hard for Eric – for a canine, he sure likes – *liked* being on the water.' For a moment he looked grief-stricken. 'I used to tease him that he was more like a Newfoundland than a wolf.'

I gave his arm a sympathetic squeeze. 'Maybe Virginia will know more.'

'We'll call her in and talk to her. How was their relationship?' Gunnar asked.

Jim shrugged. 'As I said, it was pretty volatile.'

'Did she live with him?'

'Have you seen his place?' Jim scoffed. 'No, she refused to stay there. He'd go stay at hers when they were on.'

Gunnar and I exchanged a look. Maybe there wasn't anything suspicious about Eric's missing paperwork and it was at Virginia Tide's place. Maybe she was super organised and had a filing cabinet stuffed with it. Maybe – but I didn't think so.

'Were they together recently?' Gunnar asked.

'I think so. I'm pretty sure he's been staying at her place.'

'What do you know about his dog?'

'Loki? He's a good boy.'

'Do you want him? Would Virginia want him?'

'No way!' Jim exclaimed. 'She hates animals. I wish I could take him, but I'm gone a lot so it wouldn't be fair.'

Gunnar raised his eyebrows. 'I'm surprised you don't want him.' Jim gave an uncomfortable shrug. 'If you don't, I'm thinking of keeping him,' Gunnar said.

'You ready for a dog again?'

'Yeah, I think I am. I miss having a dog. Killer left a big hole in our life when he passed. Besides, Loki's at my place. Sigrid's taken a liking to him.'

A small smile cut through Jim's grief. 'Eric would have approved.'

'I hope so. I'll call if we can think of anything else. We'll go check in with Virginia. She still over by the old Wanlier place?'

'Yeah, still there.'

Gunnar clapped him on the shoulder. 'Thanks, Jim. You take it easy now.'

Once we were back in the vehicle, I turned to Gunnar. 'If Eric was living with his girlfriend, why didn't she let us know he was missing?'

Gunnar smiled approvingly. 'You've got cop instincts. Maybe they were in an off phase and she didn't know he was missing, or maybe she knew and didn't care. Don't read anything into it. The truth is, around here if we have a secret, the whole town probably knows it. She's probably already heard Eric is dead. Let's talk to her before we start making assumptions.'

Chastened, I nodded. Still, everyone knew it was always the spouse who did the murder. Ring on her finger or not, I'd be taking a hard look at Virginia Tide.

Chapter 27

We drew up outside a neat, clean bungalow, not large, but clean-lined and cute. The garden was tidy, the windows were sparkling and even the paint was freshly applied. It looked quintessentially *American*.

An old four-door sedan was parked up in the driveway. It had recently been washed, and there was none of the usual detritus you got in a lot of cars. There was no sign of Eric's truck.

Gunnar knocked on the front door. A diminutive red-haired woman opened it and peered out cautiously. 'Virginia Tide?' he asked. Maybe he didn't know her well, or perhaps it was a standard conversation opener.

'Yeah.' She looked at us with dread in her eyes. When she spoke, her voice trembled. 'What brings you to my door, Nomo?'

'We have some questions to ask you about Eric Walker.'

She sagged against the doorframe and closed her eyes. 'God damn it. I've tried calling him so many times,' she breathed. 'My friend told me the rumours. It's true? He's really dead?' The last word came out as a whisper.

'Yes,' Gunnar confirmed simply. 'I'm sorry for your loss.'

I watched as she closed her eyes and buried her head in her hands. After a moment, she pulled them away and blew out a long breath. Her expression was resigned; she'd heard the rumours and a part of her had already accepted that he was gone. She sighed. 'I suppose you'd better come on in.'

Virginia smelled faintly of cleaning products and it was no wonder: there wasn't so much as a speck of dust inside her house. She and Eric truly had been yin and yang. She showed us into her pristine living room and gestured for us to sit. On the walls were a number of pieces of art depicting werewolves. They weren't my idea of cosy, but each to their own. Maybe it was a way of making Eric feel at home and to show she'd accepted his wolfy side.

Virginia looked at Gunnar as she fiddled with a ring on her hand. 'What happened?'

'We don't know precisely but we're working on it. He was stabbed – it looks like he bled out.'

'But he's a werewolf.' She was obviously confused. 'They don't bleed out – they *can't*. They heal too quick.'

'That bothered us as well.' Gunnar was evidently going to be close-lipped about our suspicions of magic being involved. 'If you can answer some questions, it might help us find the culprit.'

'Of course. Anything.'

'Was he staying here?'

'Rarely at the moment,' she admitted. 'We have an on-again, off-again relationship and I suppose we were in an off phase. He kept some things here but most of the time he went home, even when we were on an on-phase. He needed to take care of Loki.' I noticed that her lips pinched at mention of the dog.

'Any chance his phone or wallet are here?'

She frowned. 'No, I shouldn't think so. He kept them on him.'

'If you get a chance, will you look around your house?' Gunnar asked.

'Sure.' She gave a wan smile.

'Did he keep his paperwork here?' I asked.

She blinked. 'No, why would he? He has his own home for that.' Hmm.

Gunnar shifted the gears. 'Where were you Tuesday night?'

She shifted in her seat. 'Am I a suspect?' she asked, eyes wide.

'Just eliminating you from the list,' Gunnar soothed. 'Standard procedure.'

She relaxed a little. 'Right, okay. Um, Eric and I went to dinner at the Pizza Kodiak Kitchen. We finished up between eight and nine. I had to go to bed early because I had an early shift at the fish plant.'

I leaned in. 'I thought you were off-again?'

She smiled faintly. 'Eric was trying to persuade me to give it another go.'

'He didn't succeed?'

Her smile vanished. 'No, he didn't. And now he never will.' Her bottom lip wobbled.

Guilt pricked at me; questioning newly bereaved people sucked. I moved on to something less personal. 'Did he drive his truck to meet you?'

'No, we met in town. I drove but he'd walked.'

'When did you last see his truck?' I asked.

'I don't know – a week or so ago?' She shrugged. 'He's not the neatest, even with his vehicles. It'll turn up parked down some random side street, I expect.'

Gunnar had said it was hard to hide a stolen vehicle and the truck hadn't shown up yet. If it wasn't here or at Eric's residence, maybe someone else had it – the murderer. Maybe they'd used it to escape the scene.

'How long have you and Eric been together?' Gunnar asked conversationally.

This time Virginia looked stricken. 'Pretty close to three years. I thought he was going to give me everything I'd ever dreamed of.' She blinked back tears but even so a stray one fell and she swiped at her cheek. 'Sorry,' she muttered. 'Go on.' She took a deep breath.

'Do you know anyone who wanted Eric dead?' he asked.

She clenched her jaw and leaned forward. 'Yes, I do,' she said vehemently,

Gunnar and I slid a glance at each other. 'Who?'

'That bastard of a shifter leader, Stan Ahmaogak, that's who!'

I waited for Gunnar to say something, but he was obviously too surprised. 'Why him?' I asked, picturing the handsome man. I recalled Stan studying the body in the morgue; there had been no malice in his voice as he'd identified Eric, but perhaps he hadn't felt any because he'd already succeeded in killing him.

'Eric wanted to go work for the Mayor,' Virginia continued. 'He was hurting for money, as was everyone else that wasn't fishing.'

I recalled the fight in the council chambers; to me, fishing seemed like a dumb reason to kill someone, but Stan and Mayor Mafu had gone at each other pretty hard. I could imagine tempers flaring and someone getting killed – but Eric had been stabbed, not torn apart by another shifter. At least, that's what I assumed shifters did.

'Why would Stan *stab* Eric?' I asked, confused. 'Didn't he have claws? What is he? A mouse shifter?'

Virginia gave a quick bark of laughter. 'Stan's a damned polar bear. I wish I could put him on ice,' she said fiercely. Her hatred of him was clear; Eric must have complained about him bitterly for her to have such a reaction.

Even so, the body had been stabbed rather than slashed. The stab wounds hadn't been uniform, nor had there been parallel marks like you'd get from claws. But there was nothing to stop Stan using a knife; just because he hadn't carried one to the council meeting didn't mean he didn't have one.

Gunnar stood. 'Thank you for your time. I'm sorry for your loss. We'll be in touch if we have more questions.'

'Of course.' She walked us to the door and shut it firmly behind us. I didn't blame her; we'd just delivered the worst news of her life.

Once we were in the car, I asked, 'Could Stan have made those wounds in his bear form?'

'No, those were most definitely made by a knife, though that doesn't mean Stan didn't carry one,' he said grimly.

Snap, I thought. 'Are we talking to him next?'

Gunnar started the car. 'Yeah. Between you and me, I can't see Stan doing it, especially over fish. He might slug someone – heck, he got Mafu good at the council meeting – but if he was feeling murderous over it, it would have been Mafu's corpse on the dock, not Eric's. Not one of his own.' He frowned. 'It doesn't add up.'

I thought the same, but fish and fish prices seemed to be a huge deal here, so what did I know? Hell, people back in London killed each other because of road rage.

'I've been thinking about the cause of death,' Gunnar added. 'Besides bespelling him so his healing wouldn't take effect, he could have been stabbed so fast that his body didn't have a chance to heal between the wounds. If he lost enough blood all at once, he'd die before he could heal.'

I gave a barely audible sigh. If Gunnar was right, that expanded our range of suspects from three possible magic users and Stan to an unknown number. I wondered how we could whittle it down. 'Does it have to be a land shifter, or would the sirens and mermaids also be suspects?'

Gunnar sighed too. 'It was right on the water.'

'Shit.'

'Yup. We just increased our suspect list by two-fifths of the town.'

'What do we do?'

'We talk to Stan and hope he can narrow it down for us – one way, or another.' He looked at his watch. 'It'll have to wait, though.'

'Why?'

'Because Stan is at the fish processor right now, negotiating for that higher price.'

'His plan worked?'

'I guess we'll know when he gets back.'

I bit my lip. 'I know the negotiations are important, but doesn't murder take precedence?'

'More than half the town is involved in the fishing industry here. Murder can wait.' Small-town priorities seemed weird to me, but what did I know? 'Come on, let's go get some food,' Gunnar said. 'I'm starving. You want to come over for dinner? Sigrid would like to meet you.'

'I'd love to, but I should check on Fluffy first.'

'Bring him with you. We can pick him up on the way.'

I smiled. 'Perfect.' I was intrigued to meet the mysterious Sigrid. Having seen Liv throw herself repeatedly at Gunnar, I was interested to see the woman who had clearly captured his heart.

Chapter 28

We collected Fluffy from the office and Gunnar greeted him warmly. 'Evening, Fluffy.' Fluffy gave a bark back, which I chose to interpret as, 'Evening, Gunnar.'

Gunnar's house was the last in a row at the edge of town. It was a charming two-storey building with wooden walls painted brick red with a light-green trim, and with stylised flowers and birds decorating the windows and doorways. The window boxes were full of flowers in all colours. I felt like I'd stepped back in time a few hundred years.

Gunnar pulled up and the three of us tumbled out. Fluffy sniffed around the front and grinned up at Gunnar, tongue lolling out. I heard a 'woof' from inside the door and, as Gunnar opened it, Eric Walker's dog bounded out.

Loki ran over to greet Fluffy before skidding to an abrupt stop, flopping onto the grass and offering his belly. Fluffy gave him a polite sniff then a gentle lick on the face. Greetings over, Loki leapt up and bounded around Fluffy, tail wagging happily. Now that he was cleaned up, Loki was a handsome fellow with black and light-grey fur. He was about the same size as Fluffy. 'What kind of dog is he?' I asked as we all went inside.

'Appears to be a malamute husky,' Gunnar said. 'He's a good dog, well-behaved and grateful for attention. He's really taken to Sigrid.'

'That's nice. It was kind of you to take him in.'

'Happy to have a dog back in the household,' he admitted. 'I've missed it.'

Inside, the house was just as quaint and bursting with healthy plants. Either Sigrid or Gunnar had a green thumb – my money was on the former. I followed Gunnar through the living room; the dining area was little more than a table in the spacious kitchen, but it was homely and warm.

Sigrid was humming over the stove and I took a moment to study her. She was tall and solidly built, though next to Gunnar she looked quite small. She had long hair in a thick braid down her back; where mine was ash blonde, hers was golden like wheat. There was a little grey around the edges, but on her it just looked like highlights.

I'd put Gunnar at around fifty if he were human, but I had no idea how demi-gods aged. For that matter, I wasn't even sure I believed that he *was* a demi-god because I'd never seen anything particularly magical from him. Sigrid looked about the same sort of age, but from Gunnar's comments I assumed she was a magic user, and I didn't know the lifespan of the other supernaturals in town. They could both be fifty or five hundred. Despite the curiosity gnawing at me, I didn't ask. I'd been raised to be polite, and asking someone's age was rude.

Gunnar cleared his throat to announce our arrival and she turned and smiled welcomingly at us both.

Her smile widened further when her eyes met her husband's, the affection in them unmistakeable. He crossed the distance between them and swept her into a hug, lifting her off her feet and kissed her soundly.

Feeling uncomfortable, I looked away. My parents weren't big on public displays of affection and much more than a handshake in public had me ready to run. I was about to sidle out of the room when Gunnar put her down. 'Sig, this is Bunny. Bunny, Sigrid.'

'Pleased to meet you, Bunny.' Her smile was genuine.

I waited for the usual question about my name. I always had an answer prepared, and today's was a good one: I was going to say that it was because I had a habit of rearranging food on my plate in the shape of a rabbit. The question didn't come and I was vaguely disappointed; I'd been all prepared to re-enact *Watership Down* with my veggies.

Whatever Sigrid was cooking smelled divine and my stomach rumbled. I'd swigged a cup of blood back at the office but now I craved a hot meal, something new to tempt my palate. Fluffy and Loki were also looking at the food, both sitting nicely and staring expectantly. 'Thanks so much for inviting us,' I said. 'We don't eat many home-cooked meals and Fluffy gets so bored with dog food.'

Sigrid gave a tinkling laugh that belied her size. 'Everyone eats well here, as you can see.' She waved a hand down her body; she was shapely and not overly large, just a big woman and, in my estimation, a lovely one.

I thanked her again. 'Can I help with anything?'

'You can set the table.' She pointed out where the dishes and cutlery were. My mum had insisted that I knew the right way to set a formal table so I could do it properly if I landed a man who couldn't afford to pay for catering for a party. I had a lot of useless skills that my mother had insisted I'd need to succeed in 'society'.

'Oh! That's lovely,' Sigrid said with surprise. 'Flower napkins, how beautiful.'

I'd folded the paper towel napkins into flowers and placed them at the top of the knives. Not knowing what she was serving, I'd also put out two forks.

The crockery and utensils were mismatched, but I'd organised them as prettily as possible. I gave an awkward smile. The fancily folded napkins were probably a bit much; my mum had skewed my sense of what was normal. I made a mental note: no more flower napkins.

Sigrid placed a large roast, a casserole dish and several different vegetables on the table. My mouth watered. 'This is a moose roast and the casserole is a cheesy-potato concoction.' She winked. 'One of my own recipes.'

'It smells wonderful!' I said. Fluffy yipped agreement.

'Let's feed these hungry boys first or we won't have a restful meal with all of those puppy-dog eyes!' She gave each dog a plate piled with dog biscuits mixed with roast meat and a few potatoes.

Fluffy moaned – literally moaned – with pleasure as he gobbled his meal.

Once Sigrid was sitting down, we passed around the food and chatted. I'd never had moose before, but Mum was always getting me to eat outlandish posh foods like Densuke watermelon, oysters, and caviar. The meat was a little dry but the flavour was wonderful and I devoured everything.

'I made pie for dessert,' Sigrid announced and I wanted to kiss her. I loved pie!

Gunnar's phone rang. Sigrid frowned but nevertheless he answered it. We could only hear a faint, tinny voice at the other end so we waited until he was finished. His answers were short and perfunctory as his gaze strayed to his wife.

'Work?' I asked, when he'd hung up.

Gunnar nodded. 'Yeah, we gotta go.'

I got a chill. 'Not another murder?'

He grinned. 'Nothing so depressing, Little Miss Glass Half-Empty. Someone's found Eric's truck.'

Chapter 29

Once we were on the road, I asked, 'You were a bit cagey when you were on the phone. What didn't you want to say in front of Sigrid?'

Gunnar grimaced. 'If you thought I was cagey then so did Sig. Dammit. It was Stan that called – he found Eric's truck. On paper it doesn't look good after Virginia Tide's accusations. Sigrid thinks Stan is wonderful and she treats him almost like a son. He's often in our home – I don't want her to worry about him until we can clear him.'

Despite Virginia's accusations, I still had trouble visualising Stan as the killer. He'd struck me as straightforward: he'd thought I was attractive, so he'd given me a wink; he'd thought Mafu was annoying, so he'd given him a punch. I could imagine him beating up Eric, maybe even to death, but stabbing seemed out of character. I guessed that Gunnar agreed with my assessment because he'd said 'until' we clear him, not 'if' we clear him.

'On paper?' I asked.

'Stan's not an idiot. If he was the killer, he'd have set the truck on fire or taken it out of the state. He definitely wouldn't have called it in. If anything, that makes me even more certain of his innocence.'

'Unless he's counting on you thinking that,' I suggested.

'Maybe,' Gunnar conceded but he sounded unconvinced.

We pulled up in the car park of the fish processing plant next to a beat-up, navy-blue Chevy. Stan was leaning against a red-and-white Ford truck parked alongside it. 'It's a funny thing, Gunnar,' he started as we approached. 'I swear this wasn't here when I went in for the meeting. I chose a space next to two empty bays on purpose because I didn't want to scratch Bessie.' He patted his truck with affection.

'Bessie?' I grinned.

'You gotta name your vehicle.' He winked at me. 'Only crazy people don't name their vehicle.'

My grin widened. Stan was growing on me.

Gunnar gave one of his noncommittal grunts and Stan got back to the point. 'It wasn't here before. I mean, look at it – I'm parked *right* next to it, but I know I parked next to two empty bays. Besides, I would have noticed Eric's truck.'

If he was right, then my bet was that the killer was fucking with him – either that, or someone was trying to lose the truck amongst the factory employees' vehicles. It was more likely it had been deliberately parked by Stan's car in a clumsy attempt to frame him – or to ensure it was discovered.

'Thanks for calling it in, Stan,' Gunnar said. 'Could you come by the office tomorrow? I have a few more questions.'

'Sure.' He frowned. 'Am I a suspect?' For once, he sounded a little uncertain.

'Not in my book, son, but you know I have to follow protocol.'

Stan nodded, though he looked a little upset as he climbed into Bessie and left. There was no innuendo or winks for me; he was off his game, and I was surprised to feel a glimmer of sympathy for him. 'How come we didn't question him more now?' I asked nosily.

Gunnar nodded at the car. 'We need to dig into the vehicle and we can't do that with a possible suspect sitting idly by. What if he interfered with the evidence?'

'He'd already have done it before he called,' I pointed out.

Gunnar grimaced but didn't deny it. He passed me a pair of nitrile gloves and the camera; as we examined the outside of the truck, I started snapping away. I was beginning to get the hang of this crime-scene thing.

There was mud in the tyre treads and on the sides of the truck; either the murderer had been having fun off-road, or Eric hadn't washed his truck recently. After seeing his home, I suspected the latter. The truck was an older model, probably from the nineties, and it had dents and rust everywhere.

Fluffy was sniffing around Eric's truck and he whined at the rear driver's-side tyre. I assumed another dog had peed on it, probably Loki, so I shushed him. He sat and gave me sad puppy-dog eyes. 'I can't bring you with me anymore if you pee on the evidence,' I warned him sternly.

At my firm tone, he dropped to his belly, rested his head on his paws and looked dejected. My heart sank. He'd been through God knows what before I'd rescued him from that bin, and my firm tone had clearly triggered bad memories. Shit. 'I'm so sorry, boy,' I murmured. 'You aren't in trouble, I promise.'

He sat up slowly, eyeing me with a caution that stabbed my heart. After a moment he pointedly sniffed at the tyre again and looked at me expectantly.

I felt like a total idiot. Fluffy was a *dog,* and here I was acting like he was Skippy the bush kangaroo. '*What's the matter Skip? There's trouble?*' Feeling stupid I took out a swab kit, read the instructions on the outer packet then carefully swabbed the tire where Fluffy had been sniffing. The smell of the fish plant was permeating the air, so I couldn't catch anything else.

As I swabbed, Fluffy gave me a doggy grin with his tongue lolling out. I patted his head then marked the bag as 'rear-driver tyre' and threw it in the evidence box. It was probably an abuse of resources to send it to the lab so I'd have to toss it before it got sent out, but at least I'd made my dog happy.

We didn't see anything suspicious on the outside of the car so Gunnar went to open the doors. They were both locked. Bummer. He slid me a look then returned to the driver's side and tried again. This time the door opened. Huh? The same thing had happened with the back door at Eric's house. I could only conclude that Gunnar had some sort of lock-opening magic. Maybe it wasn't the most exciting skill but it would give a less-moral man a long career in burglary – yet here was Gunnar on the side of the law. Despite his love of moonshine, he was a good man, I was certain of it.

'I mustn't have pulled the handle hard enough,' he remarked airily.

I nodded. If he wasn't comfortable confessing about his magic, that was his concern. Still, I'd put money on Gunnar being a magic user.

The question was: why didn't he want me to know about it?

Chapter 30

Gunnar unlocked the passenger door and grimaced. 'Dammit,' he muttered. 'Smells like bleach. If the car has been bleached, we're not going to be able to tell if there was blood here or not.' He pulled a spray out of his kitbag. 'This is luminol. It's used to detect blood at a crime scene, even if the scene has already been scrubbed clean. It also reacts positively to the presence of bleach. Get ready to take some pictures.'

He sprayed it a little on the seats and instantly there was a blue glow. I took some pictures. Gunnar sprayed some more and the blue glow spread. 'The whole car has been scrubbed with bleach and that invalidates the reaction. Let's get searching.'

I took more photos as we started to look through the truck. Unlike Eric's house, the interior was pristine. I was fairly certain by now that the killer had stolen Eric's car and used it to leave the murder scene, then cleaned it to within an inch of its life so there were no prints, hair or blood to link them to the car. Thanks to shows like *Law and Order* and *CSI,* everyone these days thought they were an expert on forensics.

But if the killer had stolen the car, why dump it here rather than torch it? To point the finger at Stan? Or to plant something they wanted us to find?

I moved behind the passenger seat: no phone, no wallet, no murder weapon. It didn't look as if Gunnar had found anything useful either. No 'ah-ha!' moments for either of us.

There was a large console between the two front seats. Since Gunnar had started on the back seat, I climbed into the front and started wading through its contents. There was some loose change, a few old cassette tapes (who still had those?), and a phone charger that fit into the cigarette lighter.

I carefully checked each item and placed it in a bag. Finally, I reached the bottom and felt around the dark recess with my hand. Under the rim of the console was a folded piece of paper and I yelped in surprise as I felt a corner of it prick me. I pulled it out and unfolded it carefully. 'I found something,' I called excitedly.

Gunnar stopped searching and waited for me to read it. '*Dear Eric*,' it started. I flipped to the back to see who it was from, it was signed, '*Virginia*.'

I went back to the note. '*I don't think this is going to work out. Come and get your things, or I'll bag them up for you. I'm sorry, I thought we could work it out this time, but I'm done. After you get your things, I think it's best if we don't see each other again. Sorry, Virginia.*'

No date; nothing to say which of their many break-ups this related to.

I passed it to Gunnar and he scanned it, his expression unreadable. 'Not a note I'd hang on to,' he remarked. Did that mean it was recent?

'Me neither,' I said, 'but it was tucked into this hidden space. Maybe he shoved it in here and it got lost.'

'Maybe. Or maybe it was planted.'

'Or that.' Was someone trying to make us look more closely at Virginia? She hadn't been in floods of tears at the news of Eric's death, but we all grieved differently and she had seemed upset. But the most important thing was that she was human; she had no magic and therefore no means to kill him and, as far as we knew, no motive. I hadn't dismissed the idea of her hiring a hitman. I was unliving proof that people did shit like that in real life, not just in the movies.

I took back the note and studied the writing. It *looked* feminine – all loops, rounded edges and oversized – but who was I to judge? My handwriting looked like that of an angry serial killer. 'Do we have any samples of her handwriting to compare it to?' I asked.

Gunnar gave me another of his piercing looks. 'You're pretty good at this for someone with zero experience.'

My stomach fluttered a little with pride. I'd always thought I could be good at something like this, and it was a thrill to think that Gunnar thought so too.

'Virginia will be living on a human schedule, so we'll get a handwriting sample tomorrow,' he said. 'Something to add to your list. There should be a form we can get her to complete,' he mused.

'How about we get her to complete a witness statement by hand about the last time she saw Eric?' I asked.

He smiled. 'Two birds, one stone?'

'Exactly.'

We finished searching of the car but didn't find anything else interesting: no suspicious syringes or cloths smelling of chloroform. There was nothing to link the vehicle to any part of the murder, other than it possibly being used by the murderer to escape. But that didn't tally with what Virginia had said; she'd claimed Eric had walked to meet her on the night he had died. If that was the case, he must have gone back to his house and got in the truck – but why? Who was he driving to meet?

Gunnar called Burden's tow-truck company and arranged for the vehicle to be towed to the Nomo's office. We'd keep it there for a while, look through it again and then release it to the next of kin. 'We're still missing his keys, wallet, phone, and the murder weapon,' he said. 'Let's hope something shows up soon. Meanwhile, I'll see if we can get a psychic to look over the truck.'

'We have psychics?' I asked. I wondered why we hadn't asked them to look at Eric's house.

'There is one in town but she's a bit – eccentric. There's no guarantee she'll agree. She doesn't like to leave her home, so we'll have to take the truck to her and that will mess with the mojo. We'll see.'

I guessed that was why she hadn't been asked to check out the house. An agoraphobic psychic? I shook my head. One thing I was learning about Portlock: no one was quite what they appeared to be.

Chapter 31

I called Virginia at 8am. It wasn't my favourite time of day, even before I became a creature of the night, and apparently Virginia wasn't a lark either. She snarled, 'Who is calling this early? It's my day off!'

'I'm so sorry, Ms Tide, but I was wondering if you could come down to the Nomo's office and fill out a report.'

She sighed. 'I'm sorry, I'm not a morning person,' She paused a beat, 'I'm not an evening person either, but I can rock 11.30am like you wouldn't believe.'

That made me grin. 'I'm not a morning person either.'

'Well no, you wouldn't be,' she replied, her tone still humorous. 'Do I have to come in? Can't I do it online?'

'No, sorry. It's a paper form,' I said. We did have it online, but I needed that handwriting sample so I didn't regret the lie.

'How prehistoric,' she muttered. 'Fine, I'll come by at eleven.' She hung up without a goodbye.

Mum would have chewed her up for breakfast for those terrible manners. 'Rude,' I muttered. Fluffy yipped his agreement.

By noon Virginia still hadn't showed up and my good humour had worn off. I'd staggered up in *daytime* for this – and she hadn't strolled in yet? I was struggling seriously with tiredness and I'd even had a catnap on my keyboard. Fluffy had nudged me awake before my drool could damage the electrics.

I picked up the phone and dialled Virginia again. She didn't answer but this time I did get a terse text message that confirmed she was coming.

Sidnee walked in just after noon with two huge chai lattes and lunch. I was starving. I quickly microwaved some blood to line my stomach. Sidnee laughed as she watched me hold my nose whilst I chugged it down. 'I think you must be the least bloodthirsty vampire I've ever seen,' she teased. 'My neck has never felt safer.'

I stuck my tongue out in response and she giggled. We sat down together and ate. The food and the company really helped lift me out of the doldrums of daytime exhaustion. The blood had filled me more than I'd expected, so I gave Fluffy half of my pastrami on rye and sipped happily on my chai latte.

'Oh my God,' I said happily, 'I never thought I'd be able to get a chai latte in this t– town.' I cut myself off before I could say something scathing about the tiny, rustic place in which I now resided. That was my mum talking, not me. I cleared my throat. 'Where did you get this drink? From the gods?'

Sidnee laughed. 'The hardware store.'

'The *hardware* store?'

'Ernie makes a mean chai.'

'He sure does. Is there anything that Ernie *doesn't* do in this town?'

She giggled again. 'Nah, he's pretty much confined to the store and the radio station upstairs. But if you catch him between eleven and one on a lucky day, he works the coffee counter at the store and no one makes a chai tea like he does. It's almost ... magic.'

'What *is* he? *Could* it be magic?'

She frowned. 'It's considered a bit rude to quiz people on what they are, so just be careful who you ask, especially if you're not on the job with Gunnar.'

I nodded to show I'd taken her warning to heart; I could see how quickly I could get into trouble unintentionally.

'I think Ernie is some sort of magic user,' Sidnee mused. 'Not sure what kind, though. I guess his drinks could be magic, but he may just be great at steaming milk.'

'That's a super-power in my book.'

Sidnee laughed, then checked her phone and sighed. 'I've loved hanging out but I've gotta go. Have a good day!' She gave me an air kiss goodbye.

My face hurt from smiling. Being around Sidnee was always uplifting.

As two people approached the door, I tried to cling on to that feeling. One of them was Virginia; the other was technically my other boss: Connor MacKenzie.

Lucky me.

Connor held the door for Virginia and she preceded him in; boss or not, since she was first in, I dealt with her first. Besides, I was still a little miffed with Connor for insulting me – *twice*.

I gave her the paperwork to fill out and sent her to one of the waiting-room chairs before turning to Connor. Next to me, Fluffy let out a low growl. I loved my dog! 'How can I help you?' I asked, my voice saccharine sweet.

'Why aren't you at home? It's daylight.'

'Gosh,' I said, wide eyed, giving him my best blonde-bimbo impression. 'Thank goodness I have you to tell me the time. I still haven't worked out what the little hand on the clock means.'

He ignored my sass. 'The daylight exhaustion must be killing you.'

'That's what coffee is for,' I sniffed.

He frowned at me. 'You haven't checked in. It's irresponsible.'

Oh, wonderful: now he'd added irresponsible to my list of negative attributes. Unfortunately for him, I had no idea what he was talking about. My face must have shown my confusion because he expanded. 'The check-in. You never answered the email my office sent you and you've missed your first vampire mentor check-in.'

'I check my email every day – I have to for work. I never got an email from you or your office.'

He pulled out his phone and rattled off an email address. My heart thumped wildly. 'That's my old email,' I managed. Fuck. The vampire king had been monitoring my emails before I disappeared; was he still doing it? I hated the thought of him knowing about my new life, and I worried about him coming here and dragging me back to Europe by my hair. 'I shut that account down. It was compromised.' I licked my suddenly dry lips.

'Compromised how?' Connor folded his arms.

'My sire and the Vampire King of Europe were monitoring it. Once I got my secure email here, I shut down the old account and I haven't looked at it since.' I grabbed a Post-It note from my desk and wrote my new email address. 'Here's the one you should be using.'

His frown eased a little as he studied me. God knows what he was thinking – probably that I was a timid mouse as well as an irresponsible idiot. I forced myself to square my shoulders and look him in the eye. New town, new Bunny; I couldn't let the fear I'd felt in London follow me here. I'd been helpless then but I wasn't helpless now; I worked for the Nomo now. I was part of Team Law.

Connor's mouth tightened. 'Unfortunately your mentor has left town for a little while, but you still have to complete the intake and classes. I'll fill in until she gets back. Meet me at my office at Kamluck Logging after sunset.'

'If I don't get called on a crime I'll be there,' I promised.

The frown was back. 'You don't understand,' he said darkly. 'If you don't show, you won't be working here anymore.'

I blanched and took a step back. Some unidentifiable emotion danced across his face then was gone in an instant. When he next spoke, his tone was softer. 'You have to meet your obligations because you are a new vampire. We don't make you stay in a conclave here, but you have to check in once a week. Once you've completed a year without any issues, we can move you to a monthly check-in.'

Weekly check-ins were better than a hundred years in a conclave, but even so the restriction chafed. I had moved to the other side of the world, but I was still being controlled and constrained just like I had been by my mum all my damned life. Was *I* ever going to be the boss of me?

I clenched my jaw. Damn right I would be.

I asked Connor for the address of his office and he told me to Google Kamluck Logging. I guessed he'd become a vampire in an era when chivalry had already died. He walked out, all six-foot whatever. No matter how much he was annoying me, I could still enjoy those sharp cheekbones and the way that he filled his jeans... I sighed. I had *horrendous* taste in men.

Virginia was still scribbling away but with my sharpened supernat eyesight, I could already tell the handwriting looked *very* similar to the note. I texted Gunnar: *Virginia's writing looks same as note at cursory glance.*

We'll send it off for a formal examination, he texted back.

The rest of the day was slow and tiredness pulled at me, but as the sun dropped a new energy surged through me; I guessed I'd got my second wind. At least the long afternoon had been productive and I'd caught up on the paperwork from the murder. I had invoices to attend to and umpteen forms to fill out; luckily they were straightforward, and Sidnee had already shown me how to complete, copy and file them before I scanned them onto the electronic system and attached them to the relevant case file.

Gunnar walked in as daylight started to fade. It gave me a warm glow that he already trusted me to manage the office by myself; obviously, it might have been a case of necessity rather than trust, but I chose to take it as the latter.

He looked like death warmed up. 'What's the matter?' I asked right away. '

'Thomas Patkotak identified the werewolf.'

I blinked. 'Patkotak?'

'He has resources,' Gunnar said vaguely. 'Quicker ones than state ones.'

I frowned in confusion. 'But we'd already identified Eric Walker?'

'Not Eric. The other one.'

Ah: the one that had red eyes and haunted my dreams. Great, now we'd given my nightmare a name. I licked my dry lips. 'Well?'

Gunnar looked unhappy. 'It was Jack Taylor.'

'But Taylor was human,' I protested blankly.

'Born and raised, but werewolves are *made* – and Jack disappeared on the full moon,' he said grimly.

The penny dropped. 'Someone turned him.'

'And it didn't turn out right.'

'What makes you say that?'

'That thing that attacked us ... that wasn't Jack. Werewolves maintain their personality on a shift – they're the same person, but on four legs instead of two. But that thing...' Gunnar fell silent and we both looked at the boarded-up front door.

Fluffy rested his head on my knee in support. I broke the heavy silence awkwardly. 'Have you told the family?'

'No, I'll go and notify them now. They deserve closure. I just wanted to get the office keys from you before I go.'

'I can come with you,' I offered.

'That's okay,' he responded gently, but his eyes gave away his thoughts. He wasn't going to take me, their son's killer, to announce his death.

'Of course,' I managed. I packed up my stuff blindly and threw on my jacket. 'I'll leave you to it,' I passed him the office keys and scarpered. Gunnar was looking at me too knowingly, and I couldn't face it.

With Fluffy by my side, I all but ran home.

Chapter 32

I burst into my house, slammed the door and collapsed to the floor. I turned to my panting dog, 'Thank God you're here,' I murmured, throwing my arms around him. 'The werewolf I killed ... it was a boy, the missing boy – Jack. His name was Jack.'

Now I could let go, I started to cry in earnest. Fluffy laid his head next to mine, whining softly whilst I sobbed my heart out. When the tears slowed, I took a shuddering breath. 'It's okay,' I said to my still-whining dog. 'Don't be sad. It was just a shock. It's one thing to kill a scary beast that was attacking me; it's another to have killed twenty-one-year-old Jack. It's just going to take a while to settle in. That's all.'

I gave a shaky smile. 'Come on, let's feed you before I have to go and meet the lumbering lumberjack.'

I was feeling raw and vulnerable; the last thing I wanted right now was a meeting with Connor – who literally might be the boss from hell. Who knew where vampires originated? It didn't feel heavenly to have to ingest blood to survive, that was for sure. But wherever he was from, he was my destination tonight so I'd have to like it or lump it.

I tried to count my blessings. At least I wasn't dead like Jack or going to meet with the Vampire King of Europe. Connor was grumpy and insulting, but he hadn't tried to hurt or punish me. So far, the grass really was greener.

I drank some blood, popped a frozen dinner in the microwave to cook then filled Fluffy's dishes. We took a short walk while my meal cooked. 'I want to take you with me,' I assured my dog, 'but I'd better check out the lay of the land first. Connor might be more of a cat person. Are you okay staying here, bud?' I asked as we walked back inside.

He barked once but looked sad. I hated the time he spent locked up in the house, though it was much better now that I could take him to work with me. 'I promise I'll take you next time if I can.'

That seemed to cheer him up. I gave him a treat and he lay down on the floor to eat it while I wolfed down my meal. It wouldn't win any culinary awards but it filled a space.

I Googled the address of the logging office and saw that it was ten miles away. What was Connor thinking? I could probably walk or run there, but it would take ages and I didn't want to arrive all sweaty and gross. I didn't even know if Portlock had a taxi, so I called Sidnee to ask. 'There sure is,' she promised. 'You just dial 907 followed by 2. You'll be good,' she promised.

I hung up, dialled, and ten minutes later a green mini-van pulled up in front of my house. I patted Fluffy, grabbed my phone and went outside. I recognised the taxi driver right away: it was Thomas Patkotak. Now, what in heck was he doing driving a taxi? Unease stirred in my gut. Gunnar had said

Patkotak hunted naughty supernaturals and I'd killed Jack...

I remembered the armoury that he had brought to the council meeting; no doubt he was similarly armed now. If I ran, I could get a tomahawk in the back.

Fuck. Be brave, Bunny. Gunnar hadn't arrested me; he hadn't even made a note on my file. It had been a justified killing. Maybe Patkotak was here to shake my hand. Yeah, right.

Trying to appear calm, I started towards the car. At least being repeatedly dragged into Mum's soirees had given me the ability to fake it till I made it. Hopefully Patkotak wouldn't even know that I was shitting myself.

The man behind the wheel gave a friendly smile that instantly eased some of my tension. I tried to smile back. 'Mr Patkotak?'

He chuckled. 'One and the same. You have a great memory – you only met me for a heartbeat that one time.'

'You made an impression,' I said drily. 'You had quite the array of weapons with you. I was impressed.'

'Always best to be armed. You never know what will try to kill you in Portlock.' Suddenly all hints of good humour were gone.

A shiver ran down my spine. I thought of poor Jack – and Eric – and found myself agreeing with him.

'Where to?' he asked, once I was sitting in the front seat next to him. Maybe he really was just here as a taxi driver. Huh.

'Kamluck Logging office, please.'

'Ah, off to see the big vamp boss.'

'Yeah.' I sighed. 'The one and the same.'

'So... Bunny is an unusual name.'

He didn't ask the question, but I answered it all the same. 'During a camping trip I put on my bunny slippers and refused to take them off around the campfire. I got too close and an ember flew out and landed on one of them. I had to take it off and hop around for the rest of the trip,' I lied.

Patkotak smirked, but his expression said clearly that he wasn't buying the BS I was peddling. He struck me as someone in the know, and finding out he'd managed to identify Jack before the state team reinforced that. 'Can I ask a question?' I asked.

'You go for it,' he grinned. 'But I reserve the right not to answer.'

'Noted. At the council meeting, what was all that chatter about the barrier and the cairn?'

He was silent for a few moments. 'Gunnar didn't fill you in?'

'No,' I paused. 'I think he's afraid he'll scare me off.'

Thomas studied me for a second. 'You seem solid. You're still here after being attacked by a werewolf.'

I appreciated him not calling Jack by name; humanising my victim made it so much worse. 'Thanks.' Since I was feeling bold and reckless, I added, 'And you're not afraid to be alone in a car with a vampire.'

He barked a laugh. 'Darlin', I could kill you ten ways before your fangs dropped.'

I didn't doubt that, and for some strange reason it made me like him more. He wasn't in the least bit afraid of me, but even he looked nervous talking about the beast beyond the barrier. 'So, what *is* out there beyond the barrier?' I had questions, important questions like what sort of beast was it? Could it be killed? And did it think vampires were tasty?

'Long ago, this was just a normal town, as ped as it comes, even smaller than it is now. People did three main things here for employment – fishing, logging and mining. One day, a man was out working. When he didn't come back, people went looking for him. He'd had his head stoved in by some logging equipment, a piece of metal weighing more than five hundred pounds. Someone had picked it up, bashed his head in and left him there to die.' He looked at me to see if I was still following.

'A vampire could do that,' I suggested.

'True, but at the time no vamps lived here. There were a couple other supernaturals, and a shaman from the Alutiiq tribe, but it wasn't as cosmopolitan as it is now.' He turned up a road with nothing but forest on both sides. The trees hid the moonlight and our route darkened. I shivered; it was atmospheric, to say the least.

Patkotak continued. 'Then a group of miners didn't come back. A few days later their bodies washed down the river into the bay. They hadn't been cut up or chewed on – something had *torn* them apart.'

The hairs rose on the back of my neck.

'People were spooked. They quit coming to work and businesses had to have guards. Finally the shaman said it was a nantinaq and told his people they had to leave. The natives left.'

Thomas appeared to be native or part native and I wondered if he was also Alutiiq. I didn't ask; I didn't want to be impolite to someone who claimed he could kill me ten times before my faulty fangs dropped. 'What's a nant-ee-nok?' I asked hesitantly.

'A vengeful bigfoot.'

'Vengeful?'

'Vindictive. Malevolent. We had encroached on his territory and he was pissed off. Only this didn't seem to be a normal bigfoot – he was larger, scarier and meaner than our woodland brothers. Frankly, I'm not even sure it was a bigfoot.'

We turned onto a street I'd never been on before.

'Anyway, the few supernaturals that were here joined forces and came up with the barrier. They begged the Alutiiq to come back, and some did. A few humans stayed or came to work here, but the barrier keeps most away, particularly those that want to investigate a spooky "ghost town". We just live our lives, keep our noses clean and we have this little patch of paradise to ourselves.'

'Wow, that's some story. So the barrier has kept the bigfoot creature away for how long?'

'Nearly a hundred years. It went up in 1931. We have a celebration each year when the spell is strengthened and renewed. You'll get to see it soon.'

'And humans can't see Portlock through the barrier?'

'Not unless they've been formally invited in or they have some supernatural blood.' We turned and stopped in front of a log building. 'We're here.'

'Thanks so much Mr Patkotak. I really enjoyed the ride.' I opened the door and climbed out.

As I shut it, Patkotak rolled down the window; evidently he wasn't quite done with our conversation.

'You're welcome, Bunny. Call me Thomas.' He shifted in the seat to look out at me. 'I'm not usually a taxi driver these days but I wanted to talk to you. Since I own the cab company, I had the driver take off early.'

I gave him a sharp look. 'Why?'

'I wanted to take your measure since you killed Jack,' he said evenly. 'You have hidden depths, I think. You intrigue me, Bunny from England, and I think I can help you.'

'Help me? With what?'

He smiled faintly. 'With murder.'

Chapter 33

After my encounter with the enigmatic Thomas Patkotak, I was more than a little on edge for my meeting with Connor. My nervousness may have stemmed in part from my perception of vampires – but they *had* turned me without my permission and forced me to discover a whole new magical world. Okay, so magic was kind of cool, but forcing me to drink blood for the rest of my life not so much. That shit should have come with a permission slip.

I forced myself to put one foot in front of the other. Connor had warned me that my job was on the line and I loved it enough to stick my head into a lion's gaping maw – or stroll into a vampire's lair. Besides, the whole thing with Jack had unnerved me and I needed to prove to myself that I could still do this. This was a *new* Bunny, dammit, not one who turned tail at the first sign of danger.

The office was a single-room cabin with four desks and chairs, shelves, filing cabinets and, of course, Connor MacKenzie. He was looking through the filing cabinet when I walked in. 'Just a minute,' he said without looking up. How charming: I didn't even warrant eye contact.

Still, there was a silver lining: he was bent over so I could shamelessly ogle his fine figure. At times like these, it was hard to remember that he was a total arsehole. Then I remembered that I'd arrived punctually *and* I'd had to take a cab, and here he was making me wait in some sort of childish powerplay. I refused to be riled.

Mum would have made me sit demurely while I waited, legs crossed at the ankle, hands resting on each knee, head slightly bowed. Since I was feeling churlish and was trying my best to be the antithesis of all she'd taught me, I sat down and slung my legs over the chair arm.

It had been a long, emotional day. I'd been fighting daylight exhaustion all day, plus there's been the emotional upheaval of the whole werewolf attack. Stick a fork in me, I was done. I closed my eyes for a little catnap. Connor could wake me when he finished being powerful with his filing.

I opened my eyes abruptly, certain that the noise of my own snoring had woken me. Connor was studying me with an unreadable expression. I yawned. 'All done with your paperwork?' I asked.

'Some time ago,' he said drily. 'That's quite the snore you have.'

I refused to blush. 'A sign of healthy lungs.'

'No doubt.' He looked amused. I studied him; his dark hair was a little long and curled around his ears. His blue eyes studied me right back. 'Shall we start?' he asked softly.

Still half-asleep, I blinked. Start what? A tempestuous affair? Because I was pretty sure that's what I'd been dreaming about, and I was game if he was. He might be obnoxious but he was pretty, and he didn't need to *talk* during sex...

'Start the meeting,' he clarified. 'Thank you for arriving on time. I apologise for keeping you waiting.'

I waved one hand dismissively. 'No problem.'

His lips twitched. 'You managed to keep yourself occupied.' His tone was warmer than it had been previously and I wondered what had changed. 'I have some forms for you to fill out.'

'More forms? Why?'

'Because we like to keep good records on our people in case of emergency.'

'The borough already has all my information,' I explained.

'We aren't part of the borough, we're a separate entity and we report to the world vampire council.'

My mouth went dry. 'There's a world council?' I squeaked, thinking that my escape from the Vampire King of Europe might not have been an escape after all. If Connor reported my info to the vampire council, could they make me go back to him?

He frowned at me as my breath started coming thick and fast. 'What's wrong?' He looked around, alarmed.

'I...' I didn't know what to say to him. Could I tell him that I'd fled from my sire, that I'd run away to avoid the conclave and one hundred years of indentured servitude? Would he send me back if he knew I'd flouted the rules? 'I can't do this now,' I said lamely.

His frown deepened. 'What's the issue – can't you write?'

I glared. I'd had one of the finest educations money could buy and I knew all sorts of truly useless shit; I could talk about Monet or Descartes until the cows came home. 'I can read *and* write,' I said through gritted teeth. 'But I have enemies in Europe. Vampire enemies. I don't want them to know where I am.'

'So how would your info get back to them?' Connor looked confused.

'Surely if you file it with the world council, my enemies can find me?'

'No, they only need to keep track of you if you do something you shouldn't, like expose the supernat world to the humans or kill another vampire. If you're on the Nice List then the paperwork gets filed locally.'

He shrugged. 'The world council is a little behind on modern technology.'

The council might be, but the vampire king had monitored my phone and computer so closely that I'd ditched them once I got here.

'What about if you kill a werewolf?' I asked faintly. 'Am I still on the Nice List then?'

'There's enmity between vampires and shifters, for all we currently have a truce. So yes, you're still on the Nice List.' He leaned forward and studied me. 'How are you feeling about dispatching the werewolf?'

I bristled. 'What are you? A psychologist?'

'No, but I'm responsible for you. It is my job to take care of you.'

'I can take care of myself.'

'Evidently so – or the werewolf wouldn't be dead.'

I flinched. 'It was Jack Taylor,' I said softly.

He froze. 'The werewolf?'

'Yes.' I bit my thumb and thought of Kivuk. 'Can a vampire be turned into a werewolf?'

'No,' Connor said decisively. 'We're already dead.'

I sighed. 'I don't *feel* dead.'

'Neither do I. Now, the paperwork?'

I sighed. 'You promise it won't leave your office?'

'I'll even shake on it.' He held out his hand.

I looked at the calloused hand being held out to me; it felt like he was offering me more than a handshake, more than a promise. I swung my legs to the ground and took it.

As we touched, an electric zing blasted through my hand. I think Connor felt it too, because he let go just as abruptly. I looked up at him, ready to ask what had happened, but my words died in my throat.

He was looking at me like I was lunch. His pupils were incredibly large, making his ice-blue eyes appear black. The tension between us was suddenly overwhelming, and I itched to lean over the desk and kiss him. With herculean effort, I scuffed my toe on the floor, using the action to look away from him and break the spell.

'I must have built up an electric charge or something from the carpet,' I mumbled. I looked down at the worn and grimy commercial carpet beneath my trainers. 'Sorry I shocked you.' He was still staring at me. I cleared my throat, 'So, where's this paperwork?'

He blinked, and whatever moment we'd had was broken. When he turned back, he was all business. He handed me a file. The forms inside it were pretty basic – they weren't asking my bra size or my favourite meal.

I sat down and started filling it in. Connor was back in his chair, looking at his computer, but I knew his eyes were on me when I was looking down at the forms.

I wrote until my hand ached, then gave Connor a copy of my passport and visa. Once the paperwork was done, he studied me again. 'You don't know anything about vampire culture, do you?'

'Other than the whole drinking-blood thing, no. Is this the part of the meeting where you tell me I should be sleeping in a coffin?'

His lips turned up. 'If it gets your rocks off. Personally, I prefer a bed.'

Talking about beds with him felt far too intimate. 'Can I go now?' I asked abruptly.

'Are you in a hurry to leave, little rabbit?'

I glared. 'It's Bunny, and you know it.'

His smile widened. 'It's a hard name to forget. Much like the woman.' He sobered. 'Do you know how long it's been since someone slept in my presence?'

'Like, last week?' I asked sarcastically.

'A century or more. Amongst vampires, sleeping – *just* sleeping – is a sign of great trust. Whether you meant to or not, I promise I won't treat it lightly, Bunny.'

It could have been worse; I could have proposed to him or something. 'Great, thanks. That's swell. If we're done here, I'd like to go home.'

'Just a few more things.' He handed me a paper with a list of websites on it. 'You have to take vampire classes. You should know the basics.'

'Like don't go to sleep in other vampires' offices,' I muttered.

He smiled. 'Like that,' he agreed. 'We don't teach the classes here, but someone has taped them. You need to complete one video from each of the ten categories, and there's a paper test when you're done. Let me know when you're ready and we'll set it up.'

I groaned. 'Seriously? Surely all I need to qualify as a vampire is to be undead and drink blood? This isn't a driving exam – there doesn't need to be a theory portion.'

He smirked. 'You have thirty days.'

'Fine. Great.' I pulled out my phone.

'Who are you calling?' he asked curiously.

'I don't have a car, and your lodge is ten miles from my house. I'm calling a taxi.' I pressed dial.

Connor reached over lightning fast and hung up the call. 'No.'

I stood up in a snit. 'No? What the hell do you mean, no? I'm not bloody well walking.'

'Obviously not. You're newer than a week-old lamb. You can't ride with humans because their blood is too tempting. The cab company is owned and run by humans, and we can't risk an incident.' He picked up some keys from his desk. 'I'll give you a ride.'

Much as I appreciated the offer, I hated that I had no choice. I was never putting myself in that position again. 'Look, Mr MacKenzie—'

'Connor.'

'Connor, then. I came here in a taxi, and the driver is still very much alive. I've never been tempted to drink human blood – or any blood that doesn't come from my fridge. I can barely make myself drink *that*.' I grimaced. I hated that it tasted good and I needed it to survive. It was still *blood*...

His jaw dropped a little. 'Are you kidding?'

'No, I'm not,' I said grumpily. 'And I'm not keen on accusations that I'm about to go on a bloody killing spree!' My sire had made much the same irritating – and erroneous – statements.

'Okay, calm down.'

My glare intensified. I'd calm down one of my feet in his crotch if he wasn't careful. 'Why does everyone assume I'm one second away from a bloodbath?'

'Because you're a new vamp and most new vampires are driven by bloodlust. The smell, the pulse, the beating heart of a living thing – they're hard to resist.'

I could hear heartbeats, but I tuned them out like I would an irritating toddler. 'Then call me Job and watch me walk away from temptation. I drink my three cups of blood a day and I eat regular food. I'm fine. Can I call a taxi now?'

'I'm happy to drive you home,' he said mildly, though he was still looking at me like he thought I was lying.

I didn't particularly want to be alone with Connor for any longer than possible. We had all this chemistry and tension – and I didn't know what the fuck that zap had been – I still wasn't over my last date with a vampire. One moment I'd been kissing Franklin, the next I'd been undead.

Connor was handsome, and I was attracted to him like a magnet to iron, but it was just science. I just needed to reverse my magnetic field and I'd repulse him and it'd be fine. End of story.

I risked a glance at him. His jaw was set. I sighed. 'You aren't going to let me call a taxi, are you?'

'No. I can't.'

I despised that he was giving me no choice but I saw no option other than walking home and I was tired. I swallowed my pride with difficulty. 'Fine, let's get this over with.'

Chapter 34

The silence in the car was thick and oppressive, hanging in the air like a third, uninvited passenger. It felt awkward to me and evidently Connor felt the same, because after a difficult five minutes he shattered the silence with something predictable. 'So, Bunny, how did you get your nickname?'

I hated it when people relegated my name to 'nickname' status, so I pulled out one of my most bullshit responses. 'I was born with a congenital tail. Even though it was removed, my parents insisted on calling me their little Peter Rabbit. Eventually it got shortened to Bunny.' I could tell from his face that he wasn't sure if I was lying or not. I kept my expression bland.

'Is there a reason you don't use Elizabeth?' he asked finally. 'That's a nice, solid name.'

'Yes,' I said drily. 'My parents gave it to me.' Besides wealth, an excellent education and a nanny to raise me, that was about all they'd given me. Hashtag poor little privileged white girl problems. I mentally played myself the world's smallest violin and I couldn't stop the bitter smile that rose.

'Who was your cab driver?' Connor asked, obviously trying his best to keep some sort of conversation going. Obviously he didn't like the cloying silence any more than I did.

'Thomas Patkotak.'

'Ah,' he said, like it answered a million questions.

It didn't answer any for me. 'What does that mean?' I asked when curiosity got the better of me.

'Nothing, I was just curious.'

'Bullshit! Just tell me you don't want to tell me. I hate lying.'

He sighed. 'You're very prickly.'

I folded my arms defensively. That silence rolled out again for a while, thicker than a bank of fog, until he asked, 'What's your dog's name?'

'Fluffy.'

'Bunny and Fluffy?' A smile tugged at his lips.

'Yeah, so?' I sounded like a mulish teen but he was pressing all my buttons.

'Have you had him long?'

'I got him after I was turned. Someone had locked him in a bin.'

'People are animals,' he growled.

At least we could agree on that, and I grudgingly gave Connor a tick in the plus column. If he liked dogs, he wasn't a complete arsehole. 'Yeah, they suck.' I agreed. 'Fluffy was starving, and filthy. I saved him and he saved me right back.'

I cursed the second I confessed that vulnerability but it was true. It wasn't just that Fluffy had attacked my sire for me, he saved me every moment he was next to me with his pure, unconditional love. It was a constant balm to my soul. Maybe one day, he'd help me heal the gaping fractures in my heart.

'Vampires rarely have pets,' Connor warned. 'Unless the vamps are really old.'

'Why not?' I asked, incredulous.

'Bloodlust. They end up juicing their pet and can't live with the guilt. Having Fluffy is going to raise eyebrows in the vampire community – it says a lot about you and your self-control.'

'I'd never hurt Fluffy.'

'I believe you.' He sounded faintly surprised.

We turned into my street and I grabbed the door handle before we'd even rolled to a stop outside my house. I couldn't get away from him quickly enough. I pushed open the car door.

'Bunny, wait.'

I froze.

'How about dinner some night?'

He wanted *more* of this uncomfortable situation? 'Umm,' I managed. How the fuck did I turn him down without offending him? He was my *boss*.

He smiled ruefully. 'Too soon. Sorry, maybe another time. Have a good night.' He was trying to hide it, but his eyes looked a little vulnerable. Oh bollocks. I didn't want to upset the local vampire head honcho – and maybe I didn't want to close the door to a date in the future. He *did* like dogs, after all.

'My last date was with my sire,' I blurted out. 'And you know how that turned out. I'm not ready to date yet, but thanks for the lift home.' I jumped out of the car without waiting for his response.

I ran to the door – and froze. Tacked to my front door was a note: *Make sure Eric's death becomes a cold case, or I'll make sure you become as cold as him.*

My eyes narrowed. Sonofabitch – someone was threatening me. We must be doing something right.

The front door was still locked and there were no signs of a break-in. 'Fluffy, are you okay in there?' I called. He barked in response. 'I'm not touching the door until we've had the chance to do prints and stuff. Stay there.'

I looked back; sure enough, Connor was waiting to check I'd got inside okay. When I didn't unlock my door, his eyes sharpened and I saw his lips move in a swear word. He pulled out his phone, made a brief call then turned off the truck engine and joined me. 'Are you okay?' he asked with concern.

'I've been threatened before. As threats go, this one's pretty weak,' I said lightly. 'Threatening me with being cold? I'm cold all the time – Alaska's pretty chilly at this time of year.'

Connor obviously picked up on my need not to show fear. 'It gets warmer, though probably not what *you'd* call warm – forty to sixty Fahrenheit in summer,' he said lightly.

'I'm a Brit. I work in Celsius.'

'Four to fifteen Centigrade.'

'In summer? That's awful! I should have done my research before I hopped on a plane. I was too busy thinking about two months without daylight. Being restricted to night time in London sucked.' I touched the charm around my neck. 'But this helps.'

'The charms are incredibly rare and very expensive. Don't expect all vampires to have them, and be wary of other vamps trying to take yours. It's like wearing a diamond the size of a fist around your neck.'

'Gunnar didn't mention that.'

'Gunnar doesn't mention a lot of things,' he muttered, frowning. 'Speak of the devil.'

My boss's SUV drove up. He parked and slid out of the car looking grim. 'Bunny, Connor,' he greeted us. 'What have we got here?'

'Just a note,' I said as nonchalantly as I could. Maybe I'd be scared later, but for now I was keeping my emotions tucked in tight.

The note had been written in block capitals on ordinary white paper. Gunnar was wearing nitrile gloves. He took a few pictures of the door then slid the note into an evidence bag. 'I'll send it to the lab and get it checked for prints.'

'Make sure it's expedited,' Connor growled.

'Obviously.' Gunnar frowned. 'I take care of my own.'

'Evidently not.' Connor gestured to the note. 'You need to find the killer.'

'We're working hard on it,' I interjected before they fell into a pissing contest.

Connor's eyes softened. 'I know. Open up, let's do a walk-through.'

As I unlocked the door, Fluffy rushed to me barking repeatedly. 'I know,' I murmured comforting him. 'Someone came to the door. Did they come in?' Fluffy let out a low growl that promised violence and his hackles rose. 'You saw them off, huh?' He barked again. 'Good boy.' I gave him a full body cuddle. 'Who's my good boy?'

'Lucky mutt,' Connor muttered under his breath. I looked at him, but he clearly hadn't intended me to hear his comment. He was still standing on the front step. 'May I come in?'

'Oh! Is the needing to be invited in thing for real?'

He looked amused. 'No, it's just polite. You need to watch those videos I gave you.'

I flushed. 'Right. Well, sure, come on in.'

The two men checked the house whilst I stayed in the hallway with Fluffy. After a few minutes, Gunnar rumbled, 'All clear. No sign of an intruder.'

'Great,' I said, but the adrenaline was leaving me and my bravado was going with it. 'Thanks.'

Gunnar gave me a nod. 'We'll head out. See you tomorrow at the office.'

'Will we have any prints?'

'Tomorrow? No. Maybe the day after, if there are any. We have to be realistic – they probably wore gloves.'

I grimaced. He was right, the same as with the car. The killer was annoyingly switched on; it was just my luck to get a smart killer. Gunnar drove away but Connor hesitated. I gave him an awkward wave and he smiled; with the smile, those blue eyes looked less like ice and more like the sea.

I fucking love the sea.

When he'd driven away, I turned to Fluffy who was waiting patiently in front of the door. I wondered if he'd been sitting there the whole time waiting faithfully for my return. I hoped the killer had got the scare of a lifetime when Fluffy growled through the door.

I gave him another full body cuddle. 'Thanks for watching out for me, bud. I'm sorry I didn't take you, but I'm pleased as hell you stayed here.' I kept on patting him because the action soothed me, too. 'Let's talk about other stuff. If I think too much about the note, I'll freak out. Let's talk about Connor instead. Let me tell you, that meeting was so awkward. Be glad you didn't go,' I murmured into his thick fur.

'Half the time I want to go full Buffy on his ass, the other half I want to go full Faith. This time, though, he tried to make conversation. It was almost nice.' I sighed and scruffled Fluffy's ears. 'Will I ever fit in here?'

At least one person wanted me gone; the killer thought that I was a weak target, weaker than Gunnar. But I was a vampire for God's sake – I drank *blood*. I needed to toughen up; no self-respecting vampire would quake in their boots because of a damned note. It was paper and ink, nothing more.

Fluffy jumped all over me, pulling me out of my reverie. He licked my face and neck until I giggled. He thought I was doing just fine.

Maybe one day soon I'd believe it, too.

Chapter 35

I awoke after a sleep fraught with dreams to a weird text message: a list of five names from an unknown number.

I replied straight away: *Who is this? What's with the list?* I was sharp because the note was still freaking me out. What if this message was from the killer, a list of their next victims? I discarded the thought immediately; only a genuine idiot would tell the police their next targets.

I looked out of the window and my heart stopped when I saw a truck parked out front. It started again when I realised the truck was Connor's. He'd been guarding me whilst I slept? A tiny feminist part of me wanted to be outraged because the suggestion that I couldn't take care of myself pissed me off, but mostly I was incredibly grateful to see him there. He probably protected all of the new vampires like this. Uh-huh.

My phone beeped with another message. *It's Thomas. It's a suspect list. Hunt them down.*

Aren't you the hunter? I sassed back.

Aren't you the police? There's no bounty, so it's all yours. The thought that I was the police made me snort. But why help *me*? Why hadn't he given the list to Gunnar? Was there history between them?

I replied: *I'll go through your list, but only if you tell me where you were the night of the murder.*

The only thing he wrote back was: *Ha!*

That was *not* an alibi, but Thomas was human. From what Gunnar had told me, he could definitely kill a werewolf but not in the way in which Eric had died – no human could do that. We were looking for a magic user or a shifter.

The list seemed endless, but perhaps with Thomas's help we had a solid place to start. It felt a little like cheating but the real police worked with tip-offs all the time. Besides, if the killer now had me in their sights, I suddenly felt a whole lot more motivated to find the fucker.

Excited that we might actually get somewhere, I showered, dressed and hustled into work as the sun was setting. Gunnar was waiting at my desk; Sidnee must have already clocked off for the day. 'What's up?' I asked. 'Prints back?'

'No, nothing yet on that front, Bunny. But our tech guys had a look at the phone we found in the drink. It was Eric's all right, but it had recently had a factory reset. Nothing helpful on it.'

'Damn.'

'Yeah. So after that disappointment, I took the car to our psychic, Marguerite, but unfortunately she didn't get anything from it. She said its energy had been cleansed.' He sighed. 'I've been chasing dead ends all day. Now you're here, let's go and meet the first magic user on our list of suspects.' He scanned my face. 'Are you okay after that note yesterday? If you need a day in the office, it's not a problem.'

'I'm fine,' I promised airily. 'Were you sent the same list?' I asked curiously.

'*I* compiled my list after talking to Sigrid about the powerful magic users in this town. What list are you talking about?'

I showed him Thomas's message. Gunnar looked surprised. 'Why would he do that?'

'He drove me to my meeting with Connor last night and said he'd help me find Eric's murderer. How can he know anything if he isn't involved?'

'Thomas is a force of nature,' Gunnar said begrudgingly. 'He has resources we could only dream of. Anything coming from him is worth checking out,'

'Okay.' I waited a beat. 'He wouldn't tell me where he was the night of the murder. In fact, he laughed when I asked him.'

Gunnar grimaced. 'Patkotak is a *hunter*. If he'd murdered Eric, we'd never have known because the body would have disappeared.'

I nodded, trying not to show that I was a little spooked by that titbit. I changed the subject, 'So which magic user are we visiting first?'

'Anissa Popov, the Alutiiq shaman.'

'What do you want me to do? Take notes?'

'Keep that bright mind working, those excellent vampire eyes looking, and that great memory memorisin',' he said with a chuckle.

I hadn't told Gunnar about my memory, so I guessed he had his own deductive skills too. 'How does Thomas's list compare to Sigrid's?' I asked.

'Completely different,' he admitted. 'We'll run down Sigrid's list first and deal with the three magic users first. I want to get them done quickly – if we take too long, we'll have to deal with Liv, and I make a point *not* to deal with Liv,' he said drily.

'Who else are we covering today?'

'Shirley Thompson and Freya Sigurdson, both witches.'

I didn't know anything about witches or shamans. 'Can shamans and witches hurt us?' I asked nervously. The note had put an itch between my shoulder blades.

'You're safe with me,' Gunnar promised fiercely, though it was notable that he didn't confirm that they *couldn't* hurt us.

'Is that a "they wouldn't dare" safe, or an "I can out-magic them" safe?'

He laughed – but once again he didn't answer. I liked Gunnar but he was very private about his powers, whatever they were.

'Should I take Fluffy home?' If he was home, he would guard it but he was also vulnerable. Then again, the killer hadn't attempted to go inside.

Gunnar looked at him and scratched his beard thoughtfully. 'Let's take him with us. You never know when we'll need a little intimidation.'

'Fluffy isn't mean,' I protested.

'Of course not, but he looks like a police dog. I think it's time we get him a K-9 vest and use him properly. That okay with you?' he asked Fluffy, who gave him a wag.

'Hang on. He's not a trained police dog – I don't want him getting hurt.' It was one thing taking him to the office with me while I did paperwork; it was another thing to trot him out with us to question suspects.

'I have a vest for him. He'll be fine, but it's your call. We can leave him here,' Gunnar offered.

Fluffy gave a low whine and looked at me pleadingly; he wanted to ride shotgun. I sighed. 'Where's the vest?'

'Same place everything is, in the back room, top shelf, in a box labelled "Killer".'

I found the black bulletproof vest. It read 'Nomo K-9' on the side in gold lettering. When I pulled it over Fluffy's head and did up the Velcro fasteners, it covered his chest, his sides and down to the base of his tail. A perfect fit.

We walked back out and for a second Gunnar froze before pulling a smile onto his face with a real effort. 'You look like a real police dog now, Fluffy,' he said, but his voice was tight.

Even though I'd only had Fluffy for a matter of weeks, the thought of losing him one day made my heart constrict. Maybe that was another reason why vampires didn't have pets: having something to love with a mortal lifespan was a recipe for heartbreak. Nonetheless, I reached out to touch Gunnar's arm in silent sympathy for his loss. He might have Loki now, but Killer would always be padding around after him in his heart and his memories.

Fluffy broke the heavy moment because he got distracted by chasing his tail. Moments later he was spinning round and round in a tight circle, making me laugh. 'Stop! You're making me dizzy! Dumb dog.' I gave his head an affectionate ruffle. He gave a sharp bark followed by his doggy smile.

Gunnar patted his head again. 'Let's get this show on the road. We've got suspects to question and a killer to catch.'

Amen to that.

Chapter 36

We loaded up the SUV and drove to a neighbourhood I hadn't seen yet. I was slowly building up a nice visual map of Portlock in my head, but there were still blank spaces. I'd get there.

Whilst we were driving, I got a message from Sidnee: *Gunnar told me about the note, you're welcome to stay with me anytime.* That warmed me.

I'm okay, I tapped back, *but I really appreciate the offer.*

The car rolled to a stop. The shaman's house was different from the other houses I'd seen so far; in fact, it looked older than any building I'd seen so far in America. It was built of logs and it was low – almost eye-level for Gunnar – and had what appeared to be a sod roof.

'I didn't know anyone still lived like this,' I murmured, eying the house with trepidation. It looked like a sneeze might send it tumbling, and being smothered by tonnes of earth was not my preferred way to go.

We knocked on the door and a few seconds later it swung open. A small, ancient woman waved us in without comment and a chill ran down my spine. She'd been expecting us but I knew that Gunnar hadn't called in advance. That didn't bode well.

The house was partially dug into the hill that it rested against. It was warm, dry and very cosy, and it looked modern. The magnolia paint, wooden floors and big TV on the wall were in complete contrast to the outside.

'Are you Anissa?' Gunnar asked, and I fought to keep the surprise off my face. I thought he knew everyone in Portlock, though logically in a town of a thousand inhabitants – maybe two – he couldn't know them all. Maybe he was only familiar with the movers and shakers.

The old woman shook her head and left us in the living room. Soon a younger woman came out, drying her hands and looking faintly harassed. 'Hi, I'm Anissa. What can I do for you?' The old woman sat down in front of the TV.

'I'm Gunnar, the Nomo. This is Bunny, my assistant, and our K-9, Fluffy.' Fluffy sat and did his best to look fierce. I stifled a smile. 'We have some questions for you regarding the murder of Eric Walker.'

Anissa's brow wrinkled and she looked confused. 'Why are you asking me? I didn't know Eric Walker. I heard he'd died on the docks, but that's all.'

'Routine. We have to talk to all magic users with the strength to kill a werewolf, and you're on the list,' Gunnar said. 'Where were you the night of—'

She put up a hand to stop him. 'Look, before you get into your questions, I just had a baby. I've been in Anchorage for the past three weeks. If your werewolf died during that time, that should give me a great alibi.' A baby started crying. 'She's up again,' she muttered tiredly. 'Wonderful. Just give me a moment.' She slid out of the room.

Gunnar and I looked at each other and waited awkwardly. Anissa returned five minutes later with a wailing baby on her shoulder, bouncing and patting her rhythmically on the back. I didn't know much about babies, but this one looked new and tiny. The racket she was making from such tiny lungs was truly astounding.

'Here's the hospital number and names of the doctors who attended to me. I had a C-section and then I got an infection, so I only got home yesterday.' She held out a note to Gunnar.

The old lady stood and held out her hands for the baby and, with relief, Anissa surrendered her. 'Thanks, Mom,' she murmured. 'I'm just so tired.' Her mum patted her hand understandingly and started gently swaying with the infant, who stopped crying abruptly. If anything, that seemed to upset Anissa even more.

Gunnar cleared his throat. 'Sorry to have disturbed you, ma'am. We'll let ourselves out.' He paused. 'We'd be grateful for your discretion about this visit.'

Anissa nodded wearily. 'You were never here.'

As Gunnar went to the door, I lingered and touched Anissa's arm. 'You're doing a wonderful job.'

Her eyes filled. 'I don't think I am. She hates me.'

'She doesn't. I'm new to this world, too, and it's sharp and loud and a bit crazy. She probably feels just as overwhelmed. You'll get there. You've just had major surgery – it's insane that you're even walking about. Relax and cut yourself some slack. She's alive, clean and fed. Nothing else matters. You're doing great.'

She sniffed. 'Thank you, Bunny.' She suddenly reached over to hug me and I patted her awkwardly on the back.

Gunnar was waiting for me on the front step. He raised an eyebrow in question but I shook my head. He didn't need to know that I'd once found a book on post-natal depression in my mum's stuff. I'd read it cover to cover, mostly because I was nosy, and wondered if mum had ever been diagnosed with PND. They weren't so aware of mental health back in the day. Hopefully Anissa was full of hormones and she'd settle and find her way. I made a note to check on her in a few weeks' time.

'The doctors in Anchorage should be easy to verify in the morning,' Gunnar said gruffly.

I agreed, but we both knew that Anissa wasn't a real suspect any longer. The only thing she was going to kill was an afternoon nap.

Chapter 37

Next on Sig's list was Shirley Thompson. Her house was small, painted sunshine yellow, with carefully tended gardens in front. 'Gunnar,' I said as I looked at the plants. 'A lot of these are poisonous.'

I'd been to the Alnwick Poison Gardens when I was at university in Edinburgh. The idea of poisons had fascinated me for a while, and I'd picked up a book on toxic plants. 'She's growing monkshood, also known as wolfsbane, water hemlock, foxglove and bog rosemary. They can all be deadly.'

'Really? How are you so knowledgeable about poisons?'

'You said something about my memory. I remember everything I see,' I admitted. I braced myself for the strange look that was sure to follow.

Instead he surprised me with a broad grin. 'That's brilliant.' He clapped me on the shoulder. 'I *knew* you'd be an asset.'

He started down the path. 'Hold on.' I cleared my throat awkwardly. 'I just wanted to remind you that the body showed some signs of poisoning. I know you dismissed it at the time, but Eric had a lot of liquid around his face – saliva – and his pupils were really wide. He could have been poisoned before he was stabbed. And – here we are in a poison garden.'

He looked back at me. 'I'll call the lab tomorrow and have them add checks for the poisons you just mentioned.'

I smiled; relieved he was taking me seriously. 'Thanks, Gunnar.'

'Let's go. Keep your wits about you,' he said gruffly.

I held Fluffy's lead tightly so he wouldn't accidentally brush the plants with his fur or tail. Gunnar knocked loudly on the door and we waited.

When it was opened, a polished, professional looking woman took one look at us, reared back and hit Gunnar with a fireball square in the chest.

'Get back!' he roared to me.

Feeling beyond useless, Fluffy and I hurried back down the steps. Gunnar was still standing by the door. The witch flung another blast at him and this one blew him off his feet, sending him flying back into the centre of the very poisonous garden. Fuck. Some of those plants would be highly dangerous if his skin so much as touched them.

'Gunnar!' I yelled in panic. I started forward. I couldn't let him face this bitch alone.

'Stay!' he barked at me. Feeling like a dog, I obeyed. He knew what was going on better than I did.

When Gunnar stood up, he was truly livid. The first fireball had annoyed him, but the second one had made him furious. With his cheeks flushed red, he stomped back to the front door.

The witch had started to gather another fireball when he pulled her out by the arm. The fireball stuttered and died. She continued to try and fling spells at him, but it was like nothing would stick and she was too close to knock him down again

She was screeching swear words as he hauled her down to the SUV. 'Get the magic cancelling cuffs, Bunny. Quickly!'

I opened the rear door and sifted through the contents of the black duffel bag until I found the green zip ties – green for magic cancelling. I ran back to Gunnar. He pulled Shirley's hands behind her and zipped the cuffs shut. She sagged.

'You wanna tell me what that attack was for?' he demanded after he'd placed her in the back seat. I put the black bag well away from our prisoner as Gunnar secured her in the car with ankle restraints; he wasn't taking any chances. She glared and didn't reply.

'Why'd you kill Eric?' Gunnar asked.

'I want a lawyer,' she snarled back.

'You can call one from your cell.' I waited for him to read Shirley her rights, but he didn't. I guessed the American system was different to ours.

Gunnar was still royally pissed. He was the most even-tempered guy I'd ever met and I'd never seen him angry before, but I guessed fireballs were beyond most people's limits. He jabbed some numbers into his phone. 'Sig? I need you to come to the station to search a female for me. Five minutes out. Thanks.'

We drove back in silence, Fluffy on the floor at my feet watching the witch behind us. Back at the office, Gunnar left her in a cell to be searched thoroughly by Sigrid. The cell was the one marked green, so it had magic cancelling properties too. 'Well I think we have a suspect,' he said wryly.

'Me too. How come Sigrid is searching her?' I asked.

'She's trained in searching female suspects. I do the men. If you stick about, I'll send you on a course so you can take over. Sig's deputised for things like monitoring the cameras and doing searches, but it's not what she loves doing – she's just been drafted in over time. I'd like to ease the burden on her.'

The idea of searching a woman's cavities didn't set my world on fire, but I could see it might be necessary. 'Sure,' I shrugged. 'Are you okay?' His clothes were scorched but his skin didn't look burned.

He waved away my concern. 'I'm fine – though she singed my beard.'

'It still looks magnificent' I assured him, only partly tongue in cheek. 'So, what now?'

'We process her paperwork and wait for her to meet with her lawyer.'

'What are we charging her with?' I asked curiously.

'For now, we can charge her with attacking a Nomo. She did that with a witness present – you.'

'What about Eric's murder?'

'I'll get a warrant to look at her place tomorrow. If we find anything linking her to the murder, we'll charge her. If not, we might have to wait for those lab findings. If Eric was poisoned with something she's growing in her garden, we can build a circumstantial case. It's not ideal but...' He sighed. 'There's nothing we can do tonight. Why don't you take Fluffy home and get some rest?'

'Don't we still need to talk to the third suspect?' I asked.

Gunnar rubbed the back of his neck. 'Dammit, yes. No one has gotten to me like that in years, I'm a little off my game.' He scratched absently at his arm. 'We'll do it tomorrow. We both need a rest, and I need to wash this stuff off my arms and hands. I'm starting to itch.'

'Good idea. Some of that stuff can be really irritating – it can even cause your heartbeat to slow and give it palpitations. Go to the hospital if that happens, okay?'

'Yes, Dr Bunny. Can you get yourself home safe?'

'Of course,' I promised airily.

He gave me a hard look. 'Bunny? Stay sharp.'

I gave a cheeky salute that made him smile and shake his head, then snapped on Fluffy's lead. The two of us had the tensest walk home ever but, despite my agitation, nothing jumped out at me.

I hated that the killer had made this town feel unsafe and I couldn't wait to bring them down. Then again, maybe we already had.

Chapter 38

The next day when I peered out of my curtains, I felt weirdly disappointed not to see Connor's truck parked outside. I guessed he thought the danger was gone; I wished my gut agreed.

I walked quickly to work; only when I arrived at the Nomo building did the tension ease from my shoulders. Walking around with a target painted on my back wasn't a pleasant sensation.

When I checked in with Gunnar he assured me he was fine, though the skin on one of his arms was still red, then he spent five minutes bitching about Shirley Thompson and her slippery lawyer. He gave me carte blanche to spend time running down Thomas's list; he was going to work on Kivuk's case for a while.

I called all of the names on the list that Thomas had sent me. Two answered and I made appointments for them to come in to the station in the next couple of days; it didn't feel as urgent now we had Shirley in custody. Three people didn't answer, so I left messages. Fingers crossed they would call back before we had to go looking for them.

After that, we loaded up and headed to the last magic user's house on the list. Freya Sigurdson lived close to the medical centre in the middle of town. With Shirley's blasts fresh in our minds we approached more cautiously this time, and Gunnar made me stay back from the door and the front window. Fluffy and I waited dutifully in the driveway as he knocked on the door. A little boy, about four or five years old, answered it and we both relaxed.

Gunnar beckoned me over to the porch then crouched down. 'Hi, little man, is your mommy home?'

The boy ran off. A few seconds later, a frazzled looking woman came to the door, another toddler on her hip. She clearly recognized Gunnar. 'How can I help the Nomo's office?' she asked.

'We wanted to speak to you regarding the murder of Eric Walker,' he said.

She scrunched her eyebrows together. 'I doubt I have anything to offer. I only saw the man in passing.'

'Do you mind if we come in for a few minutes?' his voice was at its mildest.

She hesitated, then sighed. 'The house is a mess but sure, come on in.' She ushered us into the living room. It was clean, but there were toys and children everywhere. Never had I been more grateful for the de-cluttered state of my own home.

'I run a daycare for the witches in town,' she said as I counted at least six kids.

Gunnar gave her a kind smile as I sat down and held Fluffy close by his lead. Finally a child noticed us and squealed, 'Doggy!'

Immediately we were beset by small wild beasts who climbed all over my dog. I was tense for a moment because I'd never seen Fluffy with kids, but it was clear that he was in his element. I unclipped his lead so he wouldn't inadvertently strangle someone, and he promptly laid down. He let the children sit on him like he was a horse, he played dead when they asked to, and he even shook hands. I was a terrible owner; I didn't even know that he knew any tricks. He was far better trained than I'd suspected.

I tuned back in to Gunnar and Freya. 'I don't have the time or energy to murder anyone,' Freya was saying. She did look exhausted. 'Freddy!' she called out. 'Be careful with the knife!'

My heart stuttered but then I realised the kid was wielding a wooden knife on a chopping board, cutting Velcro fruit in two. He threw the wooden knife, narrowly missing another child. Freya pocketed it and Freddy collapsed into a wailing heap.

'Sorry,' she said to us. 'What did you ask? Oh, where I was when he died.' She tapped her lip thoughtfully. 'It was a TV night, I think. I watched shows until maybe 8pm and then I went to bed. People start bringing me their kids at six when they go to work so I always go to bed early. You can speak with my husband – he was with me.'

'We'll check in with him,' Gunnar promised.

She gave us his phone number and we stood to leave. Fluffy gently extricated himself from the pile of kids and trotted to me. I clipped his lead back on.

Freya didn't bother following us to the door; she had to juggle toddlers who were crying because the doggy had left. She looked even more frazzled.

'We'll check with the husband, but my gut says no. That was a bust,' Gunnar remarked as we climbed back into the SUV. 'But at least we have one suspect. Shirley Thompson definitely has the magical power to have killed Eric, and the poisons add a whole new angle. Her attack on me doesn't exactly protest her innocence, either.' He looked pleased. 'I sent your list of poisons to the lab so they can check the bloodwork for them.'

'Any itching today? Heart palpitations?' I'd been slightly worried about him all night.

He gave a huge, booming laugh. 'I'm perfectly sound, no worries, Doc. I had the council sign a warrant. Want to go check out Shirley's place?'

'Absolutely!'

We turned out of Freya's driveway and headed back to the perfect yellow house with its beautiful garden of death.

Fluffy started growling the second we pulled up. 'It's okay, boy, the bitchy witch is in the lockup,' I reassured him. He looked at me with a flat expression and growled again. I sighed. 'I don't speak dog.'

'You don't need to because I do,' Gunnar said. 'We need to be on our guard. Eyes peeled and stay behind me.'

Since we had a warrant and no one opened the door when he knocked, Gunnar twisted the knob and we walked in; he *definitely* had some door-opening mumbo-jumbo. He called out, 'It's the Nomo, we have a warrant.'

No one responded. A quick glance told me that Shirley lived alone – the photos on the mantel were of her in various poses and there was only one coffee cup and one plate in the sink.

Because of Fluffy's warning growl, we checked the house from top to bottom before we started our search. Once we were sure the place was clear we started at the top, looking for anything that indicated she knew Eric Walker. We both wore double gloves because of her poison garden – and it was a good thing we did because her fridge was stuffed with labelled bags of plant samples and bottled extracts from her garden, all deadly poisons. The labels had a motif of a skull with flowers growing out of the eye sockets, which was vaguely cute in an emo way though I thought she could do with some re-branding.

I wondered how she dared store food in the same fridge, but it didn't look like she ate very often; besides the poisons, it mainly contained condiments. I reminded myself not to borrow her mayo. 'What does she need this volume of poisons for?' I wondered aloud, as we tagged and bagged everything carefully.

'I'm betting she's dealing on the black market,' Gunnar said grimly. 'This amount will get her locked up for a long time if we can prove she's selling it.'

Annoyingly, we didn't find anything related to Eric Walker: none of his missing paperwork, no wallet, no note in her diary to meet him, nothing. It was frustrating, but if the bloodwork *did* reveal that Eric was poisoned, we could cross-reference the type with the ones here and build a circumstantial case. As Gunnar had said, it wasn't ideal but it was possible. But we were missing a motive. Why kill Eric? Shirley wasn't involved in the fish dispute.

Gunnar snagged her laptop; we took that and the poisons and left. We'd finished booking her in earlier and later we'd be charging her with distributing a deadly substance. Shirley Thompson was about to have a shit day, slippery lawyer or no. No amount of grease could get her out of having a fridge full of poison bagged and ready to be sold.

Gunnar's phone rang as we were walking out of her home. He answered briskly, 'Gunnar.' His frown was immediate. 'I'm in the car,' he said shortly. 'I'll call you back.' He hung up and tucked the phone back in his pocket, then started the SUV. 'It's a good thing we talked to everyone and finished searching the house. That was Liv and she was *not* happy.'

As the head of the magic users, she was probably angry that we hadn't gone to her before we questioned her people. I was glad I wasn't Gunnar; Liv made me feel nervous, and he was going to get her full wrath.

I thought of hot sands and didn't envy him a jot.

Chapter 39

Instead of waiting for the promised call back, Liv was at the Nomo office when we arrived there almost incandescent with rage. Her eyes sparked with it. 'Your office,' she snarled to Gunnar. She ignored me; I'd never been more grateful in my life to be a lowly minion.

She stalked into Gunnar's office and slammed the door shut when he'd joined her. That didn't stop me hearing her diatribe. 'You have singled out the magic users!' she screeched. 'And after I helped you with the body! I would expect this from the other council members, but you're supposed to be neutral!'

'I *am* neutral, Liv, but I have to follow the leads I've been given.' Gunnar must have been getting upset because I could hear him too.

'And they only led to magic users?' Her voice went up another notch.

'No, of course not. We've talked to several people in town.'

'But you've arrested a witch!'

'Shirley tried to blast me to smithereens when we went to ask her questions!' he protested. He was getting frustrated.

I didn't catch Liv's response but a moment later the office door opened. 'Bunny, can you come here for a moment?'

I could, but I didn't want to. 'Yes.' I stood reluctantly. Fluffy whined, but he stayed put. 'Coward,' I whispered to him. 'What can I help you with?' I asked calmly when I reached the door.

'Could you please let Magic Leader Liv know what poisons we identified at the Thompson residence?'

I pictured them in my mind. 'Aconitine, alkaloids, digoxin and andromedotoxin.'

'And how do you get those poisons?' he asked.

'From synthesising the plants monkshood, hemlock, foxglove, and bog rosemary.'

'And where did Ms Thompson get her plants?'

'She grows them in her front garden. Almost everything I saw was native to this area of Alaska, so she probably told everyone they were wildflowers. Monkshood is quite lovely – purple flowers on long stems. Bog rosemary looks a little like a fuchsia from a distance, foxglove can be bright pinkish purple, and hemlock is white. All very pretty when they flower.'

'Thank you, Bunny.' Gunnar was dismissing me, but I stood there for a moment to make sure he wanted me to leave. He turned back to Liv. 'And another thing. Eric may have been poisoned. There were signs on the body that we are waiting to have verified by the lab. Do you still think I'm not being neutral?'

She was quiet a moment then, suddenly looking weary, she blew out a harsh breath. 'No, those are valid points. I'll drop my complaint with the council.' I noticed that she offered no apology for her accusations.

'I appreciate that. You have a good day, now,' Gunnar's voice was back to being even.

Liv brushed by me as she left. I watched to make sure the main door shut behind her. 'I thought you were a goner.' I smirked.

Gunnar laughed. 'Me too. Liv terrifies me.'

'She throws a better temper tantrum than Freddy,' I joked about the toddler we'd met at Freya's place.

'Thank God she didn't have any knives to throw!'

The door dinged to let us know someone had stepped in and I hurried to the front desk. A man in a suit with a briefcase in one hand was there. 'Hi, how may I help you?' I asked.

'Laughton Giles to see Shirley Thompson.'

'I'm sorry, she isn't cleared for visitors,' I said regretfully but firmly.

'I'm not a visitor. I'm her new lawyer.'

Gunnar joined me at the desk. 'She retained Ted Finigan.'

'She has revised her legal needs, as is her right. The latest charges are above Finigan's paygrade. I'd like to see my client now.'

'Fine,' Gunnar said brusquely. 'Bunny, see Mr Giles to interview room one. I'll go get his client.'

We only *had* one interview room, but I nodded. 'Please follow me,' I said and used my keys to open the door to a small room which contained a table and two chairs. Nothing exciting.

When we had processed her earlier, Shirley Thompson's clothing had been searched and placed in storage until her release. She'd been given green scrubs and slippers. Now her hair was loose from its tight chignon and her face was scrubbed clean of makeup she looked younger – but no less threatening. Her glare could have felled a man at a hundred paces.

Gunnar unfastened her cuffs, leaving one secured around her wrist so she couldn't do magic. He told the lawyer to knock twice when he was done, then locked the door after we'd stepped outside 'The lawyer doesn't look like he's from here,' I remarked.

'He's not. He flies in from Homer, although I think he lives and practises in Anchorage. He's too fancy for our little town – but he's supernatural and knows our laws, more's the pity.'

I picked up on his disquiet. 'Why?'

'He's known to be utterly ruthless and he gets the guilty off. He will twist everything. We have to make sure our case is airtight.'

I couldn't think of any mistakes we'd made so far in Eric's case, but I was new and I didn't know the local laws. I should probably learn them, read a few books to give me a solid grounding. 'Gunnar, is there a law book for Portlock?'

'I think there's one in the back room. You're welcome to study it on slow days, but it has to stay here in case we need to refer to it.'

'That's fine. It's just that I don't know much about American law and I'm getting the feeling that Portlock is a law unto itself.'

'You'd be right. We have our own systems and laws because of our unique situation. They're based on American law – but loosely. Connor asked me to remind you of your vampire classes. You're welcome to do them here after your shift. I don't imagine you have a computer at home.'

'I appreciate that.' Inwardly I groaned. I was already working long hours which I didn't mind because I loved my new job and I wanted to impress but adding studies into the mix meant I'd be pulling ever longer shifts. Plus I really struggled to focus in the day as the daylight exhaustion was dragging me down. Still, the classes were the lesser of the two evils; I liked my job here and I wanted to keep it – and I didn't want to go back to the Vampire King of Europe. Ever.

I checked my phone. One of the people from Thomas's list had called so I hurriedly set up an appointment for them to come in and answer some questions. Three down, two to go.

Just as I was completing the remaining paperwork for Shirley Thompson's arrest, two knocks from the interview room interrupted my concentration. I fetched Gunnar and we approached the door. As he opened it, Shirley came barrelling out and startled him. He lost his balance and fell against the doorjamb – and the witch came right at me.

I did something I'd only practised in self-defence classes: SING. I jammed my fist in her solar plexus then smashed her instep with my foot. When she bent over, I slammed the base of my palm into her nose and kneed her in the groin. It was less effective for a woman but a kick in the lady garden still hurt, especially when delivered with vampiric strength.

Shirley went down with a groan, blood spurting from her nose. To add insult to injury, the cavalry arrived in the form of Fluffy, who jumped on her and pinned her down, his teeth clamped around her throat to hold her still.

By then Gunnar was on his feet, swearing loudly and vociferously. 'Good boy,' he praised Fluffy, 'but off you get now. I've got her.'

Fluffy carefully removed his jaw before turning, farting and climbing off Shirley. Gunnar flipped her on to her stomach, cuffed her and hauled her to her feet none to gently. 'I'm taking her back to her cell,' he said to me. 'Check on the lawyer, will you? He's on the floor.'

I hurried into the room where the lawyer lay crumpled on the floor with his papers strewn around him. I panicked for a moment, thinking he was dead, but thankfully his eyes fluttered opened and he groaned. I hurried around the table to help him up, and he gave me a grateful smile. 'What happened?' I asked.

He smiled ruefully. 'Client confidentiality.'

I blinked. 'Seriously?'

'Seriously,' he confirmed.

I wasn't pleased with the stance he was taking but maybe I didn't need to know the ins and outs. Shirley was clearly desperate and she'd taken out her lawyer in a bid to escape. She *must* be guilty. I doubted he'd continue handling her case now – and it wasn't like there was a tonne of supernatural lawyers around. 'Are you okay?' I asked.

'I'll be fine. I need to gather up my stuff and make some calls to the council on behalf of my client.'

My jaw dropped. 'You're still representing her?'

'I'll be more wary when we meet again, but she's paid my retainer and I'm under contract.'

'Surely attacking you breaches that?'

He grinned. 'Absolutely – but she's going to be one heck of a challenge.'

'No kidding,' I said faintly. 'She's guilty as hell.'

'Allegedly.' He put the papers back in his briefcase and left with a spring in his step. Lawyers were fucking weird.

Chapter 40

'Did she say anything to you?' I asked when Gunnar returned.

'The usual. Called me a pig and spat derogatory remarks. How's the lawyer?'

'He's staying on the case. Total bollocks, if you ask me.'

Gunnar shook his head in disbelief. 'Well, at least we have some more charges to add.'

'Don't we need *him* to press them?'

Gunnar smiled. 'Nope. I got knocked over, too. Besides, we can charge someone if it is in the public's best interest and I think it is, don't you?'

'Oh, absolutely. I'll fill out the paperwork and bring it to you to check.'

Gunnar left soon afterwards but I decided to stay and complete one of the vampire classes on my list. I took Fluffy out to do his business then came back and pulled up the first class on the computer.

'*How to Control Your Bloodlust 101*,' I read out loud to Fluffy, who whined. 'I know,' I agreed. 'It sounds as boring as hell, but I have to do it. The least *you* can do is keep me company.' He rested his heavy head on my lap in response and I laughed. 'Thanks, bud.'

It was one of those classes with a number of short videos interrupted by extremely stupid questions that you had to get one hundred percent right before you could move on. You could make as many attempts as you wanted to get the right answer, so the test was effectively meaningless.

At least I could click through it as fast as I wanted. The questions were ludicrous, like: *If a human cuts themselves and begins to bleed, you should: a) call an ambulance and hope they get there before you suck the victim dry; b) lick the wound, no blood should ever be wasted; c) exit quickly so you aren't consumed by*

bloodlust; d) hand them a plaster and hope you don't
succumb to bloodlust.

I rolled my eyes; the right answer was blindingly obvious. I hoped that vampires dumb enough to need these classes didn't end up mixing with ped society. I flew through the videos, answered all the questions correctly and finished the 'recommended to take one hour and forty-five minutes' class in fifteen minutes.

'It won't be too bad if they are all like that,' I said triumphantly to Fluffy. 'Let's do one more before we go home.' He laid his head back down with a doggy sigh.

The next one was a gem: *What to Do in the Event of a Blood Shortage*. I looked down at my dog. 'What do you think? Rob a blood bank?'

He gave a sharp, amused bark that sounded like a yes. It was a good thing he wasn't taking the tests for me because I'd probably fail and have to turn in my fangs. Not that that would bother me; they dropped down when I didn't want them to and stayed up when I did. They'd been useless for defence; as far as I could

315

see, they were just an extra cleaning fee at the supernat dentist.

I skimmed through the introductory paragraphs. 'Oh, you'll love this Fluffy! *"In an emergency, seek blood from farm animals, even pets, before you consider your neighbours."*' I patted his head. 'No chance. You are more important to me than other people. I promise I'll eat my neighbours first.' Well, all of my neighbours except Sidnee; friends definitely weren't food.

His tongue lolled out in a doggy grin.

The second class took a little longer, but even so I was done in half an hour. I shut down the computer and left the building. As I locked up the office, I suddenly felt like someone was watching me. *Don't be ridiculous Bunny,* I told myself. Even so, I looked around. No one was loitering in the lingering darkness.

The horizon was lightening a little; daybreak was coming. I shivered and, despite the charm around my neck, I moved quickly. A waxing gibbous moon burst through the clouds and an eerie howl filled the night.

It sounded like a wolf, which was all I needed. Sidnee had said the other howls had been real wolves, so it might not be a *were*wolf.

Fluffy was looking around warily, tension in every line of his body. 'You reckon it's a werewolf or real wolf?' I asked him. Naturally, he didn't answer.

We walked quickly through the deserted streets towards home. Fluffy stayed close to me, though I wasn't sure if that was to reassure himself or me.

Abruptly a howl rent through the air close to my left side – far too fucking close! I whirled around and my slow heart actually beat hard and fast for a moment. Fluffy growled as my fear spiked, and for once my damned fangs did what they should do: they grew.

I looked in the direction of the noise and immediately spotted a huge figure hunched in the shadows of the trees at the side of the road. A werewolf then, not a real wolf. Patkotak's comment about always being armed suddenly seemed incredibly wise and I wished I'd brought Gunnar's machete.

I looked around for somewhere to run. I hadn't quite reached the residential section, so I'd have to head for home – but chances were the hulking creature would catch me first.

Fuck it. I straightened. I had fangs. Fake it till you make it. 'Who are you? What do you want?' I snarled, trying to sound tough. I didn't really want to know the answer to either question – I wanted to be left alone but that was no longer an option.

The figure stepped into the streetlight and it took every scrap of my self-control not to step back. Yes, it was a werewolf but, unlike the previous one I'd seen, this one's eyes were human rather than red. It was huge, eight feet tall if it was an inch, and covered with sparse, straggly hair. Its ears were tall and pointed and its muzzle was clearly canine, though shorter than a dog or wolf's. Its arms were longer than a human's and hung almost to its knees, and its huge paws had an elongated human-like heel. Those paws were tipped with gruesomely curved claws.

No; no, no, no. I regretted my decision not to run like fuck. Fear made heat sink into stomach; flames flickering into existence in my gut.

It opened its mouth. 'Back off.' Its voice was guttural and threatening.

'Back off what? Was it you who left the note?'

That seemed to surprise the creature. 'What note?'

'The one on my door?'

The werewolf made a sound that I realised was laughter. 'You have many enemies. Good. If we kill you, the Nomo will have many suspects.'

So this wasn't my note-writer; anyway, it would probably be too difficult to hold a pen with those claws. I folded my arms and stood my ground. Fluffy, bless him, stood between me and the monstrous creature and gave a warning growl.

'Stay away from the pack,' the werewolf continued.

Pack? I was completely confused. I'd thought all shifters in Portlock were under Stan's control. Was it a werewolf term? 'What pack?' I asked but he had already backed into the shadows and melted away. I didn't wait for him to return with his pals.

Someone had turned Jack into a werewolf, and Kivuk was still missing. Maybe he'd seen something he shouldn't have, or maybe his disappearance had nothing to do with Jack. All of those thoughts whirled in my head as Fluffy and I jogged home.

For the first time since my first night in Portlock, I locked all the doors and windows and rolled down the metal blinds. It wasn't overkill if you thought someone was after you – and I knew that someone definitely was after me. But I was home, I was safe and I was *not* going to be intimidated.

I repeated my mantra firmly as I slid into my bed – but in my dreams I saw the glow of red eyes.

Chapter 41

When Fluffy and I hurried into work the next day there were no creepy monsters lurking in the trees – not that I was aware of. But I knew that monsters existed everywhere and they didn't always wear fangs or wolf coats.

Sidnee was still at the desk and she jumped up and gave me a huge hug. I was about to tell her about the werewolf when Gunnar called me into his office. He looked agitated. 'What's up?' I asked.

'Shirley has demanded a council ruling rather than a trial by a jury of her peers.'

I frowned. Surely the council wouldn't be easily swayed by whatever sad tale she concocted? It seemed a strange choice, though. Maybe she was snooty and thought she had no peers to match her?

'The trial will be next Friday. You can come with me and see the legal system in action.'

'Great. I'll try and read those law books beforehand,' I promised. 'What charges will she face? We haven't accused her of Eric's death yet, have we?'

'No. The council will rule on the attack against me and Shirley having poison in her possession. I won't be voting, obviously.' He looked serious. 'That note has come back with no prints on it, Bunny. I'm sorry.'

I sighed. 'It would have been too good to be true if there had been. Has Shirley given a statement? We still don't know her motive.'

'She's pleading the Fifth,' he shrugged. 'Maybe Eric ordered some poison from her and didn't pay up. Hopefully between now and Friday we'll find more evidence so we can charge her.'

The front door beeped and I nearly jumped out of my skin. 'What's the matter, Bunny?' Gunnar asked. 'You're as twitchy as the critter you're named for.'

I grimaced. 'Fluffy and I had a chat with a werewolf on our way home last night.'

His jaw worked. 'What happened?'

I described the confrontation as succinctly as possible, including the werewolf's brown eyes.

'He said "the pack"? Are you sure?' Gunnar demanded.

'Positive," I replied. 'He was pretty scary. I wish I'd had your machete.'

Fluffy yipped agreement and Gunnar grinned at him. 'Good boy for keeping her safe. We'd best think about giving you a weapon besides those gnashers. And I think we need to talk to Stan again, see what he'll tell us about "the pack". You game?'

'Sure thing.'

Following the discovery of Eric's truck, Stan had come to the office and given a full statement about the vehicle and his relationship with the dead man. There hadn't been any red flags, and I'd believed him when he said the truck had appeared after he'd parked up. Gunnar had checked with the fish plant's CCTV;

annoyingly, the area where Stan had parked fell just outside its remit.

Gunnar smirked. 'You do realise Stan turns into an 1800lb bear?'

I knew that he was a polar bear shifter, but I'd had no frame of reference. Eighteen hundred pounds was a lot, right? I mostly worked in stones. 'Uh, no.'

'Don't worry, he's a total teddy bear.' Sure – a gigantic one. Gunnar continued, 'Just give me half hour to finish up some stuff and then we'll go speak to him.'

I went back to see who had walked in when the door pinged. Luckily, Sidnee was already dealing with their complaint and they left once they'd filled out a form. 'I'm clocking off,' she yawned. 'It's been a long one.'

'Be careful walking home,' I urged and quickly filled her in about the werewolf.

She looked at me worriedly. 'Maybe you should think again about staying with me?'

I smiled back. 'I'm fine, honestly. I have Fluffy.' And my stiff, unyielding pride.

'Okay, if you're sure,' she replied dubiously. 'Stay safe, Bunny.' She made tracks and I lost myself in a sea of paperwork.

I'd been working for a solid hour when my phone beeped and I saw a text from Sidnee. *We can't let this note and werewolf stuff bring you down. Clearly, you need to get some friends and allies. I'm throwing you a 'welcome to Portlock party'. How about Saturday at eight? I'm trying to book a place so I don't have the where yet. You in?*

Hell yeah! I didn't even have to think about my response: this somewhat reformed party girl was itching to go dancing and pound some shots. I wasn't sure how that worked in a small, damp town, but surely I'd be able to get some shots somewhere. If push came to shove, I could always down the little bottle of moonshine I'd gotten from the Grimes brothers.

Almost instantly she replied: *Fab. I'm on it. It's going to be awesome!*

I laughed and put away my phone feeling much lighter.

Chapter 42

Stan lived on his fishing boat. I didn't know what to expect because I'd never been on a fishing boat before; the only boats I'd been on were billionaires' yachts when Dad had taken me to business deals to make sure he came across as wholesome and nice.

Gunnar and I drove to the other end of town where the fishing boats were moored near the fish plant. Instead of turning into the plant car park, we pulled into another one that was full of trucks and empty trailers.

For a moment I missed the glitz of London so much that it hurt. God, would it kill these people to wear some heels and some nice dresses occasionally? Whack on some false eyelashes and get their nails shellacked?

But I blinked and then London was gone, as dead to me as my own body. I couldn't go back there, not now, not in a hundred years. I was stuck in Portlock –but on Saturday, you could bet your arse I'd be wearing nails longer than the werewolves' claws.

I followed Gunnar down the ramp to the harbour and we turned onto a boardwalk aisle between two rows of boats. He stopped about ten boats down at a large aluminium one with a painted blue stripe and a blue cabin. It was named *Bear's Honeypot*, and I snickered at the name.

Gunnar called out, 'Stan, it's Gunnar. Can we come in?'

The door opened and Stan stepped out. The boat smelled like fish and I rubbed my nose; it was an effort not to hold it. Taking Gunnar's hand, I stepped on board. 'Stan, can Fluffy come with me?' I asked.

He looked at my dog. 'Sure. We don't have any fish on board right now anyway. Come on inside, where we can sit.'

There was a table with bench seating for four small adults, the steering and the captain's chair, and another bench next to it. I wondered how many people were needed to run the boat; it didn't look like it would sleep more than two, unless you were *really* friendly. It was homey, I decided, determined not to be my mum's snobbish daughter.

Stan motioned for us to sit at the table though it was a tight squeeze because of Gunnar's size. 'What's up?' he asked, once we were settled. 'I thought we were done with all the Eric stuff. I've answered all of your questions.'

'We are,' Gunnar assured him. 'We have another suspect in custody. Bunny will fill you in – she had an unsettling experience last night.'

Stan's eyes swung to me. I noticed the flicker of interest in his eyes but I ignored it. 'Fluffy and I were approached by a fully-shifted werewolf. He gave me a warning. He said, "Back off and stay away from the pack." Does that mean anything to you?'

Stan frowned and ran his fingers through his unruly hair. 'He told you to stay away from the pack?' his brow furrowed.

'Yes.'

'That's odd. We don't go by "pack" anymore. We adopted 'shifter group' to make it an all-inclusive term.' He thought for a minute. 'Thank you for bringing it to my attention. I'll get to the bottom of it.' His tone was dismissive.

Apparently we were done here. We stood up to leave but then Stan stopped me. 'Bunny, could I talk to you privately for a second?'

I froze, but Gunnar threw me a smile, and walked out. Stan waited until he was out of earshot. 'I was wondering if you wanted to go out sometime?'

I blinked. I thought he was handsome but, like I'd said to Connor, I wasn't ready to date yet. I needed to find out who I was first.

'How about dinner Saturday night?' he pushed.

I was relieved that I had the perfect excuse. 'I can't. Sidnee is throwing me a party on Saturday.' He looked disappointed. 'I'm sure she'll invite you,' I continued, 'so by all means come along. It's at eight, though I don't know where. I'll let you know.'

He grinned. 'It's a date.'

Oops. I really hadn't meant to imply... I gave a feeble smile. It would be fine. It was just a party; what could go wrong?

Fluffy and I climbed back into the SUV. 'I've been thinking about the list of names that Thomas gave me. None of them are on Sigrid's magic user list. Do you know any of them? Do you know what they are?' I asked.

'Contrary to common belief,' Gunnar said drily, 'I don't know *everyone* in the town. I only recognised one name – Reeve. He's a werewolf.'

I bit my lip; my gut was saying 'yahtzee'. 'That's who I'm interviewing first. Do you think the names Thomas gave me are members of this so-called pack?'

Gunnar's eyebrows shot up. 'What makes you say that?'

'I rang all the names on the list and left messages. Later on I was threatened by a werewolf warning me off the pack. If Reeve is a werewolf and he's on the list...'

He nodded slowly. 'You've got good instincts. It's possible. Maybe Patkotak is giving us a lead on who turned Jack Taylor.' He looked at me sharply. 'You've got a few meetings lined up with them, haven't you? When's the first one?'

I checked my phone. 'In a couple of hours, after lunch.'

'I'll be out but I'm contactable if you need me.'

I felt a wave of panic. 'You want me to take the appointment by myself?'

'He won't try anything in the Nomo's office. Werewolves respect authority figures. Besides, it's not a full moon so he can't turn anyone. You'll be fine – Reeve is gruff but he's a good man. Besides, if you're sticking around you need to start building your own reputation in town, Bunny. In a town like this, reputation is everything. Who are you going to be?'

Wasn't that the million-pound question? We rode the rest of the way to the office in comfortable silence.

Fluffy and I settled in at my desk. When I'd finished the paperwork, I did a bit more work on Connor's vampire videos. I was going to meet Sidnee at the diner for food in an hour – my lunch time, and her very late dinner time – before my first interview on Thomas's list.

I still itched to bring Thomas in and pick his brains. How had he got these names and why had he given them to me? How could he know I would be perceived as a threat to the pack? Were they the names of suspects or something else entirely? Gunnar had left this in my hands and I was nervous about getting it right.

When it was nearly time to meet Sidnee, I walked Fluffy home to leave him there, much to his obvious displeasure. I had a cup of blood then hustled to the diner. I could see Sidnee's dark head in a booth in front of the window. She already had menus waiting.

I hadn't eaten there before, partly because I didn't have any money to spare and partly because I hated eating alone in a restaurant, but the food smelled divine. 'Hey, Sidnee!' I slid into the booth across from her. 'So, what do you recommend?'

'I usually get the halibut and chips – but then I love fish. Part of being a mermaid.' She grinned ruefully.

'If it's good, I'll try it.' I was game for something new. I loved a good chippy at home, although I'd never had halibut.

When the waitress came, we both ordered the fish and chips and a chocolate milkshake, and I ordered an extra coffee to get me through the day. The waitress was so friendly that it felt alien; British customer service tended to be either surly or begrudgingly polite. Her effusiveness made me wonder is she was going to spit in my coffee before she brought it over. No one could be *that* nice.

Whilst we waited, I brought up the mysterious 'pack' and Thomas Patkotak's list. 'If he gave you a list, it'll be for a reason,' Sidnee commented. 'He's very smart.' Her tone was just a shade too admiring; yes, Patkotak was a total silver fox.

'But what *is* the reason?' I asked in frustration. 'I tried to call him but he didn't answer.'

'You can trust him. He's odd and a little scary, but he keeps an eye on everything in this town. He misses nothing.'

'What would you ask the people on the list?' I asked. 'I don't know how to run an interview, and Gunnar is leaving it all to me.'

She thought about it. 'I don't know, but I'm not good at the detective thing like you are. Gunnar says you've got great instincts. I'm sure you'll do fine.'

I wasn't sure; I was worried that Patkotak's reason for sending me these names was because he had his own agenda.

The food was good and Sidnee looked pleased that I ate with gusto. It was always awkward when you recommended something to someone and they didn't like it.

The waitress came over 'How is everything? Is it amazing?' We assured her that it was. 'Great! I'm so pleased to hear that. Can I warm that for you, honey?' She nodded at my coffee.

Warm it for me? Was she going to microwave it for me? 'No, thanks.' When she'd gone, I turned to Sidnee. 'Why would she warm my coffee? What was she going to do – boil it up again?'

Sidnee laughed. 'Is that why you looked at her so weird? It just means "do you want a top up?". You know, more coffee?'

I felt my skin warm. 'Oh, right.'

Sidnee grinned broadly at me. 'Any other Yank differences you need me to translate?'

'I'm good,' I mumbled. 'I thought there wouldn't be much culture shock coming here – I mean, I've watched US TV all my life – but there are loads of differences.'

'Like what?'

'Everyone drives a truck or a huge car – your vehicles look like they're on steroids. Everything is super-sized. The roads are wider, the houses are bigger.' I paused. 'And your toilets flush differently.'

Sidnee burst out laughing. 'Oh my goodness, well that's confirmed it. Brits and Yanks are just totally different.'

I stuck out my tongue at her good-natured teasing. I caught the eye of the waitress and asked for the bill. I had one eye on the clock, so I had to dine and dash.

I thanked Sidnee for inviting me, gave her a one-armed hug and made tracks to pick up Fluffy. Back at the office I had just settled Fluffy, and put away my bag when my first interviewee arrived.

Game on.

Chapter 43

Wilds Reeve – yes, that was his actual name though in my opinion it was cruel to name a kid "Wilds" – looked like he'd walked off a mountain. His long dark hair was streaked with silver, and his bushy beard didn't look like it had ever seen a brush. He wore camouflage trousers, a matching shirt and sturdy hiking boots.

He towered over the counter. When I asked if I could help him, he gave me a scathing look. 'I'm reporting to some interview today, as requested.'

'Follow me, Mr Reeve.' I led him into the interview room and asked him if he wanted something to drink. When he declined, I asked, 'Do you mind if I record this?'

His eyebrows shot up. 'Where's Gunnar? I thought he was doing this.'

'Sorry, Mr Reeve. I'm conducting the interview.'

He gave me a long look, his distaste evident, then he shrugged, 'Fine, whatever. Let's get it over with.'

I turned on the recorder. 'Please state your full name.'

'Wilds Robert Reeve.'

'Mr Reeve, did you know Eric Walker?' I'd decided I'd start by talking about Eric, lull him into thinking that Eric's murder was the reason he was there. Then I'd ask about 'the pack'.

'Of course. He was a wolf in my shifter group.'

'Please tell me about your movements on the seventh.'

His look was savage. 'I didn't kill Eric.'

'I didn't ask if you did,' I said mildly. 'Your movements?' I prompted.

'I worked, I went home, I watched TV, I went to sleep.'

'Is there anyone who can corroborate that?'

'Yeah.' I looked at him and waited for a name. 'Molly Vaughn,' he said begrudgingly.

I recognised the name immediately because it was on the list. Had he really been with her, or were they giving each other alibis? 'How long have you and Ms Vaughn been involved?' I probed.

'A while.' He folded his arms. 'It's none of your business.'

Really? There'd been a murder and I was interviewing him about it; I'd expected him to take it a bit more seriously. But it wasn't the murder he wasn't taking seriously, it was *me*. If Gunnar were asking these questions, Reeve would have answered.

I calmed myself with effort and changed tack. 'Did you and Mr Walker get along?'

'Yeah. As I said, I didn't kill him.' When I didn't reply, he huffed and elaborated. 'We weren't close, but I didn't have anything against the man.'

'Is there anyone you know who wanted Mr Walker dead?'

'No.'

I paused again then asked, 'Are you a werewolf, Mr Reeve?' I knew I was being rude.

He bared his teeth at me. 'Why is that important?'

'It's just a question and it'll be easy to find the answer,' I said coolly. 'I can ask Stan or I can ask you. It'd be better coming from you.'

He sighed. 'Fine. Yes, I'm a werewolf.'

I leaned forward, 'And are you a member of the group that calls itself "the pack"?'

When he leapt up, his chair slid back and slammed into the wall. I sat quietly, making no sudden moves. *I am a vampire. I can handle myself*, I told my lizard brain which wanted to cut and run. Fear had my fangs dropping, but I kept my top lip still so he couldn't see them; I didn't want the situation to escalate into violence because I knew I'd lose.

Reeve was panting and I was suddenly concerned that he'd start shifting, 'Where did you hear that?' he growled.

'From your reaction, I'm assuming that you *are* part of the pack?' He glared but didn't respond. 'Did you threaten me last night?'

'I want a lawyer!'

I kept my breathing even and I felt my fangs retract. *Shit, come back*! I wanted the fangs. 'Why do you want a lawyer, Mr Reeve? You haven't been charged with anything.'

'Then I'm leaving.' He threw open the interview room door and stalked out. When I followed him, I saw Gunnar in the doorway of his office leaning against the jamb, his massive arms crossed over his chest. I guess he'd changed his mind about leaving me alone to deal with Reeve. Had it been a test to see how I'd handle the interview?

Reeve stormed out of the building. If it was a test, I guessed that I'd just failed. Damn it.

Gunnar came and sat with me. 'What happened?' he asked evenly.

'Reeve didn't want to say whether he belonged to the pack. We've definitely uncovered something but I've no idea what. It certainly raised his hackles when I mentioned it.'

'Interesting,' Gunnar commented.

I glanced up at the clock on the wall. My next interview was in fifteen minutes. 'I guess we'll ask the next interviewee if they are in the pack too then judge their reaction.'

'Sounds like a plan.' He looked at me appraisingly. 'Reeve was a bit loud. Are you all right, or do you want me to take over?'

I was pleased that he was giving me the option. I squared my shoulders and gave him my most confident smile. 'I'm absolutely fine. If you're happy with me handling it, I can absolutely handle it.'

'Okay, it's yours. I'm here if you need me.'

I was a vampire now; I didn't need my hand held. When Reeve had gotten loud, my fangs had come out to play. Yes, they'd run away again, but for a moment I'd been ready to kick ass. That counted as an improvement, right?

I toyed with the idea of bringing in Fluffy with me for the next interview but I didn't want him getting hurt, and bringing him in for back-up sent the same vibes as having Gunnar there. It didn't say I was tough and independent. Gunnar had asked me what reputation I'd wanted around Portlock, and that was it. Having my pet sit in might undermine that a tad.

Chapter 44

Molly Vaughn swanned in fifteen minutes late. She was providing Reeve's alibi and I wondered if he'd called to warn her. If I'd been better prepared, I would have had them come in at the same time. Live and learn.

Molly had attitude. She was a smallish woman with bleached-blonde hair, heavy makeup and very fake boobs – she was too thin to have the gigantic, unmoving cantaloupes that were fixed to her chest. She wore a tight, hot-pink tank top, black sports bra, leggings and flip-flops. Cold temperatures didn't bother me as much now that I was a vampire, but even so I wouldn't be strolling around like that anytime soon. Maybe werewolves ran hot.

I'd assumed she was a werewolf, but you know what they say about assumptions – I was an ass. If she was a werewolf, I wondered what happened to those fake boobs when she shifted. If they stayed, in place she must look hilarious.

I ushered her into the interview room, careful to keep my irreverent thoughts off my face. 'I'll be recording our discussion.' I didn't bother to ask nicely because the set of her jaw told me she was determined to be difficult. I hit the record button. 'Please state your name.'

'Molly Maguire Vaughn.'

She was wearing a set of rings on her engagement finger. 'Is that your maiden or married name?'

Her eyes grew sharp and she looked like she wanted to lie. 'Married,' she admitted grudgingly. 'It's my married name.'

Interesting: she was married to a guy named Mr Vaughn and bonking Wilds Reeve. Poor cuckolded Mr Vaughn. I might not have uncovered a grand conspiracy, but I definitely had something to pressure her with. 'Did you know Eric Walker?'

'Yeah, in passing. He was a werewolf in the shifter group with me.'

'Are you a werewolf, too?'

'Yeah. What's it to you? Doesn't mean I whacked him.'

Whacked? Were we in a bad mafia movie? And that was almost the same thing that Reeve had said. 'Where were you the night of the seventh?'

She gave a saucy grin. 'With Wilds. He's...' she gave a wiggle in her seat and a groan of pleasure '...wild in the sack.' She flashed me a grin, trying to provoke a reaction. I delighted in giving her none.

'Is your husband aware of the affair?'

'Don't know. He's oblivious about everything,' she muttered. 'Including me.'

'I might have to call him in and ask him some questions.' I watched her face to see if that would encourage her to change her story. She blanched, but said nothing.

'Do you know anyone who would want Eric Walker dead?'

'Lots of people I'm sure. He was a bit of a dick.'

'Does anyone in particular come to mind?' I pressed.

'I'd say his little human girlfriend. She begged the p— the other werewolves to change her but they refused. Stan has a whole big application process if a human wants to be turned, and I think he's only accepted one in ten years. She'd applied before and been refused.'

Now that *was* interesting. Virginia wasn't exactly heartbroken when we'd told her Eric was dead; I had assumed that was because she already knew, but maybe she wasn't all that cut up about it. I thought about the note in the car; maybe it had been a recent note, in which case, she'd lied about their current relationship. Shirley was still looking good for the poisoning and murder, but had she been hired? It was time to take a harder look at Virginia Tide, human or not.

'Is it a difficult process to be turned?' I asked, thinking of poor Jack.

'It's not too different from you vamps. Someone has to bite you and exchange bodily fluids.' She shrugged. 'Doesn't always take.'

I frowned. I was very drunk when I was changed, but I remembered it was traumatic. 'What happens if it doesn't take?'

She smiled. 'They die.'

'But that didn't happen with Jack? When he was turned he didn't die, did he?'

Her mouth worked. 'I don't know what you're talking about.' She moved uncomfortably in her seat.

Yes, you do, lady. Yes, you do, I thought. 'Are you a member of the pack?'

She grinned slyly. 'There is no such thing, honey. There's only the shifter group in these parts.' Her smirk belied her lie. 'Unless you're charging me, we're done here.' She stood up and sauntered out before I could reply.

Her pride had made her tell me more than she'd meant to. If I wasn't sure before, I was now: Wilds had coached her in the thirty minutes between his interview and hers, but she'd still slipped up and almost said she was part of the pack – as were Wilds Reeve and Eric Walker. And the pack had *definitely* been involved in turning Jack. Had it been Eric's idea? A practice run before he turned his girlfriend?

That brought a whole new set of questions. Could Jack's family have found out? Was Eric's death revenge for his? My gut was telling me that we were on the right track – I just had to get the pack members to give the game away. I hoped the others on my list didn't talk to Reeve or Vaughn before I got to them, but I wasn't holding my breath.

Luckily, as a vampire, I didn't need it all that much.

Chapter 45

Gunnar had watched my interview with Molly Vaughn through the camera in the corner of the room. He agreed with most of my conclusions but shook his head when I suggested that Jack's family might be involved and hired Shirley.

'No,' he said firmly. 'They were devastated when I told them about Jack's death. They were praying he was okay – they'd been holding out hope that he'd gone off travelling. Telling them the truth crushed them. Unless they're Oscar winners, they're not involved.'

Damn, I'd loved that theory. And didn't that make the guilt I'd been feeling over Jack's death almost overwhelm me? I battled my own feelings, trying to make sure none of them showed on my face.

Gunnar's phone rang. 'Hold on, calm down,' he ordered when he answered. 'Say that again.' He grimaced. 'I'm on my way, don't touch anything. Get inside, lock the doors.' He hung up. 'There's been another murder. Let's move!'

We ran to the SUV, Fluffy leapt into the boot and we roared off. 'Who's dead?' I asked.

'Mrs Wright didn't know – she didn't get close enough for an ID, just spotted the body,' Gunnar replied tersely, careening down the country roads.

'The old lady with the creepy cairn?'

'The old lady with the creepy cairn,' he confirmed.

'Shit.'

The drive felt like it took ages but less than five minutes later we screeched up to her house. Gunnar pulled out two handguns. Clicking the safeties off, he passed one to me. 'I don't know what to do with this,' I pleaded.

'Grip the handle, point the barrel at the bad guy and pull the trigger if they threaten you. No more bad guy,' he said drily. 'Come on.' We plunged around the side of the house to the cairn. Where the creepy doll had rested on top of it there was now a man, a stake plunged through his heart. Just like what had been done to the doll. I recognised the body from his file.

'Kivuk,' Gunnar breathed, and swore vociferously. 'Stay here, keep your eyes peeled.' He moved into the undergrowth as I stood holding the gun out like I knew what to do with it.

'Fluffy,' I said softly, 'stay by me.' It wasn't for his safety but my peace of mind; I was shitting myself. Kivuk was a vamp like me and something had picked up his body, snapped his back across the cairn and shoved a stake into his heart. A stake to the heart would kill us.

I realised I was trembling. I took some deep breaths and tried to stay calm, but a branch snapped and I spun, raising my gun in the direction of the noise. 'Easy tiger,' Gunnar called. 'It's just me.' I lowered the gun with relief as he lumbered towards me.

'The killer's gone.' He grimaced. 'I checked the barrier. There are signs of a recent tear, but any rift has already healed.'

'Is that good?'

'Not particularly. If the nantinaq knows how to make a rift – no matter how temporarily – we could be in real trouble. Mrs Wright's house is one of the cornerstones of the barrier. We have to look at strengthening it – and soon.'

'Shall I get the camera?'

He shook his head. 'There's no need. We know who the killer is.'

I blinked. Law and order in Portlock seemed a bit fast and loose. 'But what if it's someone pretending it was the...' I stumbled over the name '...nant-ee-nok?'

'That's why I went to check for rifts. There was one, so no doubt it was the beast of the barrier. I'll call Connor. He'll probably want to deal with the body himself.'

Minutes later, Connor arrived in his truck, his expression grim. He nodded acknowledgment and – to my surprise – held out his hand for Fluffy to sniff.

When Fluffy seemed happy, he patted his head. Then he seemed to steel himself. Jaw set, he walked to the cairn. He went down on one knee, grasped Kivuk's lifeless hand and bowed his head. It was too intimate a moment to witness so I looked away and petted Fluffy instead. The action soothed me a little.

When Connor was done saying goodbye, he stood up. He returned to his truck, grabbed a large tarp out of the back and laid it on the ground. He was preparing to lift the body alone but I hurried forward to help; it didn't seem right to make him jiggle his friend's body about in an undignified manner. 'I'll get his legs,' I murmured, grasping Kivuk's muddy boots.

Connor's expression was unreadable but he nodded. He slid his arms under Kivuk's shoulders and lifted the sizeable man easily. Together we walked the body to the tarp and Connor wrapped him up. When the tarp was secured with rope, I picked up Kivuk's feet again and we carried him to the bed of the truck. Connor pulled a plastic sheet over the back of the truck, obscuring Kivuk from view.

'I'm sorry,' I said.

'We weren't close,' he said.

'Not now, perhaps. But you were once.'

'Yes.' His eyes clouded with grief. 'We were once.'

Chapter 46

I tried to talk Sidnee into cancelling my 'welcome to Portlock' party – it seemed in bad taste with Kivuk's body only just discovered – but she wouldn't hear of it. She insisted that the town needed a party now more than ever; we needed to come together as a community and I was a good excuse.

I wasn't churlish enough to argue so there I was, winding my hair up into a messy chignon, leaving curled tendrils framing my face. I finished with a slash of bright-red lipstick. Despite myself, I was feeling excited and a little nervous at the same time – excited because it was a party, nervous because it was also my inadvertent 'date' with Stan.

I studied my reflection. I'd gone to town and I was London ready: fake eyelashes, manicured nails and a full face of makeup. My light-blue dress ended mid-thigh. I would probably stick out like a sore thumb but I didn't care – I *needed* this. Like Sidnee had said, we all needed to blow off some steam.

I'd promised to be there at 7.30 prompt, so I headed out. Fluffy gave me a doggy sigh as I walked past, but he knew he couldn't come. I left the TV showing a wildlife show so he wouldn't be bored. I'd already drunk my blood so I could eat whatever party food appeared and maybe even enjoy a glass or two of wine if the damp town was feeling generous.

I walked the short distance to the Portlock Hotel where Sidnee had reserved the ballroom. It was downtown, just across the street from the city building, but I was tottering in heels so it took me longer than I'd expected. Still slightly wary that I might be accosted by a werewolf, I had a small switchblade in my purse courtesy of Gunnar. I tried to put such thoughts out of my head, but the moon was only a day or two off being full. The skin between my shoulder blades itched as I hustled into the hotel.

It was a square, characterless building but inside it was clean and modern. The 'ballroom' was little more than a conference room with commercial carpeting and sound- proofing. Tables were set up around the edge of it with a space in the middle for dancing. The DJ on the stage was getting things prepped and testing his equipment.

Sidnee was propped up at the bar wearing a stunning silver number that wouldn't have looked out of place at the Oscars. At least someone in this town knew how to clean up! 'Wow, Sidnee, you look amazing!' I said as I walked up to her. 'And this party was a lot more effort than I was expecting.'

'Bunny! The woman of the hour. This is nothing – I love an excuse to throw an event!'

I laughed. 'Well, I'm grateful.'

'Good, because I invited everyone in town.'

I stared at her, eyes wide. She laughed and jostled my shoulder. 'I'm joking! Relax, this room can only hold a hundred and fifty.'

Some of the staff walked in carrying food. 'Did you have this catered?' I asked incredulously. She must have spent loads of money.

'Don't worry about it. I'm charging a little for entry, so everyone will cover their own costs. It won't cost me a dime.' She was virtually bouncing on her toes. 'Plus, I have permission to serve alcohol, so we'll actually make money! All profit will go to the Nomo's office, and maybe we can get that damn door fixed properly. Again.'

'I'll just go home then!' I teased.

'No, you won't. You and me, we're going to eat, drink and dance!'

'I have to confess something. I did something stupid. Don't laugh at me.' I looked around to make sure no one could overhear. 'I turned down Connor MacKenzie for a date and accidentally agreed to one with Stan Ahmaogak. He thinks he's my date for this party.'

Sidnee laughed. 'Damn, girl.'

I groaned. 'I don't know what to do.'

'Pray?' Then she snorted again with laughter. 'I invited a date too – but just the one.'

'Is it the guy you've been seeing, the one you told me about?'

'Yes, it's Chris. He's a fisherman, he's in my siren group.'

'Is he a mermaid too? Or is it merman for a guy?'

'It's merman for a guy, but he's actually a selkie. There's a whole bunch of different water-based shifters in the siren group.'

'Oh cool,' I said blankly. I knew nothing about selkies.

'The selkies are sort of insular, so I wasn't sure he'd go out with me at first but he seemed enthusiastic. We'll see how it goes.' She shrugged like it didn't matter, but I could see that it did.

The DJ finally started playing and the room filled up. People were eating and buying drinks, and a few got up to dance. The lighting was low, but for me it was as bright as day; the best side effect of vampirism was great eyesight.

Sidnee suddenly gave a happy noise and ran off to greet someone whom I assumed was her selkie date. She pulled him over to me. 'Bunny, this is Chris Jubatus. Chris, Bunny.'

'Hey, Chris, nice to meet you.'

He looked at me curiously. 'And nice to meet you, Bunny. That's an unusual name.'

I wondered how many times my name would be commented on tonight. 'I really love carrot cake,' I said blandly. 'When I was a kid I ate so much of it that my friends called me Bunny. It kinda stuck.'

'Carrot cake is sublime,' he agreed. 'Talking of cake, I'm starving. Excuse me a moment.' While Sidnee took him off to get food, I found an unoccupied chair that faced the door. Of course, as soon as I sat down both Connor and Stan entered the room at the same time. Fuck.

They both zeroed in on me and came over. Connor arrived first. 'Hey, Connor,' I said, suddenly shy. I wasn't sure what to say to the man who had camped out on my lawn to make sure I was safe, who only yesterday had been visibly heartsore as we'd moved a body together.

'Great party,' he said, with an easy grin. 'Save me a dance later?'

'Sure.'

'Have you eaten? Want to get some food?' he asked.

Stan was right behind him, arms crossed over his chest. 'Are you trying to steal my girl?' he demanded.

I cringed: *his girl*? What century was this? I had agreed, sort of, to one date but not a permanent love connection.

'Excuse me?' Connor asked.

Here it comes, I whispered to myself.

'We're on a date,' Stan said.

My wince was visible this time and Connor noticed. 'Did you tell *her* that? She doesn't look enthused.'

'Of course,' Stan looked confused. 'What's going on here?'

I sighed and checked the exits; unfortunately I was trapped and had to deal with this. 'I meant to invite you to the party as a friend,' I said weakly to him. 'I hope that's okay. I'm not ready to date yet – but I'd love to save you a dance later. Okay?'

Before either of them could respond, I turned and headed to the bar; sometimes running away was the only answer. 'What can I get you?' the barman asked.

'The strongest thing you have.'

He grinned. 'Coming at you. I hope you can hold your drink.'

I absolutely could not, thank goodness. It was time to get shitfaced.

Chapter 47

I woke up with a groan. I'd hoped that my dose of vampirism would save me from a hangover, but maybe it didn't work if you drank your body weight in booze.

I looked down. I was still in my party clothes but at least I'd managed to take off my heels. I was lying on top of my bed where I'd probably collapsed when I came home.

'That's a good boy,' a male voice said from my kitchen and I sat up with a start. I checked the other side of the bed; it was not rumpled. No second body had been lying next to me. No drunken shenanigans. I breathed a sigh of relief. I wasn't against a tipsy shag, but if I was so drunk I had memory blanks the next day, then any bloke who rolled in the sheets with me was taking advantage.

So who the fuck was in my kitchen? Frankly, if it was a murderer, they were quite welcome. My head *hurt*.

I stood up, wobbled a bit and held my head, then looked around for a weapon. All I could find was my favourite pair of clubbing stilettos that I'd worn the previous night. I grabbed one.

I was having a hard time summoning up any panic because Fluffy wasn't barking. My fangs remained stubbornly unsheathed. Stupid things. 'Who's there?' I called, cringing as the words echoed around my aching head.

'Come and find out,' an amused voice replied.

I recognised that voice. I cracked open the bedroom door and peered out. Connor was leaning against my kitchen table, feeding Fluffy freshly cooked strips of bacon. He saw the shoe clasped in my hand. 'Fashion emergency?' he smirked.

I dropped the shoe, stumbled out and made it to the kitchen table in time to collapse into a chair. 'What are you doing here? What happened?' I asked, my head in my hands.

He laughed. 'You drank Stan under the table and you were the life and soul of the party.' He didn't seem cross at the mention of Stan. From what I remembered, Stan had ignored my rebuff and ploughed ahead as if we *were* on a date, holding out chairs, bringing me drinks. If we *had* been on a date that might have been nice, but I'd made my position clear so it had pissed me off. I remembered thinking that doing some shots would cool his ardour, then I had a sudden flashback to me dancing on the bar. Oh fuck my life: I had *Coyote Ugly*ed.

I groaned again and put my forehead on the table. 'I didn't...'

Connor was grinning. 'You did. You have a decent singing voice, too. Who knew that you could hold your own with Lady Gaga and Taylor Swift?'

I moaned again. 'Stake me now.'

'That was nothing. The highlight was when you ranked the hottest men you'd met so far in town. I was proud I made the list.' He grimaced. 'Though it was weird to be up there with Patkotak.'

'Bounty hunters are sexy,' I murmured against the table. 'Dangerous vibes.'

Connor grinned. 'Good to know.'

With remarkable effort, I got up and started rummaging through the kitchen drawers. 'What are you doing?' Connor asked.

'I'm looking for a wooden spoon that I can use to stake myself.'

He barked a laugh. 'It's not so bad. Everyone had fun – and you weren't the only one table dancing. It's fine.' He sat me back in the chair. 'You need some blood – that'll cure your pounding head. Sidnee really knows how to throw a party and the alcohol was flowing, so I think it's safe to say that not many people will remember your behaviour – they'll be too busy worrying about their own. Gunnar really cut up the dance floor with Sigrid. That was a sight to see.'

'How come you're here?' I asked ungratefully after he'd handed me a cup of warmed blood.

'Since your date was snoring under the fondue table, and Sidnee was making out in a dark corner, I figured someone should take you home before you did something you'd regret. After the table-dancing thing, I manoeuvred you home.' He paused. 'I want credit for the fact that it was like wrangling a horny octopus.'

Kill me now. I held my nose and gulped down the blood. It tasted amazing; the stuff was growing on me, particularly when it had miracle hangover-curing properties.

Connor stared at me. 'Is that seriously how you drink blood?'

'Yup.'

He shook his head. 'You are the strangest vampire I've ever met. Most vampires have to hold themselves back to keep from finishing a whole bag at once.'

'I'd be happier with a bacon butty.'

'A what?' Connor asked.

'A bacon sandwich. Don't you eat those here?'

'We make bacon sandwiches – and a BLT is the food of the gods – but I don't know what a butty is.'

Madness: I had moved to a hick town where they didn't even have bacon butties. I looked at him blearily and sighed. 'You didn't tell me why you are still here. What time is it?'

'It's morning. I stayed because you were ... not making the best choices.'

Shit, what else had I done? Dare I ask? I looked at Fluffy, who gave me a sympathetic glance. I swallowed. 'What else did I do?'

'You kept trying to go back to the party, but that was a definite no. The doors were closed and the party was over.'

'That's not too bad.' I slumped back into the chair, relieved.

Connor came over and knelt in front of me, bringing himself down to my level. Suddenly my head was pounding in a whole different way. Tension thickened in the air and his lips tipped up just a little. For a moment I thought he was going to kiss me, but then he reached towards my face – and peeled something off it. He held out my false eyelash. 'You had a caterpillar on your cheek,' he teased, getting back to his feet.

Fluffy barked pointedly and his eyes flicked to Connor. 'She doesn't need to know,' Connor muttered to him. Fluffy's tongue lolled for a moment in a huge grin then he barked again. 'Fine,' Connor muttered, running a hand through his hair. 'I guess you were a little frisky as well.'

Frisky? Was that a word from this century? I peered at him through my fingers. 'With you? Did I attack you?'

'It was like trying to disentangle a tall tree from a rainforest canopy.' His eyes twinkled. Twinkled!

This time, I pounded my forehead on the table and groaned for the millionth time that morning.

Connor laughed and pulled me up. 'It's fine. It's already forgotten. You were wasted. I just stayed to make sure you were safe, what with the note and everything else that's been going on. Since you're safe and conscious, I'm heading out.' He gathered up the dishes, put them in the sink and walked out of the door.

I had big plans for the rest of the day: I was going to sit in the shower until I'd washed away my shame, then I was going to climb into bed and not come out again. Ever.

Chapter 48

I wallowed in my embarrassment for the rest of the day, watching trashy TV and eating copious amounts of chocolate. When Monday rolled around, I realised I had to go to work and face the town. I contemplated wearing a huge scarf and dark sunglasses, but that would just draw *more* attention, not less, so I pulled out my most subdued clothes: jeans, black shirt, black leather jacket and trainers.

With Fluffy on his lead, I slunk out of the door. It was the worst walk of shame. Ever. All I could hope was that everyone else had been as wild and they were now as mortified as I was. Here's hoping.

I only passed a few people on the way in, and thankfully I didn't recognise any of them. I was about to breathe a sigh of relief when I entered the office – but there was Stan, waiting for me. I froze. If he hadn't already noticed me, I'd have backed out and run all the way home.

'Bunny!'

I skirted around him and settled Fluffy under my desk. 'Hi, Stan.'

'What happened at your party? I woke up the next morning and everyone was mostly gone. I had to call the cab company.'

'We drank too much,' I said drily.

He grinned. 'I gathered that. I just don't remember any details.'

'Apparently, you fell asleep under the fondue table, and I went on to entertain the masses. From a table top.' I groaned. 'It was a disaster.'

'I'm sorry. I don't usually fall asleep on my dates.'

'It wasn't a date. Remember?' I grumped.

'It felt like a date.'

I sighed. He was not getting the message.

'I'd like to make it up to you,' he said sheepishly. It was kind of cute and some of my annoyance dissipated, but even so I needed to set him straight.

'Listen, don't take this the wrong way. I think you're great, but it's not a good idea if I date right now. I'm sorry.'

He frowned, then smiled. 'I can respect your wishes for now, but I'm not giving up! I think we'll have a great time together one day.'

I gave a weak smile. Pushy wasn't attractive, but I didn't want to fall out with him and, from what I remembered, we'd laughed together a lot at the party. 'Sorry,' I said again.

He shook his head. 'Don't be sorry. Just let me know when you're ready.' He waved and left. I sighed and sank onto my desk chair.

'Bunny, has Stan gone?' Gunnar's voice drifted through his door.

'Yes, boss.'

'Come in here, we have some lab results.'

Finally, a distraction. I was hoping the lab had matched the poison in Eric's system with something in Shirley's garden; if they had, we could add a charge for murdering Eric in time for the council trial. I hurried into Gunnar's office and scooched a chair close to his desk as he turned the computer monitor so we could both read the results.

The handwriting on the note found in Eric's truck matched Virginia's handwriting on her statement: the note really was from her, not a plant from the murderer to make us look in her direction. There were no fingerprints on the threatening note, but that would have been too good to be true.

I felt my excitement building; my gut had said that we were right to look at her.

I read on. There were no prints or physical evidence on the truck. The swab on the tyre that Fluffy had made me take had blood and dirt on it – Eric's blood. The dirt matched the soil sample taken at the docks, so that put the vehicle at the scene. The murderer had definitely taken it, not some joy-riding teen. We were getting somewhere.

We both leaned forward as we reached the final pages: the toxicology and coroner's reports. My heart sank as I read on. 'No matches?'

Gunnar sighed. 'None. Eric was poisoned all right, but I had them cross-check all the plants in Shirley's garden, not just the ready-made poisons from the fridge, and whatever was in his system didn't come from there. I was so sure,' he groused. 'If Shirley didn't poison him then we need to go back to the drawing board. We're back to our magic users and shifters.'

Dammit. 'What's the official cause of death?' I asked.

He scrolled through the document. 'Here, read for yourself.'

When I'd done, I looked up at Gunnar. 'The heart was punctured but the cause of death was exsanguination?'

The chair groaned as he leaned back in it. 'Yeah, the stabbing killed him.' He looked away for a moment. 'Maybe we need to look closer at this pack.'

'Both Reeve and Vaughn denied being members of it, but I didn't believe them. They're involved with each other, and I'm sure Reeve coached her because some of her responses were virtually the same as his.' I leaned forward. 'I think you're right. If Shirley didn't kill Eric, maybe this pack is involved. There's a reason why Thomas gave me that list. Vaughn and Reeve used each other as an alibi for the time of the murder but that could be total BS. I have another coming in today, but the other two haven't answered.'

'Time we tracked them down,' Gunnar rumbled.

'I agree. And did you notice that Vaughn tried to point the finger at Virginia?'

'Yeah, but she's human.'

'She could have hired someone,' I pointed out. 'Apparently she wanted to be turned, and Stan said no – and she had all that werewolf artwork in her home.' Dammit, I should have asked Stan about Virginia, but I'd been eager to see the back of him.

'Hmm, maybe, but that seems like a reason to lash out at Stan, not Eric. When's your next interview?' Gunnar asked.

I resisted the urge to point out that it was on the electronic calendar we shared. 'One am, after lunch.'

'How about we round up your other two beforehand?'

'Can we do that?'

'We can.'

'Then let's go!' I gave him the names and addresses. 'Mitch Schilling, and Kelly Sykes. Ben Eielson is coming in later today.'

Gunnar tapped at his computer. 'Schilling works for Connor at the logging company. Call there and see if he's at work.' He tapped some more. 'Sykes fishes, but since the fish processor hasn't raised the rates yet he's probably home. We'll go to his residence first.'

I nodded. I didn't want to call Connor, but what were the chances he'd answer the office phone? He probably had an assistant for that. I looked up the office number and called.

'Kamluck Logging. Connor speaking.'

Fuck's sake. The universe hated me. 'Connor, it's Bunny.'

'Ah, Bunny. Did you add me to another list? Will I finally make it to the top?'

I cringed inside. 'This is Nomo business.'

He chuckled. 'Later, then. What can I do for the Nomo?'

'Is Mitch Schilling at work today?'

'Let me check.' It went quiet for a few moments. 'He is.'

I looked at Gunnar. He nodded. 'We're coming over. Could you find somewhere we can interview him in private?'

'You're in luck. Mitch is just finishing up so he'll be back to the office shortly. You can talk there while I go out and do my rounds. See you soon.'

I hung up.

Gunnar and I were quiet on the way to the logging company. I was thinking of questions to ask, though since Gunnar was there he would probably take charge. We pulled up outside the office. It had been raining and puddles had collected in the uneven gravel parking lot. I wished I had worn Sigrid's ugly brown boots. I'd looked on the website; those boots came in better colours. I was ordering a pair after I got paid. In bright pink.

Connor was in the office with another man. He was exactly the kind of guy you pictured when you thought of a lumberjack: burly, with a thick beard and shoulder-length hair. His jeans were cut off at the bottom and ragged so they didn't catch on anything as he worked. His boots had spikes on the bottom, and he smelled of diesel and oil. I almost looked around to see where he'd dropped his axe.

'This is Mitch Schilling,' Connor said. 'I'll leave you to it.' He shook Gunnar's hand, gave me a lopsided grin, then shut the door behind himself.

Gunnar raised an eyebrow at the look but didn't say anything. He sat in Connor's chair and indicated that we should take the visitors' seats. 'Mitch, Bunny here has been trying to reach you to set up an interview. Any reason you haven't responded?'

Mitch shrugged. 'I've been busy.'

'Too busy to return a call?'

'And texts,' I added.

'And texts?' Gunnar added.

'I don't have any information,' Mitch protested.

'Do you know why we want to talk to you?'

'I assumed because of Eric.'

'You assumed correctly. How well did you know him?'

'A little. He was in our shifter group.'

'Our?' Gunnar was good; he was grasping the little tells.

A bead of sweat gathered on Mitch's forehead. 'The shifter group I'm in.'

Gunnar winked at me and nodded at me to ask the next question. 'So, are you a member of the pack, too?' I asked.

Mitch's hands were shaking and he was gripping the arms of the chair to disguise it. Too late: I'd already spotted the tremors. When he spoke, it was clear he was trying to sound casual but he failed miserably. 'What pack?' His nervous laugh continued for too long. 'We don't use that name anymore now that all the shifters meet under one leader.'

'Yet the other two members of the pack already told us that you belonged to it,' I said. 'As did Eric.'

'They did what?' Agitated, Mitch stood up.

Gunnar gave me a sidelong amused look. 'Sit back down, Mitch. I don't want to have to take you in.' Mitch sat. 'Go on, Bunny.'

'Eric was part of the pack. Do you want to explain what you do exactly?'

Schilling's resistance crumpled and he slouched in his chair. 'We liked having a group with just werewolves,' he muttered sullenly. 'The other shifters don't understand. We were all turned, we shift differently.'

'That's all? You just hung out and complained to each other?' I said, my tone derisory.

'No!' he snarled. Suddenly violence was hanging in the air and Gunnar tensed.

I kept pushing. 'So, what else did you do in your "private club"?' I asked.

'It *was* like a club.' Mitch clung to my words. 'We hung out, we ran in the woods. Stuff like that.'

'So why was that different from being in the shifter group?'

'Because it was only for werewolves!'

I didn't get it, but it seemed important to him. '
What do you know about Eric's death?'

'Nothing. I don't know nothing.'

'Tell me about Virginia Tide.'

Gunnar sent me a sharp look.

'Virginia?' Mitch gave another nervous laugh. 'Why do you want to know about her? She was Eric's girlfriend.'

'Did she have a reason to kill him? What was Eric like with her?'

He licked suddenly dry lips and fidgeted in his chair, picking his words carefully. 'Eric promised her lots of things but he never followed through.'

'What kinds of things?'

'The usual relationship shit. He'd get a better job, he'd buy her things, he'd marry her, he'd turn her, he'd...'

'Turn her? Into a werewolf?'

He blanched. 'Yeah.'

Gunnar jumped in. 'Is that something the pack offers humans?'

Schilling looked like he wanted to throw up. 'When she came to us, we told her no,' he protested, but he didn't answer the question.

'When was that?' I demanded. 'Before or after you turned Jack?'

He leapt to his feet. 'I had nothing to do with that!' There was fear in his eyes; he was about to demand a lawyer or run.

I moved quickly back to Eric. 'Where were you the night that Eric died?'

'I – I was...' He thought fast but the delay was telling. He sighed. 'We were supposed to meet Eric that night. All six of us were going to run. Eric was late, so we left without him – he was late a lot. We went up there.' He pointed up the hill where they were logging. 'I swear we didn't kill him!'

Strangely, I found myself believing him. I looked at Gunnar who shook his head a fraction. We were going to cut Schilling loose to see who he ran to. 'Thanks, Mitch,' Gunnar said. 'Stay in town, we'll be in touch. If you remember anything else, call the

Nomo's office.' Schilling staggered out, haggard and pale.

Gunnar said to me, 'He was involved in Jack's turning, but I believed him on Eric's death. Did you?'

'Yeah.' I admitted.

'Let's leave him to stew and speak to the others. Hopefully they will give something up on Jack and we can start making arrests. We need more than gut instinct.' He studied me. 'Why did you ask about Virginia?'

'Because I can't stop thinking she's involved somehow. She might not have stabbed Eric herself, but she could have hired someone.'

'She doesn't have any money. I checked her finances.'

'She could have called in a favour,' I countered.

'Maybe. Let's go find Sykes. After you have your interview with Eielson, we'll call her back in. I'm willing to roll with your instincts.'

I smiled gratefully; that he trusted me... It mattered.

I was vaguely disappointed that I didn't see Connor before we climbed back in the Nomo's vehicle to go and see what Sykes and Eielson had to say about this mess. It felt like we were finally closing in on something.

I was determined to get to the bottom of this pack business. They were clearly doing something shadier than running around together and howling at the moon. I'd bet my new house they'd turned Jack – but the question was why.

Chapter 49

We pulled up at the only static caravan park in town. It consisted of about twenty vans with small gardens, all well-maintained. 'Does Sykes live with his parents?' I asked curiously as we stopped behind a truck.

'I doubt it. These mobile homes are usually only one bedroom. Why?'

'In the UK, static caravan sites like this are usually retirement places or holiday housing.'

'Here in the US trailer parks are permanent residences, usually lower in price and easier to afford.'

We went up a set of three wide stairs to a cheap aluminium door. Gunnar knocked and the door rattled. A man answered. He was tall and thin, neatly dressed, with pockmarked skin, tidy hair and glasses.

Gunnar looked at him questioningly, I assumed because the man didn't match the image we'd had of Kelly Sykes. 'Is Mr Sykes at home?' Gunnar enquired politely.

'He just ran to the store. Can I help you? I'm Steve, Kelly's partner.'

'We really need to speak to him. Do you mind if we wait?'

Steve hesitated. 'No, I suppose that's okay. You can come in.'

We walked into a hallway. To the right was a small kitchen, but Steve gestured for us to follow him to the left into a decent sized living area, complete with a sofa, lounge chair and large TV which was showing a sports programme.

Steve clicked it off and we all sat. 'What is this about?' he asked abruptly.

'We need to talk to Mr Sykes about some members of his shifter group. Are you a werewolf as well?' Gunnar asked casually, as if he were making polite conversation.

'No, I'm a black bear shifter.'

'Not a werebear?' I asked nosily.

'God, no,' Steve said a little haughtily. I wondered how that affected his relationship because I'd thought shifters and weres were a bit at odds.

'Does Kelly tell you anything about the werewolves he runs with?' I enquired.

'A little,' Steve said guardedly. 'Look, is one of them in trouble with the Nomo's office?'

'One of them is dead,' Gunnar said bluntly.

Steve frowned. 'I heard about that – the murder on the docks? I didn't know Kelly knew the man. He hasn't mentioned him.'

'He knew him,' Gunnar assured him. Steve's frown deepened.

We heard a car pull up. There was a long pause, presumably whilst Sykes was looking at the Nomo vehicle, and it took him a couple of minutes to come inside. Eventually, the door opened and we heard the rustle of plastic shopping bags in the kitchen. The fridge opened and closed, then a few seconds later Kelly Sykes entered the room.

He was the complete opposite of the refined Steve – large, rough and ready. Despite those rough edges – or maybe because of them – he was also quite handsome. He was dressed in jeans, a dirty sweatshirt and brown Xtra-tuf boots, and he had a day or two's growth of stubble on his face. He looked like he was dressed for fishing, but he couldn't be because Gunnar had said that he was laid off due to the current hold-out not yet being formally lifted.

'Kelly, the Nomo has questions.' Steve's tone indicated that he had some, too. He gave his chair to his partner and stood behind him with a hand on Sykes' broad shoulders – in warning or support, I wasn't sure.

'What about?' Sykes asked gruffly, looking at us.

Gunnar started right in. 'Where were you the night of the seventh?'

'I was...' He licked his lips and looked at Steve, whose face was stiff. Kelly knew that his partner wasn't going to alibi him. He chewed on his lip a moment before sighing. 'What's the point?' he muttered. 'You already know. You've questioned most of us.' He sighed. 'I was running with a few other werewolves.'

'Who?' I asked, eager to see if the stories aligned.

'Mitch Schilling, Molly Vaughn, Ben Eielson, and Wilds Reeve,' he said quietly.

Steve's expression was dark. I wondered what Sykes had told him he was doing that day. 'So,' I continued, 'you were out running with members of the pack? You might as well be honest. As you said, we've spoken with all but one of your little club.'

'Who's left?'

I ignored that; best to leave it alone so we could speak to Eielson without interference. I pressed on. 'Where was Eric? Didn't he usually join the group?'

'He was late so we left without him. He was late a lot and we were tired of it.'

That matched up with Mitch's statement. 'Did Eric have any enemies?' I asked.

'Not anyone that didn't hate all of us.'

'Why's that?'

'Because we're werewolves, not shifters.' His tone was bitter. 'Many of the shifter group think we shouldn't be part of their collective, and a few of us were starting to agree.' He threw an apologetic look at Steve, who squeezed his shoulder.

'Is that why you formed the pack?'

'Partly.'

'What's the other part?'

Kelly clammed up. 'I want a lawyer.' Dammit. We hadn't even had chance to speak to him about Jack.

Gunnar intervened. 'We're just talking, you aren't under arrest.'

'I'm done talking.' Kelly's jaw was set. 'If I'm not under arrest, then get out.'

'Right you are.' Gunnar gave a single nod and stood. 'We'll continue this at the station when we have an arrest warrant.' He let the threat hang there but Sykes didn't bite. 'If you have anything more to say in the meantime, you know how to find us. We'll see ourselves out.'

I followed him to the car. Looking over my shoulder, I saw Steve flick the kitchen curtains and watch us leave. Something definitely smelled fishy – and it wasn't just Kelly Sykes.

Chapter 50

There was time for lunch before Ben Eielson's interview. Fluffy was waiting patiently at the office so we walked home together, ate quickly and returned. I hadn't been this careful about mealtimes before I was a vampire, but I was afraid of what would happen to me if I forgot to drink blood regularly. No one wanted a bitey co-worker.

After we strolled back in, Fluffy wriggled under the desk to lie on my feet. I booted my computer up, forwarded some emails to Gunnar then turned my attention to the questions I wanted to ask Eielson.

I popped to the toilet for a nervous wee. As I returned to my desk the man himself walked into the building. He was a medium sized, wiry, with the look of someone who was constantly checking over his shoulder. His jerky movements gave the impression that he was always flinching, and his shoulders were hunched and defensive. My first thought was that I'd found the weakest link.

'Mr Eielson?' I asked.

'Yes, I'm here for an appointment. Call me Ben.'

'Sure thing, Ben. Please, come with me.' I held open the swing door at the end of the counter. Fluffy whined a little and I patted my leg so he knew to follow me. I was learning to trust his senses more than my own; Eielson looked like he wouldn't hurt a fly, let alone a dog, but I might as well have Fluffy with me.

'What's with the dog?' Ben asked.

'He's a trained police dog.' I was flubbing the truth a little but he *was* trained, albeit by someone else, and he was currently working with the police. I smiled blandly.

Despite my assurance, Ben gave Fluffy a wary look and stayed as far away from him as possible. Maybe he was a cat person.

I pressed record. 'I'm recording this interview.'

'What is this about?' Ben asked, shifting in his seat.

'It's about the murder of Eric Walker.' Ben flinched. Whoops, I'd gone in a bit too 'bad cop' there. I reeled it back in.

'I didn't have anything to do with that!' It was weird that his first reaction was to protest; most people asked 'What about it?'. Methinks the man did protest too much, him and the rest of his pack. They were all too quick, too eager to say they had nothing to do with Eric's death, so I couldn't help but feel they were hip deep in it somehow. Shirley might or might not have supplied the poison, but the pack members were involved one way or another.

'This is routine,' I soothed, taking a line from Gunnar's book. 'We're interviewing all Eric's known associates.'

Ben leaned back in his chair. 'Fine.'

'Where were you the night of the seventh?'

He shrugged and didn't answer. 'Ben,' I said softly, 'we know about the pack.'

Startled, he sat up straight. 'How?'

'We've met all the other members. We've had some lovely chats.'

He muttered something, but even with my vampire-enhanced hearing I didn't catch it. Damn. 'Sorry, what was that?' I asked with an innocuous smile.

'Nothing,' he glowered.

'So, once again, if I can just ask where you were on the night of the seventh?'

'I was running with the rest of the pack,' he admitted.

'And just for the record, who are the other members?'

He was starting to sweat. 'You've spoken to them already?'

'All of them.'

He grimaced. 'Eric Walker, Mitch Schilling, Kelly Sykes, Wilds Reeve and Molly Vaughn.'

'When did Eric show up?'

'He didn't. He was late, so we went running without him.'

That checked out. At least they'd all backed one another's alibis. 'What time did you meet, and why that night?' That question had been bothering me. What was so special about that particular night that they'd met to run, to be together? And why hadn't Eric shown up? If he had, might he still be alive?

Ben gave a one-shouldered shrug. 'No special reason. We meet every Wednesday night at eleven – that way, we have time when it's mostly dark and the town isn't as busy. It worked for everyone's work schedules as well.'

I remembered the calendar in Eric's kitchen with every Wednesday circled. Ben's explanation played but he was refusing to meet my eyes, so I had the distinct feeling he was leaving something out.

'The seventh was a Tuesday, Ben,' I said gently. He grimaced but didn't say anything else. 'So why that night?' I pressed.

'No reason,' he lied.

He wasn't going to add anything, so I moved on. 'One of your buddies mentioned that Eric's girlfriend, Virginia Tide, had petitioned your pack to be turned. Is that true?'

His face paled. He shrugged again, but he was struggling to appear nonchalant. 'If she had, we would have said no.'

'Why?' I was hoping he'd say because it was illegal unless a petition that went through a lot of checks and interviews had been completed by the shifter group and approved by the Nomo.

He didn't. 'Because she's crazy as f— Umm, heck,' he corrected, his voice a little shrill.

'In what way?'

He gripped the arm of the chair, his knuckles white. 'She just is. She's batshit.'

I wanted to press him further but everything in me sensed he was afraid of the diminutive woman. I tried a different tack. 'Who wanted Eric dead?'

He relaxed visibly. 'I don't know. We weren't that close. There was the fish stuff going on, but I don't know much about it. I'm in mining.' He sighed. 'Eric wasn't popular. He was weak.' That seemed a rich criticism coming from a man who cringed away from the shadows and my pet dog. He hunched in on himself.

I wanted to tell him his shoulders would stay that way if the wind changed, but when I opened my mouth I realised I was channelling my mother. Ugh. Even so, his slouching had me pulling back my shoulders and straightening my back. 'Anything you can remember at all that might be relevant? Anything suspicious?' I figured a blanket question would give him a chance to voice even the slightest thought about Eric.

He thought for a moment. 'The last fight I saw between Eric and his old lady was a couple of weeks before. She wanted him to help her put some stuff into a storage unit because they were moving in together. I don't think they ever got round to it because things got overheated and then they broke up again. She said she wished she'd never met him.'

Saying you wished you hadn't met someone wasn't the same as wanting them dead, but it was interesting that Virginia hadn't told us any of this. So now we had a storage unit to look for. I wouldn't have even thought of that because Eric had lots of space at his house, as did Virginia. Why would she need a unit? To hide some evidence, like Eric's paperwork and his wallet? I wondered if Gunnar would let me search it.

'Thanks, Ben. You've been helpful. Don't leave town.' I'd always wanted to say that. 'If you think of anything else, please call or stop by.'

'That's it? I can go?'

'Yes. You're not under arrest.'

'Great.' He exhaled loudly, stood and rubbed his hands down his pants.

'One last thing,' I said abruptly. 'Which of you turned Jack?'

Ben froze, wide-eyed, panic written across his face. 'I don't know! It wasn't me.'

'Okay, you can go.'

He almost staggered with relief then turned and ran out of the building. As soon as the door shut behind him, Gunnar stepped in. 'Nice work,' he commented.

'You were watching?'

'Sure. I liked how you punched him at the end with Jack. It's not common knowledge yet that he was the werewolf that attacked you, but Ben didn't blink. You're right – one of the pack turned him. The evidence is stacking up. I want to get Eric's murder wrapped up first, then we'll go after them.' He studied me, 'You're thinking about Virginia's storage unit.'

'I'm thinking about the unit,' I agreed. 'How hard is it to get a warrant?'

'Shouldn't be too bad in this case. I'll get things in motion. Maybe we shouldn't have dismissed Virginia Tide just because of her species.'

I hadn't dismissed her; even if she were human, she could have had someone do her dirty work. 'Ben is afraid of her,' I commented.

Gunnar nodded slowly. 'Yup, I reckon he is. I'll get that warrant.' He headed back to his office.

That was good enough for me. Things were finally heating up.

Chapter 51

Whilst we waited for the warrant, I decided it was time to check Virginia's statement that she and Eric had eaten at the Pizza Kodiak Kitchen the night he was murdered. After reading the note that said she'd already broken up with him for good, it seemed odd that they were out to dinner together. The note had been folded and worn, as if it had been opened and closed many times. My money was on it being written a few weeks – or even months – before Eric's death.

I dropped Gunnar an email to let him know where I was going, then grabbed a picture of Eric and walked over to the pizza place. A bunch of teenagers were working so I asked to speak with the manager.

A harried-looking woman wiping her hands on a dirty apron came out from the back. 'Hi, is there a problem?' she asked a little grumpily. She could do with taking a leaf out of the café waitress's book.

'No, not at all. I was wondering if you remembered Tuesday the seventh, and particularly if you saw this man.' I held up Eric's picture.

She squinted at it. 'I don't know. I don't get out front very often.' She leaned in to whisper, 'Teenagers require constant supervision. They are total horn dogs.'

Ewww. *Remind me not to eat here*, I thought. But I nodded and looked sympathetic.

She stared again at the photograph. 'Actually, I think I do remember him. He was with a small woman and they had an argument loud enough that I had to come up front and ask them to leave. I don't remember what day that was though. Sorry.'

'Do you remember what they were arguing about?'

'I only heard a few words – I was focused on getting them out. Hold on, I'll ask the girl who was up front.' She went back to the counter and told the boy there to find Jessica. When she joined us, the manager asked if she remembered the argument.

Jessica nodded shyly and threw a furtive glance at me. Thankfully she was a gossip. 'It was something about werewolves,' she said with relish. 'But I don't know any details. I was hard at work.' She slid her manager a wide-eyed, innocent look.

The manager sighed. 'Just tell her the damned truth of what you saw so we can all get on with work.'

'What else do you remember hearing?' I asked.

'Umm.' Jessica folded her arms and cocked a hip while she thought. 'They shouted about a bunch of wolfy shit … stuff, sorry, Margaret,' she added to her boss. 'They said stuff about a pack – turning, running or something – then she yelled about leaving him.'

She hesitated and looked at her boss again. 'It's against company policy to use foul language, so I'll just say there was some swearing. She was cussing him out real good. I was listening because it was a bit of drama, you know. When the argument started, me and Tim were betting whether the guy had cheated on her or not. She sure was steamed.'

'Did anything else stand out to you?' I asked.

Jessica grinned. 'She threw a drink in his face and he looked properly miserable. Then she stormed off and I had to clean up the mess. Oh! And I thought it was crazy that after all she'd put him through, he still settled her bill as well as his own. He snagged the leftover pizza in a box and left.'

'He paid her bill?'

'Yep.'

'From his own wallet?' I pressed.

She shrugged. 'I guess. She'd already gone by then. He paid both bills and left.'

'Thank you for your time. I'm going to write up a statement for you. Can you give me your telephone number and address?' She rattled both off. 'Thanks Jessica. If you can think of anything else, please call the Nomo's office and ask for Bunny.'

A smirk pulled at her lips. 'Bunny? What kind of a name is that?'

I kept my expression blank. 'The UK government treated me to a round of genetic engineering and used some rabbit DNA to make me faster and more agile, hence the name.'

Her eyes widened. 'Wow. That's so cool.'

I shrugged. 'I could do without the urge to eat carrots all the time.'

The manager sent Jessica back to work and gave me a broad grin. 'She believed you, hook, line and sinker.'

I grinned back. 'Thank you for your time. I appreciate it.'

'No worries, *Bunny*.' Margaret returned to the fray and I headed back to the office.

Jessica hadn't give me a lot of information to work on, but it had confirmed a lot of what the pack had said about Virginia wanting to be turned and being refused. Was that a strong enough motivation for murder? I guessed it could have been if Virginia thought Eric was preventing her wishes being met. If she thought he was in her way maybe she'd got rid of him – but the thing that was still bothering me was the *how*.

Back in the office, I updated Gunnar. 'Great work, and great timing,' he said. 'We've got our warrant.'

'Holy cow, that was quick!'

He laughed at my expression. 'I just needed a controlling vote from the council. Since they're anxious to have this case solved, they were accommodating. The longer this goes on, the more anxious the community gets – the last few nights, the streets have been bare at night. That's not like Portlock. A good portion of the inhabitants are nocturnal. With Jack, Kivuk, and now this... The town is spooked. We need to nail this down before more fights break out.'

'More?'

'There's been some scuffles amongst the shifters. Tensions are rising and it's going to come to a head fast if we don't solve this case.'

It was a good thing I worked well under pressure.

Chapter 52

'Let's check out that storage unit. Bring Fluffy. We might need his nose,' Gunnar ordered.

'You ready to play police dog again?' I asked him. He gave a bark and a little half jump on his front feet; he was ready, willing – and excited as hell to get out from under my desk.

We climbed into the Nomo vehicle and Gunnar drove to the storage unit. I wondered if we'd find a load of junk or a serial killer's secret stash. I was hopeful that it would contain vials of poison made by Shirley Thompson labelled with those cute skulls with flowers growing out of the eye sockets.

At the storage unit's office, Gunnar told me to wait in the car. Fluffy whined softly, anxious to be out there solving crime. My boss was back in less than ten minutes and climbed back in. 'The manager is coming with a set of bolt cutters for the lock.'

Sure enough, a minute later a balding man with a slight paunch came out carrying a set of bolt cutters. He locked the office door behind him, punched a code into a box mounted on a post and the black wrought-iron gate slid back. We drove in slowly and followed him. We went down three rows, turned and moved down about a third of the way. The balding man checked the number of a unit then cut off the lock. Once he'd done that, he took the broken lock and left us to it; the vibe I was getting was that the less he saw, the better.

Gunnar passed me a pair of nitrile gloves. When we were both ready, he raised the garage-style door and motion detector lights flickered on. We stared around the unit: it was full to the top. I groaned and Gunnar heaved a heavy sigh. 'Do we have some lowly staff that I don't know about who could sort through this?' I asked hopefully.

Gunnar shot me a sideways grin. 'Yeah – you.' I rolled my eyes and he laughed.

We started pulling out boxes, totes and old furniture. About halfway down the unit, I spied a man's wallet and my scalp prickled. 'Gunnar, look!'

He stood next to me and looked down. The floor was covered with dust, except for random footprints where people had walked through. 'Hold on, don't move.'

I waited. When he returned with an evidence bag, he had me take a picture of the wallet in situ, then he picked it up and opened it. 'Eric Walker,' he murmured, reading the names on the driver's licence and credit cards. 'Bingo.'

There was no cash and no loving pictures of Virginia, just one of Eric and Jim standing in front of one of Jim's planes. Gunnar put it in the evidence bag and went back to the car to make a note on the log and put it in a secure evidence box.

Maybe the murder weapon would also be lying around. A girl could dream. That thought made me snicker; how my dreams had changed.

Three hours later we were grubby and exhausted, and we hadn't found a bloodstained murder weapon. The contents of the unit were stacked in the aisle; now we had to search every single box and then replace them. Why did Virginia keep all this shit?

After about five boxes, it was clear that most of the contents were probably her parents' stuff. Maybe she'd cleaned up after they'd passed away, and rather than sort it out immediately she'd saved it to do later. Grief was hard enough without pawing through your loved ones' worldly possessions. It had taken me months to find the courage to go through Nana's things. Mum, of course, hadn't given a fuck about them because Nana's clothes hadn't been designer and her jewellery was mainly costume. She and Nana might have been related but the family tree had branched sharply – maybe it had been struck by lightning.

'Are Virginia Tide's parents dead?' I asked curiously. 'She has a lot of their stuff.'

'I'll get Sidnee on it.' Gunnar pulled out his phone and texted her.

We took a break. Even with my vampire healing abilities my back felt tight. I walked around for a while, giving my body a chance to mend itself when I was upright. After a few minutes, the ache was gone.

Gunnar's phone chimed with an incoming text. 'Sidnee says they died two years ago in a boating accident. Her mum had cancer so they'd gone on a "once in a lifetime" cruise. When they were on a day trip on a small skiff, they got into difficulties and both died.'

That sucked. Virginia must have been around my age – mid-twenties, max. I expected my parents to live for another forty years or more. It must be hard to lose your mum and dad so young, even if they were assholes – and there was nothing to suggest that hers had been. No wonder she couldn't face sorting through her parent's possessions. 'You said she had no money. Was there no inheritance?' I asked.

Gunnar frowned. 'I just got the last couple of months' statements from her bank. No sign of a big payout. But there again, people often struggle getting money from inheritance. It feels like profiting from a loved one's death and it's not unusual to blow it all real quick.'

'That's sad.'

He grimaced. 'That's human nature.'

My mind had been churning as we were working and I finally spoke my thoughts aloud. 'The wallet – do you think she just opened the door and chucked it in here?'

'Maybe. Or Eric helped her move some stuff and dropped it.'

Damn: that was possible, *really* possible. And even if she had thrown it in here, we couldn't prove it. We still had absolutely nothing on Virginia.

We continued to work through the detritus but there was no smoking gun – or rather, no bloody knife. The wallet was a win, but not the big win we needed.

Chapter 53

Shirley Thompson's trial day had arrived. Gunnar had explained that growing toxic plants and manufacturing poison wasn't against the law because poison had a number of legitimate uses, like killing weeds or animals that were pests. *Distributing* poison for nefarious purposes was totally illegal, however. And we also had the charge against her for attacking Gunnar.

I had asked Gunnar what sentence she could get for assaulting him and he'd said anything from six months to life, depending on the level of violence used and injury sustained. Since he hadn't been hurt, he wasn't banking on her being put away for long.

The trial would be judged by the council members, minus Gunnar who'd been excused due to the clear conflict of interest. I had to give evidence about the attack, so we sat near the front of the courtroom. The council members were opposite.

Connor stared at me and gave me a half smile when I glanced his way. I returned it. Stan was also on the council and he winked when he made eye contact, making me grimace. Winks weren't professional. We were in a courtroom, for goodness' sake.

Shirley's fancy lawyer was talking to her quietly, but however much I strained to hear I only caught mumbling. He wasn't far from us, so I should have been able to hear – had he used a spell or something? I asked Gunnar if that was allowed and he nodded. 'She's allowed to confer with her counsel. With supernat hearing, magic can be used to guarantee confidentiality. I'm not sure what type of magic but the lawyer will have sorted it.'

Finally an usher announced the case name and the parties. Once the court was called to order, the lawyers did their openings. Eric's murder wasn't mentioned at all; it seemed strange that the crime we'd approached Shirley about had nothing to do with her final arrest.

'The subject was arrested without being read her Miranda rights.' Shirley's lawyer looked a shade smug. He was going to try and get the charges dropped on a technicality.

Gunnar mumbled what sounded like cuss words under his breath.

'She was held without bail for an extended period,' the lawyer continued.

Alarm bells were ringing. Fuck: Gunnar *hadn't* Mirandized her. I'd thought that maybe arrests were done differently here, but it looked like Gunnar's emotions had got the better of him. If she walked away free, then the law was unfair.

Shirley's lawyer sat and the prosecution lawyer stood. I hoped he could do some damage control. 'The prosecution calls Gunnar Johansen to the stand.'

Gunnar stood, was sworn in and sat for his questioning.

'Can you please affirm to the court that this is your statement?' The lawyer handed Gunnar a piece of paper.

Gunnar read it. 'It is.'

'Why did you arrest Ms Thompson?'

Gunnar glared at her. 'I knocked on her door to ask some routine questions. She opened it and immediately threw a fireball at me.' Even now, he sounded outraged.

'And then what happened.'

'She kept flinging them until I restrained her with magic cancelling cuffs.'

'Did you keep her locked up without giving her chance to call a lawyer?'

'No. She got her phone call the second we had her back at the station.'

'Nothing further.'

Gunnar went to stand up, but the lawyer for the defence stopped him. 'After you cuffed Ms Thompson, did you at any time Mirandize her?'

I could see Gunnar thinking. This was it; he hadn't done it. If he lied under oath and I was called to give evidence, what was I going to do? Throw him under the bus and allow a violent woman to walk free?

I bit my lip. I had to tell the truth. Anxiety churned in my gut as I waited for his answer. If he lied, some of my faith in him would be shattered. Over the course of our time working together I'd become convinced he was the salt of the earth; I didn't want to be wrong.

'No,' Gunnar finally admitted 'I didn't. She demanded a lawyer from the beginning and refused to speak a single word.'

That shut up the lawyer and he leaned over to ask his client something. After she'd replied, he said, 'No more questions.'

When Gunnar came back I asked him what the heck was going on. 'Being Mirandized isn't a constitutional right, although it's tricky. Since she didn't say anything, it's not going to be enough to throw out the case.'

'Thank God!' I burst out. 'What a relief! Is it my turn now?'

'You might not be called,' Gunnar said reassuringly. 'If neither of the lawyers have any questions for you, they'll let your evidence stand in chief.'

'In what?'

'They'll let your statement stand. I conceded on the rights point, so I expect you won't be needed.'

We continued to watch. I waited for the defendant to be called, but it didn't happen. 'Why isn't Shirley taking the stand?'

'She hadn't filed a witness statement in her own defence.'

'That's suspicious, right?'

Gunnar grinned. 'Hard to prove your innocence if you don't file one. It all rests on the prosecution, though. They still need to prove her guilt beyond reasonable doubt.' He looked smug; he obviously knew something I didn't.

'The defendant had a large amount of synthesised poison in her home,' the prosecutor was saying, and my ears pricked back up. 'When questioned she refused to answer, as was her right. However, an online search showed that she was selling the poisons over the dark web under the handle DeadlyPotionsMistress.'

I looked at Gunnar, eyes wide with shock. 'I sent her computer to cyber forensics in Anchorage. That's it – she's going away now,' he whispered.

The prosecutor proceeded to lay out all the other forensic evidence that they'd found.

The council convened for a mere twenty minutes. When they returned to the courtroom Mafu spoke. 'Will the defendant rise?' Shirley stood. 'The council finds you guilty. The amount of poison both in your possession at home and in your garden paints the picture of a voracious businesswoman. The sales itemised in your laptop's business accounts indicate that you have more likely than not assisted in the deaths of scores of individuals. As such, you are hereby sentenced to twenty years. Court is dismissed. Council, thank you for your service.'

Shirley sank into her chair, her eyes blazing with rage. I was grateful for the green cuffs around her wrists; if she'd had her magic, I could well imagine

that various council members would be going up in
flames.

Chapter 54

I was tired after the emotional rollercoaster of the trial; all I wanted was to go home, eat and lie on the sofa with my dog. I tried to slip away discreetly but Stan was waiting outside the door of the council chambers. 'Bunny, wait!' he said as I walked briskly down the hall.

I stopped and turned reluctantly. 'Hey Stan, how's things?'

'I wanted to apologise again about the other night.'

I cringed a little. 'It's fine.' I was tempted to ask him about the pack, but talking about it might have far-reaching consequences for its secretive members. Better that something like that came from Gunnar.

'I know you said no dating just now,' Stan said hopefully, 'but it's been nearly a week. Dinner tonight? No booze, I promise.'

I struggled not to let my jaw drop. A week? Really? That's what he'd taken away from my 'let's not date' statement? I hardened my voice: some guys didn't know when no meant no. I hadn't taken Stan to be one of those, but maybe he was. Maybe I needed to draw the line a little firmer.

'I've said no. I'm not dating just now – and you're also tangentially involved in the case I'm working on. It is *not* happening.' I tried to walk past him.

'Please, Bunny? I really feel like a tool. Just one dinner to say sorry would go a long way to fixing that.'

He was going to try and *guilt* me into a date? I'd let him do that before, and I wasn't doing it again. He was cute, he could be fun, but I didn't do controlling. I'd already had enough of that in my life. 'No, thanks.'

A dark cloud passed over his eyes and I wondered if he'd press the matter, but instead he flashed me his most charming smile. 'I get that I screwed up. I really am sorry. Perhaps another time.'

'I don't think so, not right now.' I smiled tightly. Then I thought fuck it; one question that he could answer was burning me up. 'Did Virginia Tide apply to be turned?'

Stan grimaced. 'Yeah, she did. I felt awful about saying no but we have to keep to a strict psychological profile. She has anger and impulse control issues, both of which make her unsuitable for turning despite her circumstances.'

'Her circumstances?' I asked.

'You didn't know? She has brain cancer. Terminal.'

My jaw dropped. 'You didn't think that might be relevant to Eric's death?'

He looked at me blankly. 'I wasn't sure if they were together or not. Besides, she can't have killed him – she's a human and she's dying.'

'It also means that she has very little to lose,' I pointed out drily. 'I've got to go.'

'Sure. It was good to see you.' This time he let me walk past him.

Gunnar was still talking to the council members so I decided to give him a ring or drop him a text with the latest on Virginia. Home was calling my name and I wanted to check on Fluffy.

Connor was waiting by the outside door, leaning against the wall. What was this: an awkward gauntlet of men? When he saw me, he greeted me with a nod. 'Your next appointment is tomorrow at the logging office after dark. Bring proof of your online class completion.'

I'd expected something a little more personal, so I just stared at him. He gave me a small smile. 'Have a good day.' He walked out and turned towards the car park.

That man blew so hot and cold that I never knew what the fuck was going on. I headed home trying very hard to not to think about Connor MacKenzie.

Fluffy bounded out when I opened the front door. 'Hey, bud! You'll never guess what happened? Shirley went down for distributing poisons!' He barked and wagged his tail in approval. 'And Virginia Tide has terminal cancer. I am *certain* she killed Eric somehow.' He barked again, and I cracked a yawn.

'I'm exhausted, so we'll just go for a quick walk, okay?'

We had a brisk walk around the block then headed back inside. I was so tired I didn't even bother closing the metal blinds. I was definitely sleeping in tomorrow; I wasn't getting up until way after the sun had set again. I had twenty-four hours off work and, other than checking in with Connor, I was free to do anything or nothing.

My mind went back to Connor. *I don't want to date,* I told myself firmly. *Stop thinking about him.*

As I warmed a cup of blood in the microwave, I grabbed Fluffy's bowls. He needed some fresh water and dinner. He sat patiently in the kitchen watching me. I smiled at him and gave him an affectionate pat on the head.

The microwave beeped, and Fluffy whirled to face the front of the house just as something smashed through my front window. I screamed and automatically covered my face. That something had landed on my sofa.

I ran to see what it was and gaped when I saw that both the sofa and curtains were on fire.

Chapter 55

I heard a vehicle's tyres squeal as it drove off, but I didn't see it – I was too busy retrieving the fire extinguisher from under the kitchen sink and trying to put out the flames. Luckily, they hadn't had a chance to spread. The bottle hadn't broken when it struck the window and the sofa had cushioned it. Thankfully, the curtains were gossamer thin and they'd burned up in seconds without anything else catching fire.

I took a deep shaky breath and toed the bottle. It was freaking aluminium – that had to be the shittiest Molotov cocktail I'd ever seen. Okay, so it was the only Molotov cocktail I'd ever seen, but everyone knew they were supposed to be in glass bottles that would shatter. Shoving the liquid into an aluminium receptacle negated the whole point of using a fragile glass bottle.

Someone might be trying to kill me but they were inept. Either that, or they were only trying to scare me.

I now had a house that smelled like burnt plastic, people could see in through the windows and I had a smoky black hole in my sofa. I called Gunnar and told him what had happened. He insisted on calling the fire brigade, just to be on the safe side.

I sighed and debated whether to open the windows to air the place out or slam down the shutters so that no one would try to kill me again tonight. Choices, choices, but in the end I opted to open the windows. The likelihood of a second strike was low, right? Once the curtain remnants and the couch were outside, the house would smell much better; maybe then I could close the shutters and sleep.

The fire department came a few minutes later, sirens blaring, followed by Gunnar. The sirens were embarrassing – I'd told Gunnar that the fire was out. Everyone in town would think I was a drama queen.

'Are you okay?' he asked, searching my eyes for any signs that I wasn't.

'I'm fine. I'm tired. I want my bed. Is all of this necessary? The fire is out.'

'These things can rekindle so let them do their thing.' Gunnar walked away a little distance, pulled the chief fire officer aside and spoke with him too quietly for me to overhear.

'Everything okay here, ma'am?' the officer asked. I explained again about the Molotov cocktail and showed him the extinguisher I'd used to put out the fire, then the firemen took the sofa outside and soaked it. As Gunnar had suspected, the fire had burned deeper than I thought and it could have spontaneously reignited in the night. Yeesh. The firemen searched the house in case I'd missed a second attempt; once everything was clear, they finally left.

I showed Gunnar the bottle. He frowned. 'It's aluminium.'

I grinned. 'I know. I'm being attacked by an idiot.'

He shook his head. 'No, I suspect not. This was a warning.'

'Or a really stupid killer?' I said optimistically.

He chuckled. 'I think even the *really* dumb ones know you need to shatter the glass to release the accelerant.'

He had a point. 'Probably.'

'We must be getting closer to the truth of Eric's death. The pack is involved somehow.'

'I think you're right, but I still think it's Virginia pulling the strings somehow.' I told him about my chat with Stan and that Virginia had cancer.

Gunnar frowned. 'I'll press again on her financials. Maybe she paid one of the pack members to kill Eric for her, one last act before she shuffles off this mortal coil. But it's still not playing right in my mind. Anyhow, I'll send the bottle to the lab. If we're lucky and they're as stupid as you think, there'll be prints.'

'Why aren't you or Sidnee being attacked?' I complained.

'No one would dare attack me.' Gunnar laughed at the very idea. 'And Sidnee has the protection of the other merfolk. You haven't integrated into vamp society yet so you're an easy target. Besides, you've been doing a lot of the questioning. If you poke the bear, you have to expect it to snarl.'

'Wonderful.'

'Do you want to stop poking?' he asked seriously.

I snorted. 'Not on your nelly!'

'Good.' His face hardened, 'When we find out who did this, we'll make sure they know not to do it again.' He looked grim and a little bit scary. Not a man I would cross, that's for sure. 'You don't attack the Nomo's office and get away with it. Retribution is coming,' he promised darkly.

'Can retribution wait?' I asked plaintively. 'I'm tired.'

He grinned, and like that, he was back to being the Gunnar I knew. 'Sure. But you should come and stay with me and Sigrid tonight.'

'No, I'm going to sleep in my own bed. They are *not* intimidating me.'

'You have a broken front window and no sofa.'

'I'll close the metal shutters so no one can get in or throw in any more Molotov cocktails. Plus, it was a warning, wasn't it?'

He paused. 'Probably. Almost certainly.'

'Then we'll be fine.'

Gunnar thought I was a mix of brave and stupid, but the truth was I was too damned tired to pack up and move. Plus, I was a homebody and all I wanted was to sleep in my own bed. And no stupid werewolves were going to intimidate me out of it. Fuck them.

Chapter 56

I assumed no one had tried to set me on fire whilst I slept, because I woke up alive, undead or whatever I was. I allowed myself to sleep late and luxuriate in bed for a while, then got up and rolled up the metal blinds. A truck was just driving away from my road. A familiar truck: Connor's.

Maybe I was mistaken, though, because a moment later Connor texted me a time for my meeting. It wasn't until early evening so, other than taking Fluffy out, I was determined to have a day relaxing. I had a bath. I did my hair. I painted my nails. I listened to some songs. I tried to settle down and watch TV but that wasn't the best idea since I had no sofa. I brought in a dining room chair but it wasn't very comfy and Fluffy couldn't cuddle with me.

Feeling restless, I flicked off the TV. With nothing else to do, I thought about the case. I thought through the facts. Eric had been poisoned and stabbed. He'd been due to meet with the pack, but he apparently didn't show up – but the pack normally met on a Wednesday and that was a Tuesday, so why had they changed the day? The pack members corroborated each other's alibis, but they were obviously sticking together.

There was more to the pack than just wanting to hang out with other werewolves. One of them – or all of them – had been involved in turning Jack Taylor. Something had gone wrong, and he hadn't retained his humanity the way he should have done.

I couldn't shake the feeling that Virginia was involved; she was sick and she was desperate, she'd asked Stan to turn her and been told no. She'd dumped Eric. She felt like he'd let her down because he hadn't got her turned. Couldn't he do it himself?

Eric's wallet was in her storage container. She hadn't cried when we'd spoken to her; there had been no signs of grief, no red eyes or puffy cheeks. Yes, everyone grieved differently, but there had been no *shock*, no denial, no surprise. Even if she'd heard it through the town's gossip mill first, surely a grieving girlfriend – even a newly *ex*-girlfriend – would care enough to come to the Nomo's office and demand answers, or ask to see the body. Too many things pointed at her. I was missing something.

The other supernaturals that could have killed a werewolf had been cleared and had alibis. Sidnee had run down a bunch of them, and Gunnar had run down the rest. What was I missing? And yet someone had either tried to warn me off or kill me last night. I had the answer; I just had to see it.

I closed my eyes and carefully scanned the crime scene again but saw nothing new. Finally, I went to get ready for my meeting with Connor. I wanted to look professional – this was formal vamp business, after all – but I hadn't seen a soul dressed formally since I'd arrived here. If I put on a suit, I'd look wildly out of place.

I settled on day-off clothes: leggings, trainers, a strappy top and a jumper that said *Jiggle Junction*. They were more casual than professional but I didn't really have any clothes that straddled the line.

I pulled my hair back in a low ponytail, swiped on mascara but by-passed the lipstick. This wasn't a date. I ignored the pang of disappointment at that thought because I absolutely did *not* want to date Connor MacKenzie. The fact that he may or may not have slept outside my house a couple of times to keep me safe through the night was irrelevant. Nice of him but irrelevant.

I called for a taxi, hoping Thomas would drive me because I wanted to speak to him again. If he had insider knowledge, I wanted him to share. There was a reason he'd dug up the pack's names, and I was hoping he could fill in the gaps.

When the taxi pulled up, it was a driver I hadn't met before. Nuts. I sighed. Thankfully, he didn't protest when Fluffy jumped in and laid down on the seat next to me. 'Kamluck Logging?' he asked.

'Yes, please.' That was the extent of the conversation.

I had cash ready this time so I paid the driver, careful to give a tip as well, then Fluffy and I walked up to the office. I was braced for whatever snarky comments Connor would throw my way, so I was surprised – and disappointed – to open the door and see a female vampire at his desk. I looked around but Connor wasn't there. It was a good thing I hadn't wasted my lipstick.

I shut the door behind me, but I wasn't sure what to do next. Did I have the wrong time?

'Ms Barrington?' the woman asked in a familiar accent.

'Yes! You're British!'

The woman smiled. 'I am indeed.' She was tall, willowy, with ink-black hair, alabaster skin and red lips: I felt like I was staring at Snow White. She was wearing a damned suit dress and I instantly regretted my choice of clothing. I crossed my arms to cover my stupid jumper which was advertising a strip club back in London.

She held out her hand. 'I'm Hester Bennet, your vampire liaison.'

'I thought Connor was...'

'He filled in for me whilst I was on holiday. He's the vampire leader, but he doesn't usually do liaison duties,' she explained with a slightly patronising smile.

I remember him telling me that he was filling in, but I'd still expected to see him today. He'd been slumming it; he was probably thrilled to be done with me.

'Mr MacKenzie passed along the email with your finished courses,' she said. 'Thank you for those.' I nodded, still feeling on the back foot. 'I have the final test and a questionnaire for you to complete, if you wouldn't mind, Ms Barrington.'

'Bunny. I'm just Bunny. Ms Barrington is my mother.'

'Bunny, then.' Her tone didn't indicate any reaction to my chosen name. 'The survey has been sent to your mobile number. Here is the written test.' She handed me a stapled set of papers. 'Once you've passed the exam, we can continue to meet weekly or, if you wish, you can fill out the questionnaire weekly and forgo the meetings.'

'The questionnaire is fine. I haven't had any issues.'

She raised one perfectly plucked eyebrow. 'Weren't you recently turned?'

'Yeah. In London about...' I thought. How long had I been in Portlock? It seemed such a short time but long as well. I had really settled in, and I owed that in no small part to Gunnar and Sidnee. They'd thrown me into real life quickly, offered me their friendship. I'd never been to a place that felt so much like home before. Even if I did miss heels.

'Ah, I have it in your file. A matter of weeks! Goodness, such a short time. You're sure you aren't having any issues coping with the blood cravings?'

I looked at her in surprise. 'I've never had a blood craving. I just drink my cup of blood three times a day without fail. It's fine.'

She tapped something into her phone. 'How peculiar,' she murmured, eyeing me with more interest.

I sat at the end of Connor's big desk and completed the test. Like the questions in the online program, they were simple and based on common sense; in other words, don't drink your neighbour or be a twat. It took about twenty minutes.

I handed her the completed test. She glanced over it to make sure I hadn't skipped any questions and put it on the desk. 'Excellent. Once you've completed the questionnaire, you're free to go.'

I pulled out my phone and activated the form. It was pretty basic: name, address, occupation, stuff like that. Then it started on the more intense questions: how many blood cravings do you have a day?; have you ever drunk from a human?; how many losses of control have you had, things like that. I rolled my eyes. I was more than capable of controlling myself.

'How long have *you* been a vampire?' I asked Hester. The question was probably rude, but curiosity won out.

If she was offended, her face didn't show it. 'Slightly over three hundred years.'

'Oh. When did you move here? You still sound very British.'

She smiled. 'Not long ago. Like you, I'm new.'

It didn't look like she'd fitted in yet. She had perfectly coiffed hair, an immaculate manicure, tights and high heels that she'd struggle with to get around the gravel parking lot. Other than her beauty, she had all the markings of a corporate drone. I knew the look and attitude; my father's business was full of them.

I finished the survey, hit submit and called the taxi company. I didn't see any reason to stay in the office with Hester while I waited. Her attention was on her computer – and she hadn't even acknowledged Fluffy. 'I'm all done, I'll get out of your hair.'

'Do make sure you complete the questionnaire weekly. We'll meet in a month's time.' She finally looked up from her screen.

'Right, no problem.'

Fluffy and I hadn't had much of a walk, so I decided to stroll around while we waited for the taxi. We might as well get some more steps in. Fluffy watered a few weeds in the car park. As we reached a bear-proof bin, he started to bark. His hackles were up, and he was looking into the woods.

'What's wrong?' I asked him, burying my fingers in his fur as I peered into the darkness. I had excellent vision but I couldn't see anything. A bear, maybe? A chill ran down my spine as I thought about Mrs White, the barrier and the Portlock bigfoot. Fuck. Now I'd gone and scared myself. 'Let's head back to the office,' I said uneasily.

Fluffy was still going hell for leather trying to scare someone or some*thing*, off. He backed away with me but he was still facing the woods. I suddenly remembered that yesterday someone had thrown a Molotov cocktail through my window; someone was trying to kill me, and here I was going for a walk in a wood. *Not your wisest decision, Bunny.*

Heat coiled in my tummy; something tempestuous and wild, calling to be used. Fear made me reach for it, but before I could seize the broiling flames within me, a gunshot rang out. I felt like someone had punched me in the chest. Someone wasn't out clay-pigeon shooting; they were clay-Bunny shooting. Fuck. I fell backwards and suddenly the trees and stars were the only thing I could see.

'Bunny!' I heard the shout from far away, and that was all.

Chapter 57

I woke up bouncing along with the trees still above me and blinked a few times. I was being held in Connor's arms, and he was moving at a speed that shouldn't be possible whilst he was carrying another human – vampire – whatever. Fire blazed in my chest and I coughed. Blood sprayed from my mouth.

'You'll be fine,' he assured me quietly. 'Your lungs have to push out the blood.'

I had a million questions, but all that came out was a low groan. It hurt like a bitch.

'Try and stay quiet,' he murmured. 'I don't know where the shooter is.'

'Fluffy?' I managed to spit out.

'He's fine. He's on our heels.'

I twisted my head around. Sure enough, Fluffy was following, his head swinging from side to side as he watched for danger. He was no longer barking and he padded on silent paws, effortlessly keeping pace with Connor. 'Where are we going?' I asked.

'Somewhere safe. Hush, now.'

I hushed. I wondered how far Connor could carry me. I'd have offered to walk if I hadn't felt like I'd been hit by a lorry. Even with vamp strength I doubted he could carry me far, though I had no real concept of what a vampire could or couldn't do. The shitty informational videos I'd watched so far hadn't helped at all.

'We're here,' he said finally at a normal volume. 'If I read Fluffy correctly, I don't think anyone followed us.' He walked us onto a porch of a small cabin. He opened the door, held it open for Fluffy, then swung it shut behind us and laid me down on a single bed.

I coughed some more, and more blood sprayed out. Gross. 'I am so sorry,' I managed to say, feeling bad about making such a mess.

'Don't worry. Lie still.' He locked and bolted the front door, then looked around the dark room. 'I could do with a bit more light before we try and fix that wound. I'll start a fire.'

I shivered. Hopefully the fire would scare away bears, too. Bears: I couldn't believe I was living in a country where I had to worry about bears. The only bear I've ever thought about before was Paddington. *I could really do with one of his marmalade sandwiches*, I thought randomly.

I was starting to shake, going into shock. Cool: I'd never been in shock before. My mind felt sluggish and weird, and I kept replaying the moment when the bullet hit me. Having a brilliant memory was a real bitch sometimes.

Connor wadded up some paper, lit it and started a fire in the hearth. He added some kiln-dried logs and immediately they burned brightly. He lit two oil lanterns; there wasn't a lot of light, but he was a vampire so it was enough for our purposes.

Then he turned his attention back to me. Lucky me.

'I'm going to have to rip your sweatshirt, it'll be less painful than trying to get it over your head.'

'Fine,' I managed, all in favour of less pain. It felt like my brain was molasses. Why couldn't I think? I was shivering manically.

His muscles bunched and corded as he ripped my sweatshirt down the front, then he peeled it off me gently. He slid the strappy top down my body until it was bunched around my waist. Thankfully, he left my bra on – he'd probably decided he could work around it.

I couldn't move my left arm. The wound seemed to be over my heart, but it must have missed it since I was alive – unless vampires really did need to be staked to die, like Kivuk had been. If the bullet had been wooden, would I have been a goner? I shivered.

Connor helped me to sit up so that he could examine my back. He gently cleaned the area. 'Looks like the bullet went all the way through,' he said with relief. 'That's good – no need to dig around to get it out. We'll get some blood in you and you'll heal up just fine once your lungs are clear. Keep coughing.'

I nodded. I was shivering with a vengeance but oddly I didn't feel cold. Connor found a blanket in a trunk and wrapped it around me. 'Don't you dare go into shock on me,' he warned.

Too late, I thought, but I couldn't speak because my teeth were chattering too hard.

'Goddammit!' He grimaced. 'I said *don't.*' He pushed the bed closer to the fire and tucked the blanket more securely around me. 'I'll be right back.'

I wanted to ask where he was going, but I couldn't say the words. The coughing started again, and a worrying amount of blood came out of me. I felt weak and lost. Fluffy was sitting by my side as close as he could, trying to warm me with his body and his love. He gave a low whine, but I was too far gone to reassure him. I let myself drift.

I don't know how long Connor was gone – it could have been minutes or hours – but finally he was back again. He held a cup under my nose. 'Drink,' he said insistently. It sounded like he was repeating an order. How many times had he said that to me?

I sniffed obligingly. It was blood all right, but it smelled weird ... off. I turned my head away. 'Drink it for fuck's sake,' he growled at me.

I started to close my eyes and he swore again. He pried open my mouth and poured some of the blood into it. I swallowed obligingly, grimacing at the flavour. He repeated the action what felt like a million times until eventually I had the strength to push the next mouthful away. 'What *is* that?' I asked.

'Blood.'

'I know, but what kind? It tastes awful,' I complained. 'Earthy.'

'Deer. You need more. Bunny, please.' It was the please that did it. I sighed, opened my mouth reluctantly and he poured more into me. I usually drank with my nose plugged but I didn't have the strength to hold it, so I swallowed quickly and tried not to think too much about Bambi.

'Most vampires can't tell the difference. Blood is blood,' he said as he poured more and more into me.

'I'm a terrible vampire,' I sighed.

He grinned. 'I think you're okay.'

'Gee, what a ringing endorsement.'

His smile widened. 'Now I know you're getting better if you're giving me crap.'

I cried out as a sudden blazing pain lanced through me. 'Ow! Ow! Motherfucker!' Tears sprang to my eyes.

'You're okay,' he reassured me as he stroked my back. 'It's the wounds closing – it's a good thing. Your accelerated healing is kicking in. You lost a lot of blood, and it slowed everything down almost to a stop. Now we're cooking.'

It didn't feel like we were cooking, it felt like we were *stabbing*. *Ow, ow, ow*! I closed my eyes tight to ride out the pain. This healing hurt worse than actually being shot. Another spasm gripped my diaphragm and I coughed violently. Dark blood shot out, not the bright stuff this time – the bleeding must be slowing down. My lung was healing. Yay, me.

'One more cup should do it.' He laid me down gently and went out again. When he came back he had more blood. 'Get this down you.'

I wrinkled my nose. 'I'd prefer a cup of tea...' He grinned and pressed the cup into my hand. This time I could grip it with my right hand, though I still didn't want to move my left arm. I figured sipping was prolonging the torture, so I swigged the blood as if it were a warm, coppery beer. I handed back the cup. 'Next time I'm shot, give me some other type of blood,' I instructed.

'I could have gotten rabbit, but it felt weirdly cannibalistic.'

I snorted with laughter and then gasped at the jolt of pain.

'No laughing yet,' he suggested.

'Well stop being funny, then, arsehole.'

He laughed. 'No one's ever accused me of being funny before.' He paused. 'It's quite nice.'

Thankfully, the pain was starting to fade. I took a deep breath and there wasn't even a twinge. Fluffy whined. 'I'm okay now, boy,' I promised. 'I'd give you a pat, but my hands are covered in blood from all of that coughing.' He laid his head down on his crossed paws, but his eyes didn't leave me.

Connor pushed the bed back into place and propped me up on a pillow. He wet a cloth and wiped my face and hands. I tried to ignore how gently he was doing it and how tender the moment felt.

When I was clean, he sat on the trunk and looked at me intensely. 'So who did you piss off so badly that they tried to kill you?' he asked finally.

'Two options, I guess. Back in London, someone paid a vampire fifty thousand pounds to turn me. It's possible they've now hired someone else to kill me.'

Connor shook his head. 'It seems dumb to make you immortal if they wanted you dead.'

'Yeah, I know. Well, option number two, then. Eric's killer has me in her sights.'

'Her?'

I shrugged. 'I'd bet good money it's Virginia Tide behind his death. I just don't know *how* she did it yet.'

Connor frowned. 'She's human,' he pointed out.

'So were Hitler and Pol Pot,' I said drily. 'It didn't stop them killing millions. Humans can be monsters, too.'

'No doubt,' he agreed. 'That's most of the reason why the supernatural community stays hidden. Regardless, she still couldn't have killed him in the manner in which he died.'

'That's the bit that's tripping me up,' I agreed. 'I figure she has an accomplice, a shifter one.' One of the pack. 'A stupid one. The Molotov cocktail was in an aluminium bottle.'

Connor didn't make any exclamation of surprise at the Molotov comment, cementing my belief that it *had* been him outside my door that morning. For whatever reason, he was watching out for me. As a strong, independent woman I wanted to be outraged, but I was still jittery from the blood loss. I'd be a strong independent woman another time – when I hadn't just been shot.

Chapter 58

Connor took Fluffy out to look for the would-be-assassin, hoping that he could find a trail they could follow so they could put an end to this shitshow there and then. The thought was a nice one: who could ever have imagined that one day I'd be important enough for someone to send an assassin? Mum would be so proud.

I grimaced at the thought. I hadn't spoken to Mum or Dad since I'd landed, and I probably should call. They weren't the best parents a girl could have, but they were mine. With Nana gone they were the only family I had left, bar some cousins I'd never really spoken with.

I lay back on the bed and turned my mind to the case. I'd obviously stumbled on something that was close to the truth. What was it? What had changed? It had nothing to do with the poison witch, Shirley Thompson, so I mentally crossed her off the list. The pack was involved in something, but I sensed that wolves would come at you directly, fully furred and fanged, so I didn't think they were gunning for me. That left the only one who needed a gun to take me down: Virginia Tide. Everything kept coming back to her.

The wallet in her storage unit had to be a clue; no one had tried to kill me until I'd found that. There was nothing important in it, though, and it would be easy to say in court that Eric had helped Virginia move her possessions into the unit and accidentally dropped it. That would be reasonable doubt, so why was she worried about it? I closed my eyes and pulled up my memory of the storage unit.

My visual memory was nearly perfect, and I had deliberately concentrated when we were searching so I'd have clear recall. There: the wallet was lying between stacks of boxes. It was dusty, but the only tracks were small – woman's size! Virginia was the only one who had visited it recently, so she *had* to be the one who'd put the wallet there! Okay, it didn't prove she'd killed him, but she'd had his wallet. Now all I needed was to nail down the fact that Eric had been carrying it when he'd died.

I gave a mental head thunk. I'd questioned Margaret, the manager at Pizza Kodiak Kitchen, about when the couple had come in. She couldn't remember – but I hadn't asked Jessica!

I dialled the number she'd given me. 'Hey,' she answered. 'Who's this?'

'It's Bunny.'

'The genetic experiment?' she said eagerly.

I sighed; I could see I was going to regret that one. 'That's me. Listen, I have a question for you.'

'Dude, do you know what time it is?'

I paused. I didn't. 'Sorry. Vampire.'

She laughed. 'You guys are all out of whack.'

'Right. Anyway, do you remember what day it was?'

'What day what was?'

Ugh: I was the worst investigator ever. 'What day it was that Eric and Virginia had that loud argument? The couple I wrote the statement about for you.'

'Oh that. It must have been Tuesday because it was my last shift that week until I was back in again on Friday.'

'Tuesday the seventh?' I pressed.

'Yes, ma'am.'

'Great. Thank you. I'll amend your statement to include that.'

I hung up and gave a fist pump. It probably still wasn't enough to arrest Virginia, but now I was *certain* it was her. Eric had used his wallet and cards on the night that he'd been killed. Virginia had left before him and, by her own admission, she'd driven straight home to bed. How, then, could she possibly have had his wallet in her storage unit?

Oh yeah, that was why she was trying to kill me. I'd got the bitch.

When Connor returned I nearly jumped on him. 'I know who the killer is! It is definitely Virginia Tide.'

He looked at me cautiously, 'Okay, but more importantly, how are you feeling?'

'I'm fine. We need to go now! We need to tell Gunnar.'

Connor checked the time. 'It's late – or early, depending on your view. Your news will keep for a couple of hours. By the time we get to Gunnar's, it'll be time for him to get up anyway. He's been burning both ends too, and he's no vamp. Fluffy and I checked things out in the woods.' He paused. 'Is there any chance you want to rename your dog Brute, or something? I felt like a dick shouting "Fluffy".'

That made me snicker. 'No. If anything, it makes me want to extend his name to Fluffy Wuffykins.' Fluffy gave a low growl; he didn't appreciate the addition.

'See?' Connor said. 'He wants to be called Brute, don't you, Brute?' Fluffy looked at him for a moment then growled again.

'Ha!' I said triumphantly. 'See? He's Fluffy through and through.' The dog sighed a little.

I turned my mind to the matter at hand. 'Any sign of our would-be killer?'

Connor shook his head. 'The trail was cold. It led us to a road into town and I'm betting he or she had a truck waiting there. The shooter is long gone.' He checked me over. 'If you're feeling better, are you up for a walk back to civilisation?'

'I'm fine.' I said again. 'Let's go.'

'I'd better lend you my shirt,' Connor offered, pulling off his black-and-red flannel shirt. Underneath, he was wearing a plain black T-shirt.

'Thanks.' I shimmied out of the bloody strappy top, which was still rolled around my waist; tugged on the shirt and buttoned it closed.

The walk was a lot further than I remembered, but then I'd been unconscious for most of the trip. I was faintly embarrassed that Connor had lugged me so far. He must be incredibly strong. Colour me impressed.

'Hey,' I asked Connor, 'how come you brought me to a remote cabin, rather than just taking me back to the office?'

He looked faintly embarrassed. 'Instinct,' he said tersely.

'What instinct?'

'I needed to get you to safety. The cabin is safe.'

'The office isn't?'

He paused, 'Not always, no. It's full of vampires, for one thing. Remember what I said about not sleeping in front of another vampire?'

'Yeah?'

'You don't really want to bleed in front of them either.'

'In case they get the munchies?'

'In case they decide that you're weak.'

That ended our conversation abruptly. About halfway back to the logging Connor said lightly, 'I was beginning to doubt you were a vampire at all, but evidently you are. You've made a full recovery.'

I stopped and put my hands on my hips. 'What's that supposed to mean? I can vampire your arse off.' Except if he asked me to grow my fangs on command.

He laughed. 'You don't like blood, you don't have blood cravings, nor do you have to fight the desire to drink random humans. The last two are normally signs of having at least a few decades of vampirism under your belt – and you're about a minute old.'

'I'll have you know I'm twenty-three, thank you.'

He sighed. 'I'm well aware. You're a babe in the woods.'

'I am not! I'm just a babe. And I just happen to be in these woods.'

He smiled ruefully. 'You are a babe all right,' he agreed.

'Anyway, I had good motivation not to be a vampire twat. My sire was one, and he was an absolute prick...' I shuddered.

'It doesn't work that way. You don't just *choose* not to have blood cravings.'

'Everyone's different, I guess. It works just fine for me.'

We continued walking. 'So the girlfriend's Eric's murderer?' Connor asked.

'Yup. Virginia Tide.'

'How did she do it?'

I huffed: that was the one piece of the puzzle I was still missing. 'I haven't worked that part out yet, but I have proof that she had his wallet and tried to hide it from us. The second I know how she did it, I'll have it all. Right now I know that she had a motive and an opportunity. She did it.' Everyone had overlooked her. She had depended on being overlooked and underestimated.

Unfortunately for her, I was also used to being underestimated.

Chapter 59

By the time we reached the truck, I was happy to see it. I hopped in and we started to drive to Gunnar's. Daybreak was coming and I fingered my charm anxiously. 'It's still good,' Connor murmured. 'You don't need to worry.'

'Have you ever been burned by the sun?'

He laughed. 'Oh yes! I cut it fine a number of times back when I was younger. And I didn't have this.' He touched the charm at his throat.

'Hurts like a bitch,' I complained, remembering my hand sizzling in my flat in London when I'd just been turned. I wished I could say that those were good times, but the memories brought back some of the darkest despair I'd ever felt. Portlock was a second chance, and I'd never forget it.

'Less than being shot at,' Connor countered.

'Less than quickly recovering from being shot at, but more than actually being shot,' I categorised. He raised an eyebrow in question. 'I have a good memory,' I explained.

'Apparently so.'

We parked outside Gunnar's. 'It's nearly 6am,' Connor said. 'Gunnar will be up and around. You'll be safe with him. I'd better go – things to do,' he said vaguely.

Like me, he had to be exhausted. 'Thanks for your help,' I said awkwardly. 'Drive safe.' I tried to work out why I felt disappointed that he was leaving.

I knocked on Gunnar's door and in moments the huge mountain of a man flung it open. 'Bunny?' He frowned. 'What the heck happened?'

I looked down at myself. I was wearing Connor's flannel shirt, but flecks of dried blood still showed on my skin. Gunnar missed nothing. I sighed. 'I got shot. Can I come in?'

'Of course!' He stepped back.

I waved at Connor, who was still waiting. When I stepped inside, he drove off looking grim.

Sigrid fussed over me, insisting I take a shower and borrow some of her clean clothes. When I went back into the kitchen, she and Gunnar both stopped talking. 'You're looking better. Gunnar can take you home to get some of your things,' she suggested. 'We think you should stay with us for a few days.'

I shook my head. 'Thanks so much, but I'd rather go home.' Fluffy and Loki were playing with each other in a lazy way, both lying down, with one of them periodically gnawing at the other. 'Anyway, I've got good news. I've got a break on our case,' I said triumphantly.

Gunnar leaned forward. 'Did you see who shot you?'

'Well, no, but...' I told them briefly about what had happened, starting with meeting Hester at Kamluck Logging and ending with Connor dropping me off. 'But I have something to show you.' I pulled out my phone, opened the gallery and pulled up the photo of the storage unit. 'Look here.' I pointed at the wallet in the middle of the layers of footprints.

Gunnar looked at me blankly. 'The wallet, again? I don't know what I'm supposed to see here.'

'Virginia is hoping that we'll think Eric dropped the wallet when he was helping her move her stuff, but look at the dust patterns. All of the footprints are those of a small woman – she's the only one who's been in that unit. Plus, there's no dust on the wallet. It was put there very recently.'

He looked again, then ran his hands through his long, thick hair. 'Damn, Bunny. Good work. That's a fine piece of evidence – though it's still no smoking gun. She could have had it there for weeks.'

I grinned. 'Nope. I phoned the waitress that works at Pizza Kodiak Kitchen. She swears the argument took place on the night of Eric's death and Virginia stormed out. Eric definitely picked up the tab.'

Gunnar rubbed his hands together. 'Now we're cooking. When the request for Eric's financials come back, we should see that he paid the bill. Hopefully he used one of the cards in that wallet.'

'Right. And she shot me. No one else in town would have needed a gun to kill me.'

'That's a fair point, but how would she know you were going to be there?'

I groaned as I connected the dots. 'Mitch Schilling. Fuck.'

'What?'

'The appointment with Hester. I don't know how the pack is involved in the mess, but they definitely are somehow. Mitch Schilling is part of the pack—'

'And he works in Kamluck Logging,' Gunnar finished. 'He knew you were going to be there and told Virginia.'

'That's my guess.' I gave a head thunk. 'And probably Connor's guess, too. He shot out of here like a bat out of hell.'

Gunnar swore darkly and dialled Connor, but it went to voicemail. 'No vigilante justice, Connor! I'll deal with Mitch. If you confront him, it'll set a bloody inferno alight in vamp–shifter relations. You know it. Keep a cool head.' He hung up and swore even more vociferously.

'You think he'll keep a cool head?'

'I know he won't,' Gunnar growled.

'Fuck.'

He stood up. 'I'd better go and try and cool him down. I'll go to Virginia Tide's first and arrest that bitch. Connor won't kill Mitch, so we have time on that front. I'll drop you home on the way.'

'If you're going after Virginia, I want in on the action,' I said stubbornly.

'Bunny, you've just been shot. You lost a gallon of blood, and even with your vampire healing you look like a firm breeze could push you over. I'll drop you home.'

'But—'

'No buts,' he said in a tone I hadn't heard before. 'You'd distract me. Right now, you're a liability. I'm sorry, but there it is.' There was no mistaking the order.

I grimaced but nodded. I rubbed the palm of my hand over the bullet wound; it was completely healed – not even a mark remained – but a phantom ache lingered. Gunnar was right: I was exhausted and I would be a liability.

'Are you still in pain?' he asked, watching my movement.

'No. I'm okay, honest.' I dropped my hand. 'Let's just get a move on. I'll sleep better knowing Virginia is behind bars.'

'Maybe you'd better stay here.'

I thought about Sigrid. She was an innocent and a witch and, as far as I knew, she didn't have any regenerative powers like I did. I couldn't bring trouble to their house. I shook my head. 'No, honestly. Fluffy and I will be fine at home.'

I stood toe to toe with Gunnar; in the end our compromise was that he'd search my house before I went in and I'd close the shutters and lock the door the second he left. I thanked Sigrid, then Gunnar and I made tracks. He was clearly anxious to get to Virginia. I couldn't blame him; I was anxious for him to get to her too.

When we arrived at my house, Gunnar did a fast walk through then left after he'd declared it was all clear. I winced when I walked in and saw the spaces where the sofa and curtains should have been, but otherwise it was fine. I loved my little house, and I could sit at the kitchen table, or go to bed. Actually, bed sounded *really* good.

It was amazing how the stress eased once the shutters were slammed down and the house felt secure. Gunnar must have felt the same, because he honked once and I heard his engine catch and rev as he drove away.

I fed Fluffy and turned on the kettle for a much-needed cup of tea. Fluffy gave a giant yawn. I was tired but he was shattered; goodness knows how many miles he'd run back and forth with Connor. 'Go on, pup,' I gave him a gentle push. 'Go to bed. I'll be along in a second.' He gave me a lick and gratefully loped away for some much-needed rest.

I settled at my small dining table and nursed my cup of tea. The first one barely touched the sides, so I hit the kettle again and made a fresh brew. I'd just sat down to drink it when there was a knock at my front door.

I figured Sidnee had heard what had happened or Gunnar had popped back for some reason, maybe to tell me about what had happened with Mitch. I sighed and stood up.

I threw open the front door and blinked in surprise at the man on my front step. 'Jim?' I said in confusion.

He gave me a sad smile. 'Can I come in?'

'Sure!' I stepped back to let him in, and as he moved I saw who was hiding behind him. Virginia Tide was on my front step. And she was armed.

Oh fuck.

Chapter 60

'Virginia,' I said blankly, staring down the barrel of the gun.

'May I come in, too?' she asked with a polite smile, as if she were a friendly neighbour offering me a basket of muffins instead of a bullet.

I didn't see that I had a whole lot of choice: if I said no, she was going to blast me there and then. 'Sure,' I said dry mouthed. 'But let Jim go. You've got me as a hostage, you don't need another.'

Virginia let out a snort of laughter. 'I don't know what I was so worried about. You're not so smart after all.'

It was still early but my neighbours would be out and about soon. Maybe one of them had seen her on my front step toting a gun and called Gunnar – unless Jim had been obscuring the view. Fuck.

I shut the door as she waltzed in. 'I was having a cup of tea, if you'd like one?' I offered inanely. I had to stall her until I came up with a plan or help arrived.

Virginia shrugged. 'Coffee, black if you have one. Jim will have milk with two sugars.' The penny dropped: she knew Jim's coffee preferences, even though he'd acted as if he barely knew her.

I studied him; he was tense but he didn't look afraid. He wasn't a hostage, he was an accomplice. Double fuck.

The water was already hot so I made the two coffees. My brain was whirling. Two on one weren't good odds; add in the gun and I was a goner.

Virginia and I sat and looked at each other across the table. She was still holding the gun. I had vampiric speed on my side, but she had something else, something unknown. And besides, I was curious: I needed to know the *how*. *How* had they killed Eric?

Jim leaned against my counter. He had magic and he'd talked about a premonition, but he hadn't made Sigrid's list of magic users that could have killed Eric.

'So how did you do it?' I asked.

Virginia smiled and clapped her hands. 'I'm so glad you still don't know. I was worried you'd worked it all out. You've been an unknown, Bunny, and unknown variables stress me out. I have a *plan*, Bunny, and I am *not* letting you ruin it before I can execute it.'

It looked like the only thing she was going to execute was me. I kept my eyes on her, all the while praying that Fluffy, on hearing a voice, would come bounding down the hallway and bite her head off.

'I can't believe the wallet nearly screwed me. Such a stupid mistake.' She glared at Jim.

'Sorry,' he muttered again, clearly apologising for the thousandth time. 'I thought delaying the ID would help us.'

She huffed. 'It was nothing to do with that and you know it. You wanted to keep the sappy picture of the two of you.'

'He was my best mate for a long time,' Jim muttered. 'I didn't have a picture of us. Until I fell in love with his girl.' He sighed.

'I was never his girl.' Virginia's eyes softened. 'I was killing time until I found you, I just didn't know it.' She looked at him adoringly and he smiled back. Great: my murderers were in love. How sweet.

I brought the conversation back to the topic at hand. 'How did you know we'd found the wallet?'

She gave me a flat look. 'Don't you know anything? After you searched the unit, I got a copy of the warrant and a receipt for the items taken. One wallet.'

'Ah.'

'Ah,' she mocked. 'Jim wanted it for sentimental reasons, so I chucked it in the unit until things cooled down. I can't believe it nearly screwed us.'

I looked at Jim, 'We checked your alibi. How did you do your flight and kill Eric at the same time?'

Jim smiled, 'I had a buddy switch planes with me. He took my plane on my flight plan, and I followed up afterwards and took his, we switched in Homer.'

I shook my head in disbelief, we'd accepted the flight records at face value. Stupid! 'Did he know what you were going to do?' I asked.

'Of course not!' Jim scoffed. 'We do it all the time if one of us is late on a route. We've covered for each other before.'

It sounded like unwitting collusion, but the other pilot needed to change his ways. If I survived this, I'd track him down and have words.

I turned to Virginia. 'So, you and Jim wanted to be together? Couldn't you just *leave* Eric? Why did he have to die?' I sipped my tea like we were having a civilised conversation, then leaned forward. 'And *how* did you do it? That's had me stumped.'

'It's not the how that's important but the why,' she said impatiently. 'The why rather reveals the how.'

I took the bait. 'Why then? You were together on and off for years. You must have had some affection for him, even if you loved Jim?'

Virginia snorted. 'Eric was filthy, he worked erratically, he made promises he never intended to keep. He loved his damned dog more than me – even though I insisted he keep it outside, he still brought the damn thing in. By the end, I loathed him.'

'You weren't married. You could have just stopped seeing him.' My tone was a little more 'well duh' than I'd intended.

Her face contorted into a snarl and I leaned back from the visibly crazy lady. 'He *promised* me, and I had to make him pay for letting me down.'

Jim spoke up. 'We had to make sure they knew we were serious!'

'Who?' Then I answered my own question. 'The pack.'

She grinned. 'Bingo. Give the rabbit a carrot.' Charming.

'Eric promised he'd make you a werewolf, but he never did.'

'No, he never did, the fucker. He dangled it over me constantly until one day I just snapped. I told him it *had* to happen. He said he'd try to turn me, but he wanted to test it on someone else first since he'd never done it before. He didn't want to do it wrong because he *loved* me.' She sneered. 'So he grabbed Jack on his way home and turned him.'

'And it went wrong.'

She grimaced. 'Eric couldn't do anything right, not even turn someone. It should have been instinctive, for fuck's sake. He panicked when Jack's eyes went gold.'

Wait ... gold? Jack had been red-eyed when he'd attacked me.

Virginia continued. 'Eric set Jack loose outside the Barrier in his werewolf form and hoped that would be that. He assumed a hunter like Patkotak would bring him down. But no ... Jack had to come back. Something about Portlock called to him. Then, when Eric saw the Nomo's door all smashed in, he freaked out and checked in with the morgue. One unknown werewolf. He called all of his pack buddies and arranged to meet them. He was going to come clean but I couldn't allow that to happen.'

She shrugged like it was of no import. 'If Eric wasn't going to turn me, and that prick Stan Ahmaogak wasn't going to turn me, then I needed option C. If God closes a door, He opens a window.'

'The pack is option C. So what are you doing? Threatening them?'

'Coercing them,' Jim mumbled. 'It's the only way to save Virginia.' He looked grim, but his eyes were willing me to understand. He'd helped kill his best friend for love.

I shook my head. *Nah mate, don't look to me for absolution. You'll find none here.*

Virginia's smile was terrifying. 'Eric called the pack together that Tuesday after our little tiff in the Pizza Kodiak Kitchen. He was upset, but I'd made my position quite clear. They needed to turn me or one of them was going to die. He texted them about the threat and they arranged to meet that night to discuss it, only Eric never showed because he was already dripping into the bay!'

She clapped her hands happily. 'And then the others knew that I was deadly serious. Now they're going to turn me, just like we wanted.' She smiled proudly. She was psychotic. God help me.

I had the feeling I wasn't walking away from this with a pulse, not even a periodic one.

Chapter 61

Chills ran down my spine. 'I still don't get *how* you killed Eric.'

She leaned in conspiratorially. 'Did you know that werewolves don't get sick? They don't get diseases or the flu. They age slowly. Hell, I even poisoned him but it just made him tired! He didn't even keel over! Wolfsbane is a total fairy tale.'

'Did you get the poison from Shirley Thompson?' I asked.

'No. I had no idea she was such a talented horticulturalist. I got it online.' She frowned. 'You never know the quality when you buy online though, do you? I would have used her if I'd known about her side hustle. After all, it's so important to support local when you can, don't you think?'

I swallowed and nodded. 'Sure. Reduce that carbon footprint.'

She beamed. 'Exactly. I knew you were smart, I knew you'd get it.'

The only thing I was getting was very, very nervous. Why wasn't help coming? I just needed to keep her talking. 'So, you're sick?' I asked, like I didn't already know about her cancer. 'And you figured turning would save you?'

'It's the only thing that will save her from the damned cancer,' Jim said desperately. 'No chemo, no radiotherapy, no drug trials – nothing else will save her. The doctors have given up on her, but I haven't. I told Eric to turn her but he wouldn't listen. Said it was too dangerous.'

'What happened with Jack would suggest he was right,' I muttered.

'Even if she loses her mind, at least she'll be alive. I can help contain her if that happens. I'll look after her.' He looked at her dotingly.

'And what kind of life will that be, chained up in your yard?'

'That's only the worst-case scenario,' Jim snapped. 'She'll be fine – I know she will. We're meant to be. The universe is aligning so we can be together.'

'How did you and Virginia get together?' I asked nosily.

'We hung out a few times together, the three of us,' Jim admitted. 'The spark between Gin and me was so real, but we fought it for a long time. By the time we caved into it and started an affair, she already knew she was sick. I had to step up to help her – Eric could barely keep Loki alive, let alone a sick human. We knew that turning her was the only way to save her. She petitioned Stan, but when she got knocked back Eric was her last chance. It was all a matter of leverage.'

'So she kept fucking Eric in the hopes that he'd turn her?' I asked, deliberately provoking him, hoping he'd make a mistake I could take advantage of.

'Fuck you!' Virginia snarled, 'You don't know what it's like. You can't. Once I'm turned, everything will be okay.'

Jim looked at me. 'We just have to get rid of you first.'

I licked my suddenly parched lips. 'Why me? Why aren't you shooting at Gunnar?'

Jim gave a shrug. 'Without you murmuring in his ear, he'll go back to thinking a shifter was responsible for Eric's death. After one of the pack has turned Gin, we'll kill one of them and set it up as a suicide, claiming responsibility for Eric's death in a note. We just need a little more time. Gunnar trusts me.'

'More fool him,' I murmured, as if I hadn't also liked and trusted Jim before this moment. I cast around for something to say, something to buy me more time. 'So ... terminal cancer?'

'Not just any old cancer.' Virginia's lips pressed tightly together, 'Aggressive brain cancer. It's in my blood, too, so the vamps can't turn me into one of them – but a werewolf can. The protocols to do it legally take months. I already petitioned Stan and he said no. I don't have months to try another shifter group.'

'I'm sorry,' I said honestly, looking at them both.

'Don't be, I'm going to get my way. Tonight is a full moon and the pack will turn me, or I'll kill them all and everyone they love.' She smiled as she said it. Fuck, she was scary.

I did actually feel some sympathy for her and Jim. It must be terrifying to be told you were going to die and know that there was virtually nothing you could do about it. And to watch the one you love waste away was even worse. Yes, I had sympathy for them both.

'So Jim helped you kill Eric? I still don't get the how.' My curiosity was keeping my fear at bay, just about.

She mock-pouted. 'Oh I'm disappointed. You still can't work it out?'

I shook my head. 'I'm drawing a blank.'

She laughed, the laughter morphing from amused to freaking insane. 'One cool thing about my particular brain tumour ... It seems to have awakened a latent magical power.' She stood and walked to the kitchen counter, heading for the wooden knife block. Jim's eyes were glued to her like she was the air that he breathed. God save me from that kind of all-consuming love.

I heard the padding of feet and turned just in time to see Fluffy run towards Virginia – he'd taken the moment when her back was turned to try and get close to her. I wanted to shout a warning to him, but if I did I'd alert them to his presence.

But Jim had noticed my dog. 'Watch out!' he called to Virginia. 'Silly dog, now she'll kill you.' He genuinely looked regretful.

Fluffy didn't pause in his attack and pounced. Virginia plucked a large knife from the block and whirled around. She waved her knife-wielding hand and Fluffy lifted up off the ground. When she flicked her hand sideways, he slammed into the wall, yelped and crumpled. He stayed down.

My mind flashed back to a similar incident when Franklin had kicked him and I had thought he was dead. 'Fluffy!' I tried to go to him – but I couldn't move! My feet were hovering inches off the floor and my limbs were frozen, locked in place.

'As I was saying, before I was so rudely interrupted,' Virginia glared at Fluffy. 'Apparently if you put a tumour in *just* the right spot, it awakens your brain's power. Telekinesis, in my case – amongst other things.'

I struggled as hard as I could, but even with all of my vampire-gifted strength I couldn't move so much as a finger. I could breathe, I could blink, but that was it. I couldn't speak. No screaming for help for me. I was going to die for real this time, and I hadn't even found out who had ordered me undead in the first place. I hoped my death would at least fuck up *their* plans. Yup, sometimes I'm petty.

Virginia looked smug. 'You want to know how I killed the big strong werewolf?'

I floated backwards until I was pinned against my living-room wall. Fluffy's body lay prone beneath me.

'I held him still and I cut and cut until he was dead. It took more energy than I thought it would, and a lot more time. Jim had to help a little by the end – I was so tired because it was hard to hold him immobile like that. And we had to be faster than his healing powers.

But eventually he lost enough blood and he wasn't a problem anymore.'

Her eyes lasered into mine as she drew the knife across my forearm. I wished I was in *Beauty and the Beast*, and Mrs Knifey was sentient and refused to hurt me. But no: my blood welled up, and the pain was quick and biting. But even as the blood was welling up, I felt the warmth as the wound healed. This time the healing hurt significantly less than the bullet wound had done.

'Vampires heal quickly too. You recovered from my shot annoyingly fast. I thought I'd got you good.' Virginia made a tsk noise, like she was vexed.

She put the gun on the kitchen counter, raised the knife again and this time she slashed my thigh. The wound was deeper and it burned like a brand. Blood spurted out with every sluggish pump of my heart. Wonderful.

'Werewolf healing slows down when they lose enough blood and I'm sure it'll be the same for you. I wonder when the last time it was that a vampire died from exsanguination? There's a delicious irony in that, isn't there?' She beamed, then she slashed my other leg.

I felt as if I cried out but no sound left my lips. Why had I been so fucking stubborn? Why hadn't I stayed at Gunnar and Sigrid's? I was going to die in my own living room because I had thought I was stronger than this little human.

I struggled harder against her iron grip. Nothing.

She waited; calmly observing my leg wounds heal. 'Hmm, I do believe that vampire healing is actually a little slower than a werewolf's. That'll make this easier.'

I tried to speak but I couldn't. I met her eyes desperately. With a smirk she pointed her finger at me and something eased around my jaw.

'Go on,' she said, eyes sparkling with delight, 'I want to know what your last words are.'

They weren't going to be my last words if I had anything to do with it. 'Did you do this to Kivuk too?' I asked. The vampire's body hadn't been mutilated, but it could have healed after she'd sliced and diced him.

Virginia frowned. 'I had nothing to do with that vampire disappearing. Why would I? He couldn't help me. Enough chatter. You bore me.'

She plunged the knife into my belly. Air burst from my lungs and I couldn't draw breath; she must have hit my diaphragm and it was spasming, refusing to work properly to fill my lungs. My body was seizing, incredible pain flaring along every nerve ending.

What a way to die. Mother would be mortified.

Chapter 62

Virginia pulled out the knife and blood bubbled out of the wound. I felt its burning heat soak through Connor's borrowed shirt. The absurd thought rolled through my brain that Connor wouldn't be getting this one back. Why was I thinking about Connor? Stupid brain. I was dying – I needed to think about something *meaningful*, Let my last moments be profound.

Virginia pulled back her arm to stab me again but then she paused. Fluffy was stirring, trying to get his feet back under him. She clearly couldn't hold us both locked in place. She smiled wickedly at his back. 'I fucking hate dogs,' she muttered, raising her knife, ready to slam it down into his defenceless back.

'Gin, please,' Jim murmured. 'I'll get it re-homed. Just knock it out,' he pleaded. He was fine with her killing me but killing my dog was a step too far.

Virginia ignored him and raised the knife again.

A pulse of volcanic rage filled my being. My vision went red and I flushed with furious heat. *No one* was going to kill my dog. Flames filled my vision and I forced the rage outward with all of my might. I screamed as a rage that crackled like a flamethrower burned out of me.

Virginia and Jim screamed too as some very real flames struck them.

What. The. Fuck.

A wave of fire erupted in my kitchen like hell on earth. Virginia screamed as her skin crisped and burned. Jim grabbed a towel and tried to put out the flames even as he was burning himself. His efforts were to no avail, and I watched in stunned horror as they were both consumed by flames.

'I love you,' he gasped in agony as he gave up his efforts to put the fire out.

Virginia's hold on me dissipated and I slowly slid down the wall next to Fluffy. I took a full breath as my muscles relaxed. I could breathe; I could move.

I was going to live – if I managed to get out of the house before the fire took a hold. Somehow I'd turned my rage into actual fire – and this wasn't like Virginia's incompetent Molotov cocktail. This shit was *real* fire.

I picked myself up with difficulty, hobbled into the lounge and grabbed a blanket to smother the flames. Part of me knew that it was already far too late but Jack weighed on my conscience.

By the time I hobbled back in, they were both gone, crispier than the Colonel's finest Kentucky fried chicken. Jim had wrapped himself around Virginia, offering her comfort in their last moments. What they had done was horrific but he *had* loved her.

I could sense hysteria trying to take over. *Don't break down now.* I had to get Fluffy and get the fuck out. I scooped him up and ran. Once we were far enough from the house, I sat down on the grass in my front garden and cuddled him. 'You okay?' I asked softly. He gave me a tired lick in response. I knew how he felt.

I'd left my phone to burn in the kitchen but one of my beady-eyed neighbours must have seen the smoke and called the fire brigade. Before too long their sirens cut through the air. Before they could arrive, Gunnar roared up. He leapt out of the car and ran to me. 'Virginia wasn't home,' he said grimly. 'I came back here as fast as I could.'

'No, she wasn't home.' I agreed. 'She was here. Her and Jim.'

'Jim?' he reared back as if I'd punched him.

'He loved her,' I said sadly. A tear ran down my ash-covered cheek. 'Killing Eric was the only way to stop her dying.'

The fire engines screamed in, two this time. 'I'll speak to the fire chief,' Gunnar said gruffly. 'I'll be right back.' As he walked away, he pulled out his phone and dialled urgently. I didn't care who he was talking to. It didn't matter. Nothing mattered.

Fluffy had gone worryingly still. 'Fluffy?' I whispered. He didn't stir and I was too frightened to check if he was breathing. A choked sob tried to claw its way out of me. 'Don't you dare leave me,' I pleaded. 'You're all I've got.' I buried my face in his fur. 'Wake up, Fluffy, please!' I begged.

I don't know how long I sat there before Connor knelt in front of me. He gently put his arms under Fluffy. 'Let me get him checked over,' he murmured.

I released my death grip on Fluffy and hope stirred as Connor took him to the ambulance. They weren't vets but they were supernatural specialists and they had an oxygen mask suitable for a dog's – or werewolf's – muzzle.

When Fluffy's chest rose, Connor turned and gave me a thumbs up. He crossed the distance between us, sat behind me and pulled me into his arms. 'He's going to be okay.' He pressed a kiss to my temple and I felt that strange zing again.

Connor sighed softly. Not now, *zing,* now was really not the time. Connor clearly agreed.

Fluffy was alive. I was alive. Virginia and Jim were very dead. Gunnar was right: everything was going to be okay.

I collapsed into Connor's arms and bawled my eyes out.

Chapter 63

'I feel fine,' I said stubbornly. 'I'm a vampire. I'm undead anyway.'

Connor rubbed a tired hand through his hair. We'd both been up for God knows how many hours. 'You're a vampire,' he agreed, 'but you've been shot, stabbed and inhaled a tonne of smoke. You've lost a lot of blood. Don't be stubborn about this. You need to see a proper healer. I've got one on retainer.'

I folded my arms. 'The only way I'm seeing a healer is if you take Fluffy to the emergency vet.'

He opened his mouth to argue then closed it again. 'Fine.'

I blinked. 'Really?'

'Yes, but I'm checking him in under the name Brute.'

I smiled for the first time in an hour. 'You do whatever you need to do. It's not my fault you're not masculine enough to roll with Fluffy.'

'I'm a *logger*,' he said incredulously. 'I'm as manly as they come.'

I sang, '"You're a lumberjack, and –'

'"– I'm okay," he sang the last line of *Monty Python* skit back at me, making me laugh. He knew *Monty Python*, I knew there was a reason I liked him.

Connor sighed. 'I'm taking your dog to the vet and Gunnar is taking you to my healer. Deal?'

'Deal.'

Muttering, he stalked off to collect Fluffy from the ambulance. Gunnar was grinning. 'I think he likes you.'

'He tolerates me.'

His smile widened, 'No, he likes you.'

'What happened with Mitch and the other members of the pack?' I asked suddenly.

Gunnar grimaced. 'Apparently Connor has given Mitch a bit of a beat down. Mitch confessed that the pack was terrified of Virginia, and they'd agreed to turn her tonight. Connor sent men to Virginia's house, where they stumbled into me. The house was empty. They reported back to Connor and I came here. Mitch confessed that he'd told Virginia about your appointment with Hester at the logging company. Virginia was the one that shot you, but it was Reeve that chucked the Molotov into your house.'

Gunnar's jaw worked as he visibly wrestled with himself. 'Look, Reeve's a wild man, he spends more time out in the wild he's named for – no way he didn't know how to make a proper Molotov. I reckon he was trying to follow Virginia's orders in action but not in spirit. I'll arrest him if you want me to, but they were all scared of her. The pack saw what she did to Eric, and she'd already threatened that they would be next. According to Mitch, she'd even threatened their families.'

I sighed. 'Don't bother arresting him. That's what she said too. I don't blame them for being scared. She was crazy as fuck.'

'That a medical diagnosis?' Gunnar teased.

'You bet.'

He grinned.

'Jim wasn't crazy,' I said softly. 'He was just desperate. He loved her and she was dying.' What he did – *they* did – was wrong, but until your lover is dying, it's hard to know what lengths you'd go to save them. Love makes us all fools. That was why I'd never fallen in love before.

A car pulled up and Sidnee climbed out. Her date, Chris, stayed in the car. 'Bunny!' She ran across the lawn. 'What the heck happened?' She stared at my burning house. The fire department were pouring water onto the flames but it was clearly in an effort to contain the fire rather than save the place. My home was a goner.

'We got the murderer,' Gunnar said proudly.

'I *murdered* the murderer,' I corrected and shivered. 'Both of them.'

'Naw, it was self-defence Bunny. You won't face any charges,' Gunnar reassured me.

'Hold up, *both* of them?' Sidnee asked.

'Virginia and Jim. They were having an affair. They needed her to be turned to save her from cancer, so she was still stringing Eric along. It came to a head when he refused to turn her because he'd failed to turn Jack successfully, so she killed him.'

'Jim? I can't believe it. What about Kivuk?'

I grimaced. 'That wasn't them.'

'Great. So we still have a killer on the loose.'

'Let's worry about it another day,' I suggested. I was all done and I was out of fucks to give.

Gunnar filled in Sidnee about all that had happened, including the beat down that Connor had given Mitch Schilling. 'And what about Mitch? Is he going to press charges against Connor?' Sidnee asked.

Gunnar snorted. 'No chance. Connor's his boss. This is going right back under the carpet.'

'That doesn't seem healthy,' I noted.

'Have you seen our portion sizes?' he joked.

'I'll go tell Chris to go home,' Sidnee said fiercely. 'I'm coming with you to the healer's.'

'You don't have to,' I protested, but not too strongly. A friend would be welcome right now.

She jogged back to say goodbye to Chris then came back to Gunnar and me. 'Everyone good? Then let's roll,' Gunnar said, slinging an arm around my shoulders.

'Let's roll,' Sidnee agreed.

Gunnar awkwardly left the room whilst Connor's healer checked me over. Sigrid, who'd driven out especially to be with me, replaced him and held my hand through all the checks. It felt nice to be mothered a little.

The healer gave me a host of potions to take. Sigrid checked them all before giving me a thumbs up, then I took them like a good little girl. I had to admit, I felt a lot better physically afterwards but it would take a lot longer for the mental scars to fade. I could still see Virginia and Jim burning when I closed my eyes.

Sidnee looped an arm through mine as we all went outside. Gunnar had been waiting by his SUV but he launched himself off it and rumbled towards us. 'All okay?' he asked. The obvious concern in his voice warmed me.

'She's all good,' Sigrid promised.

As we went back to Gunnar's SUV, I stopped abruptly. 'I don't have anywhere to go.'

'Of course you do, dear,' Sigrid said firmly. 'We have a lovely spare room.'

I looked down at my bloody, stained clothes. I really had nothing – not even my clothes had been saved. The fire brigade had kept the fire from spreading to the homes around me, but the house itself was done for. Barely a shell remained. I felt my breath catch as the enormity of it all struck me. I was in a foreign country and I had nothing. I was worse off than before I'd come here. My knees wanted to buckle.

Sigrid pulled me into a hug and patted me on the back. 'You and Fluffy are alive,' she murmured comfortingly. 'Everything else is just stuff. We'll have you all sorted in no time. Don't you worry. Portlock pulls together.' Her comfort was heartfelt and honest, and I believed her. She was special, the kind of warm, nurturing person I wished my mother was.

'Connor just called,' Gunnar said. 'Fluffy is fine. They'll keep him overnight, but he should be good for pickup tomorrow. Connor said he'd bring him round as soon as he can.'

My panic subsided a tiny bit. I wasn't alone: I had Fluffy, my dog. Who, it turned out, I'd kill to protect. And I had some sort of fire magic, which was weird because I didn't have any magic.

I frowned as I thought back. I remembered feeling heat and seeing red when I was angry. Maybe it had happened with Franklin first, but I remembered feeling hot and seeing red with the rogue werewolf, and again with Shirley when I'd smacked her down. This was big though, bigger than I could handle right now. I'd keep it to myself for now. I was already enough of a freak as a vampire; I didn't need to tell anyone about my flambé skills.

Gunnar slung a gentle arm around me. 'When you're ready, you can tell me all about the fire.

Judgement free.' He gave me a squeeze then let me go and held open the car door.

I'd told them that I'd deliberately knocked on the gas when Virginia had arrived and flicked a lighter on when I'd had a chance. The fire chief clearly hadn't believed me and apparently Gunnar hadn't either. My house hadn't exploded; it had been set on fire. The fire chief hadn't pressed me; he lived in a supernatural town where nothing was quite as it seemed. He left me to my secrets, and I'd do my best to leave him to his. Gunnar wasn't so content to let sleeping dogs lie. I'd have to come clean to him sooner or later. My vote was later. Way later.

The longer I was a vampire though, the clearer it became that I wasn't a *normal* vampire. Someone had paid Franklin fifty thousand pounds to turn me – but into *what?*

If you've enjoyed Bunny's first adventure then keep an eye out for *The Vampire and the Case of the Secretive Siren,* coming out April 2024.

If you need something to keep you going until then, how about a free bonus scene all from Connor's point of view? Grab that here https://dl.bookfunnel.com/s6lhh4hcux and don't forget all about the prequel story, *The Vampire and the Case of Her Dastardly Death.*

About Heather

Heather is an urban fantasy writer and mum. She was born and raised near Windsor, which gave her the misguided impression that she was close to royalty in some way. She is not, though she once got a letter from Queen Elizabeth II's lady-in-waiting.

Heather went to university in Liverpool, where she took up skydiving and met her future husband. When she's not running around after her children, she's plotting her next book and daydreaming about vampires, dragons and kick-ass heroines.

Heather is a book lover who grew up reading Brian Jacques and Anne McCaffrey. She loves to travel and once spent a month in Thailand. She vows to return.

Want to learn more about Heather? Subscribe to her newsletter for behind-the-scenes scoops, free bonus material and a cheeky peek into her world. Her subscribers will always get the heads up about the best deals on her books.

Subscribe to her Newsletter at her website www.heathergharris.com/subscribe.

Too impatient to wait for Heather's next book? Join her (ever growing!) army of supportive patrons at Patreon.

Heather's Patreon

Heather has started her very own Patreon page. What is Patreon? It's a subscription service that allows you to support Heather AND read her books way before anyone else! For a small monthly fee you could be reading Heather's next book, on a weekly chapter-by-chapter basis (in its roughest draft form!) in the next week or two. If you hit "Join the community" you can follow Heather along for FREE, though you won't get access to all the good stuff, like early release books, polls, live Q&A's, character art and more! You can even have a video call with Heather or have a character named after you! Heather's current patrons are getting to read a novella called House

Bound which isn't available anywhere else, not even to her newsletter subscribers!

If you're too impatient to wait until Heather's next release, then Patreon is made for you! Join Heather's patrons here.

Heather's Shop and YouTube Channel

Heather now has her very own online shop! There you can buy oodles of glorious merchandise and audiobooks directly from her. Heather's audiobooks will still be on sale elsewhere, of course, but Heather pays her audiobook narrator *and* her cover designer - she makes the entire product - and then Audible pays her 25%. OUCH. Where possible, Heather would love it if you would buy her audiobooks directly from her, and then she can keep an amazing 90% of the money instead. Which she can reinvest in more books, in every form! But Audiobooks aren't all there is in the shop. You can get hoodies, t-shirts, mugs and more! Go and check her store out at: https://shop.heathergharris.com/

And if you don't have spare money to pay for audiobooks, Heather would still love you to experience Alyse Gibb's expert rendition of the books. You can listen to Heather's audiobooks for free on her YouTube Channel: https://www.youtube.com/@HeatherGHarrisAuthor

Stay in Touch

Heather has been working hard on a bunch of cool things, including a new and shiny website which you'll love. Check it out at www.heathergharris.com.

If you want to hear about all Heather's latest releases – subscribe to her newsletter for news, fun and freebies. Subscribe at Heather's website www.heathergharris.com/subscribe.

Contact Info: www.heathergharris.com

Email: HeatherGHarrisAuthor@gmail.com

Social Media

Heather can also be found on a host of social medias:

Facebook Page

Facebook Reader Group

Goodreads

Bookbub

Instagram

If you get a chance, please do follow Heather on Amazon!

Reviews

Reviews feed Heather's soul. She'd really appreciate it if you could take a few moments to review her books on Amazon,

Bookbub, or Goodreads and say hello.

About the Author - Jilleen

About Jilleen

Jilleen Dolbeare writes urban fantasy and paranormal women's fiction. She loves stories with strong women, adventure, and humor, with a side helping of myth and folklore.

While living in the Arctic, she learned to keep her stakes sharp for the 67 days of night. She talks to the ravens that follow her when she takes long walks with her cats in their stroller, and she's learned how to keep the wolves at bay.

Jilleen lives with her husband and two hungry cats in Alaska where she also discovered her love and admiration of the Alaska Native peoples and their folklore.

Stay in Touch

Jill can be reached through her website https://jilleendolbeareauthor.com/

Jill has also just joined Patreon! What is Patreon? It's a subscription service that allows you to support Jilleen AND read her books way before anyone else! For a small monthly fee you could be reading Jill's next book, on a weekly chapter-by-chapter basis (in its roughest draft form!) in the next week or two.

If you're too impatient to wait until Jilleen's next release, then Patreon is made for you! Join Jilleen's patrons here.

Social Media

Jill can be found on a host of social media sites so track her down here.

Review Request!

Wow! You finished the book. Go you!

Thanks for reading it. We appreciate it! Please, please, please consider leaving an honest review. Love it or hate it, authors can only sell books if they get reviews. If we don't sell books, Jill can't afford cat food. If Jill can't buy cat food, the little bastards will scavenge her sad, broken body. Then there will be no more books. Jill's savage kitties have sunken cheeks and swollen tummies and can't wait to eat Jill. Please help by leaving that review! (Heather has a dog, so she probably won't be eaten, but she'd really like Jill to live, so... please review).

If you're a reviewer, you have our eternal gratitude.

Other Works by Heather

The *Portlock Paranormal Detective* Series with Jilleen Dolbeare

The Vampire and the Case of her Dastardly Death - Book 0.5 (a prequel story),

The Vampire and the Case of the Wayward Werewolf – Book 1,

The Vampire and the Case of the Secretive Siren – Book 2,

The Vampire and the Case of the Baleful Banshee – Book 3.

The Vampire and the Case of the Cursed Canine – Book 4

The *Other Realm* series

Glimmer of Dragons- Book 0.5 (a prequel story),

Glimmer of The Other- Book 1,

Glimmer of Hope- Book 2,

Glimmer of Christmas – Book 2.5 (a Christmas tale),

Glimmer of Death – Book 3,

Glimmer of Deception – Book 4,

It is recommended that you read *The Other Wolf series* before continuing with:

Challenge of the Court– Book 5,

Betrayal of the Court– Book 6; and

Revival of the Court– Book 7.

The *Other Wolf* Series

Defender of The Pack– Book 0.5 (a prequel story),

Protection of the Pack– Book 1,

Guardians of the Pack– Book 2; and

Saviour of The Pack– Book 3.

The *Other Witch* Series

Rune of the Witch – Book 0.5 (a prequel story),

Hex of the Witch– Book 1,

Coven of the Witch;– Book 2,

Familiar of the Witch– Book 3, and

Destiny of the Witch – Book 4.

Other Works by Jilleen

The *Paranormal Portlock Detective* Series with Heather G Harris

The Vampire and the Case of Her Dastardly Death: Book 0.5 (a prequel story), and

The Vampire and the Case of the Wayward Werewolf: Book 1,

The Vampire and the Case of the Secretive Siren: Book 2,

The Vampire and the Case of the Baleful Banshee: Book 3, and

The Vampire and the Case of the Cursed Canine: Book 4.

The *Splintered Magic* Series:

Splintercat: Book 0.5 (a prequel story),

Splintered Magic: Book 1,

Splintered Veil: Book 2,

Splintered Fate: Book 3,

Splintered Haven: Book 4,

Splintered Secret: Book 5, and

Splintered Destiny: Book 6.

The *Shadow Winged* Chronicles:

Shadow Lair: Book 0.5 (a prequel story),

Shadow Winged: Book 1,

Shadow Wolf: Book 1.5,

Shadow Strife: Book 2 ,

Shadow Witch: Book 2.5, and

Shadow War: Book 3.

Made in United States
North Haven, CT
19 May 2024

52708008R00317